JENNIFER STURMAN

THE HUNT

RED
DRESS
INK
™

THE HUNT

A Red Dress Ink novel

ISBN-13: 978-0-373-89570-0
ISBN-10:   0-373-89570-4

www.RedDressInk.com

Printed in U.S.A.

11/23/07

...n's
...eries

"Why is this debut so thoroughly enjoyable?
Perhaps it's because Rachel is such a winning detective:
she sifts through clues at the reader's pace
and does so with wit and pluck."
—*Publishers Weekly* on *The Pact*

"Jennifer Sturman has bridged the gap
between Agatha Christie and Bridget Jones."
—*Akron Beacon Journal*

"Rachel returns for another smart and saucy adventure in
sleuthing and romance in Sturman's second fresh, funny,
and fabulously amusing chick-lit mystery."
—*Booklist* on *The Jinx*

"Sturman's gift for plot, characterization, and dialogue
provide a uniquely satisfying romantic romp."
—*Mystery Scene Magazine* on *The Key*

"Sturman's debut is a rare delight, and her sharp,
sassy writing is wonderfully addictive."
—*Booklist* on *The Pact*

"Sturman delivers great characters, a dash of humor and a
mystery that keeps you interested—and guessing."
—*Romantic Times BOOKreviews* on *The Pact*

"Sturman's latest Rachel Benjamin mystery has the same
delectable blend of snappy writing, chick-lit liveliness
and clever plotting as the first two books
in this delightfully entertaining series."
—*Booklist* on *The Key*

Also from Jennifer Sturman
and Red Dress Ink

THE KEY
THE JINX
THE PACT

ACKNOWLEDGMENTS

A number of friends were extremely generous with their time and their knowledge of the Bay Area as I was writing this book. These kind people include Rita and Joe Brogley, Maria and Jan Leeman, Jasper Malcolmson, Stefanie Reich Offit, Elizabeth Porteous, Raj Seshadri and Rick Ostrander, and Marybeth Wittekind Sharpe and Amory Sharpe. Many thanks to Michele Jaffe, who again served as an early reader, and to Carrie Weber for her ace translation skills. And, as always, thanks to my agent, Laura Langlie, Margaret Marbury and the team at Red Dress Ink, and my family for their continued encouragement and support.

This book is dedicated to Rulonna Neilson.

"They're so *normal*."

Luisa lit her cigarette and snapped the lighter shut. "And how is that a problem?"

"I didn't say it was a problem. But they named their dog Spot."

"The dog does have a spot, Rachel."

It was true. The dog in question had a spot. And as dogs went, Spot was okay—not too yappy or slobbery. In fact, he was a completely normal dog, exactly right for his owners, Charles and Susan Forrest, my future in-laws and the source of all this rampant normalcy.

The phrase *my future in-laws* still felt unreal to me, even though Peter and I had been engaged for several months now and in spite of the very real engagement party we were currently attending at the Forrests' San Francisco home. Or, to be more accurate, the engagement party from which Luisa and I were sneaking a break. She had wanted a cigarette, and the sight of my family mingling with Peter's family, especially our grandmothers with their heads close together, undoubtedly hammering out just how many children we should have, was enough to make a little second-hand smoke seem nearly appealing.

We'd slipped out of the house through the side door and walked the short distance to the top of the Lyon Street steps, which led down from Pacific Heights to the Palace of Fine Arts and the Bay beyond. The steps were the local hot spot for underage drinkers on a Saturday night. Clumps of kids gathered on the landings, discreetly sipping from beer cans and plastic cups and apparently unconcerned that even in June the air was damp and chill.

I heard the staccato of high-heeled feet approaching, and one of the kids looked in our direction and whistled, a long, piercing wolf whistle. Since Luisa and I had already been there for several minutes, I knew the sound had nothing to do with us. I turned, and sure enough, Hilary was heading our way. Six-foot tall women with platinum hair and a proclivity for small clothing generate a disproportionate amount of whistling, especially in a city where most people's wardrobes are comprised largely of fleece.

Fortunately, Hilary enjoyed the occasional objectification. She flashed the whistler a smile and pulled herself up to sit on the stone railing. "I thought I'd find you two out here."

"Luisa needed a cigarette," I explained.

"And you're freaking out," Hilary said.

"Not at all," I said, which was almost the truth. There was

nothing quite like being the guest of honor at an engagement party to remind a person she had commitment issues,
not to mention several other relationship-related neuroses,
but I was proud of the progress I'd made in developing emotional maturity. Between the party and the quality time
Peter and I had planned with his parents over the next few
days, my skills were definitely being put to the test, but I
was confident the Forrests would never guess just how new
I was to this whole normalcy thing.

"I don't know how you people do it," said Hilary.

"'You people?'" asked Luisa, raising one dark, well-
shaped eyebrow.

"Do what?" I asked, wishing I had Luisa's one-eyebrow-
raising skill.

"Long-term relationships," said Hilary. "You and Peter.
Jane and Sean. Emma and Matthew. You, too, Luisa. At least,
until Isobel dumped you." Luisa, Hilary and I had been
roommates in college, which was starting to become longer
ago than I cared to admit. Jane and Emma completed the
group, but they were both on the East Coast this weekend:
Jane home in Boston with her newborn son and Emma at
the Southampton wedding of her boyfriend's sister.

"Isobel did not dump me," said Luisa evenly. She stubbed
out her cigarette and lit another. "After careful consideration,
we mutually decided our relationship had run its course."

"And before Peter, my longest relationship only lasted
three months," I pointed out. Technically, it had been closer
to two and a half months, but it seemed fair to round up for
the purpose of this discussion.

"Ben and I haven't been together anything like three

months, but it's felt stale ever since I got over the thrill of being with a guy who carries a gun. And that was during the second week," said Hilary. Her boyfriend of the moment, Ben Lattimer, was an agent with the FBI's financial fraud unit, and he did carry a gun, but it didn't seem to be providing much in the way of defense against Hilary. Her blunt manner masked a deep affection and fierce loyalty where her friends were concerned, but her attention span could be short when it came to romance, and it sounded as if Ben was on his way out, whether he was aware of it or not.

"Have you considered giving a guy a chance for once?" I asked.

"I have given him a chance, and it was fine for a while, but now he's getting all mushy on me. You know how I feel about that."

We did know, having listened to more than a few discourses from her over the years on how love, like Santa Claus, the Easter Bunny and a nonsurgical cure for cellulite, was a nice idea but equally lacking any basis in reality. "Are you sure? Ben's sweet, and he seems mentally stable, and he's really good-looking," I said.

"He's taller than you, too," said Luisa. "How often does that happen?"

"And how often do all of those qualities come together in one man?" I added.

"How will I ever find out if I'm stuck with him for the rest of my life?" Hilary countered, swinging one long leg with impatience.

"Do you want me to talk to Ben?" I offered. It would be

a good opportunity to exercise my emotional maturity. "I can help you work things out."

Hilary made a noise that was somewhere between a snort, a laugh and a sigh.

"I'll take that as a no," I said, disappointed.

"Speaking of good-looking," said Luisa, "what's the story on Peter's colleague, Abigail?"

Abigail lived here in San Francisco, where she ran business development for the West Coast office of Peter's company. She'd started working for him the previous fall, and it had been a bit unnerving at first to realize he was spending most of his waking hours with someone who was both brilliant and looked like a better version of Christie Turlington, but fortunately her tastes ran to women rather than men. "I think she's single," I told Luisa. "Peter says she's sort of guarded about her personal life. Not shy so much as cautious."

"I wonder why that is," said Luisa. "You'd think somebody that beautiful wouldn't have anything to worry about."

I brightened. Hilary might not want my help on the romantic front, but maybe Luisa would. "You know, Peter and I could set you—"

"Thank you, but I can handle my own personal life," Luisa said.

"Because we'd be happy to—"

She interrupted me again. "Rachel, that's very thoughtful but not necessary."

"Since when are you so eager to get involved in other people's love lives, Rach?" asked Hilary. "First offering couples therapy to Ben and me and then trying to hook Luisa up with Abigail?"

"I need something to do. My own love life is so normal. Isn't it better to take an interest in other people's relationships than look for reasons to mess up my own?"

"Have you considered simply enjoying the normality of your own life while simultaneously staying out of the lives of others?" asked Luisa.

"I know that's what I'm supposed to do, but I have all of this free emotional energy that I used to expend on maintaining my neuroses, and now I don't know what to do with it."

"Rach, don't take this the wrong way, but you haven't exactly perfected normal yet."

Hilary was hardly in a position to be evaluating who was and who wasn't normal. "It took a while, but I'm totally normal at relationships now," I told her, trying not to sound defensive.

"Of course you are," said Luisa, but her own voice held a note of skepticism.

"While we're talking about normal, I still wouldn't describe him as such, but our old friend Iggie looks a lot better than when he lived across the hall from us sophomore year," said Hilary. "He's almost attractive, in a revenge-of-the-nerds type of way."

"Huge piles of money will do that for a guy," I said, glad of the change in topic from my relative normality to somebody else's.

"Will he really be worth that much, Rachel?" asked Luisa.

"That's how things are shaping up." Winslow, Brown, the investment bank where I worked, was competing with several other firms to handle the initial public offering—IPO— of Igobe, an Internet company founded by our former classmate, Igor "Iggie" Behrenz. Iggie had been the quintessential computer geek in college, except instead of being shy and dorky he'd been arrogant and dorky, so confident in his future success that he was frequently unbearable. He hadn't changed much since then, but I was still repairing the damage from a minor misunderstanding in which I'd ended up as the lead suspect in my boss's murder. Winning his IPO business offered a chance to shore up my position at the office, however unbearable Iggie might be. Our pitch was conveniently scheduled for Tuesday morning at Igobe's headquarters in Silicon Valley, and I'd invited him to the party tonight hoping it would improve our odds. "Iggie's stake will be close to a billion dollars when his company goes public," I told my friends.

Hilary whistled. Her admirer below turned to look, wondering if she was belatedly returning his show of appreciation, but her thoughts were somewhere else entirely. "A billion? As in a one with nine zeros after it?"

"That's obscene," said Luisa. Her family practically owned a small South American country, but even their fortune seemed modest in comparison.

I worked in an industry where the net worth of the top performers regularly topped the hundred-million mark, but I had to agree: a billion did seem excessive. "Everyone's looking for the next MySpace or YouTube, and a lot of people think Iggie's got it," I said. "This IPO should be the hottest deal of the year."

"You know the article I'm working on about the newest generation of Internet start-ups?" Hilary asked us. We nodded as if we did, but while I had a vague recollection of her mentioning a San Francisco-based assignment that dove-tailed nicely with the party, I tended to lose track of what she was working on at any given moment. A freelance journalist, she jumped from topic to topic much as she jumped from man to man. "I've decided to make Iggie's company the focus. It shouldn't be hard to score an exclusive interview with Iggie, and I've been digging up some interesting material on Igobe."

"What does the company do?" asked Luisa.

"It develops technology that masks people's identities online," I explained. "Once you download its software to your computer, your privacy is protected when you're surfing the Web."

"Which means you can visit all the porn sites you want and nobody will ever know," translated Hilary.

"Isn't that a relief," said Luisa dryly.

"A lot of people seem to think so," I said. "And they're going to make Iggie a very rich man."

"I only remember him as the geek who was handy to have around whenever that evil bomb icon popped up on my Mac," said Luisa.

"Well, he's still a geek, but he's a billion times handier now," said Hilary, her smile mischievous. "And he might just come in handy tonight."

"Why do I have a feeling I don't want to know what you're plotting?" I asked.

"Plotting?" she asked with mock innocence. "*Moi?*"

"You're incorrigible," said Luisa, something she'd said to Hilary on more occasions than any of us could remember.

"And that's why you love me," she replied easily.

"Oh, is that why?" asked Luisa, but she was laughing.

"I knew there had to be a reason," I said, but I was laughing, too.

A gust of frosty air rose up from the Bay just then, and we all shivered in our lightweight summer dresses. "We should get back to the party," I said. "It's freezing out here, and Peter's probably wondering where I am."

"And Ben's probably wondering where you are, Hilary," said Luisa pointedly.

"Probably," said Hilary, but the mischievous smile was still there. "More importantly, I promised Iggie a dance."

The Forrests' house was a three-story Victorian, painted pale yellow with glossy white gingerbread trim. It looked a lot like the house in *Party of Five,* which was rumored to be nearby—not that Peter or his parents had any idea what I was talking about when I asked. Still, I'd found myself half-expecting to run into Bailey or Charlie ever since we'd arrived the previous day, and Hilary and I debated the relative merits of the Salinger men on the walk back to the party. "Don't forget Griffin," she said. "Not a Salinger, but still hot."

"As if I could forget Griffin," I said.

"Who could forget Griffin?" said Luisa, but she was teasing us—she'd never seen even a single *Party of Five* episode. Except for college and law school, she'd lived most of her life on another continent, privy only to a sadly limited selection of high-quality American television. This didn't bother her—I guessed it was hard to miss something unless you knew what you were missing, and sometimes I thought being culturally illiterate might have its advantages. I worried about the amount of space TV characters and plotlines occupied in my brain, not to mention the lyrics from eighties pop songs, especially when I was unable to remember other very basic things, like pretty much everything I learned in high school.

The party was in full swing when we slipped back in through the side door, with people chatting and mingling as they balanced drinks and plates of food from the buffet in the dining room. Peter and I hadn't yet set a date for the wedding, but his parents had insisted on throwing us an engagement party in his hometown, particularly since we would likely get married in Ohio, where I grew up, or in New York, where we lived. Their idea of a "little" party was turning out to be good practice for a big wedding—they had a wide circle of friends, and over a hundred of them were here tonight. This didn't even include the friends Peter and I had invited or the members of my family the Forrests had urged to make the trip west.

Fortunately, nobody seemed to have noticed our brief absence. Peter's grandmother and my grandmother were exactly where they'd been fifteen minutes ago, seated together in the den and poring over old photo albums, each probably calculating whose family had more dominant genes, and Peter's parents were busily introducing my parents to their friends. No mediation on my part seemed necessary, but there was too much fodder for embarrassment lurking in my childhood for me to be entirely comfortable with extended interfamily mingling.

We made our way to the rear of the house, where French doors opened out onto the deck and yard. A tent and a temporary dance floor had been spread over the grass and a band played a mix of songs from both the elder Forrests' generation and our own. Either way, most of the "younger set," as Susan Forrest put it, seemed to have gravitated toward the music. That might also have had something to do with the fact that the line at the bar was shorter here.

I paused at the top of the stairs leading down from the deck, scanning the crowd before locating Peter's sandy head on the far side of the dance floor. Even after nearly a year together, my heart still did a little flip whenever I saw him across a room. Luisa and Hilary volunteered to bring me a drink, and I went to join him where he stood talking with a man and woman I didn't know.

"Hey," he said, leaning down to kiss me. "I've been looking for you. There are a couple of old friends from college I want you to meet. Rachel, this is Caroline Vail."

The woman, an athletic-looking blonde with a kittenish face, clasped my hand in hers. "Call me Caro—everyone does. I've heard so much about you, I feel as if I know you already." I was surprised she'd heard so much about me since I'd never heard a thing about her, but I smiled and said hello.

"And this is Alex Cutler."

Alex was West Coast preppie, dressed in khakis, a navy blazer, and a button-down shirt open at the collar. His brown hair was cut short, and his blue eyes were friendly behind round, wire-rimmed glasses. "So you're the woman who convinced Peter to cross over to the dark side," he said.

"He means New York," Peter said. "People out here have a hard time understanding why anyone would live anywhere else."

Hilary appeared at my side with a wineglass in one hand and a martini glass in the other. She passed me the wine as Peter introduced her to Caro and Alex.

"You know, Hil, these two might be able to help with the article you were telling me about," he told her. "Caro runs a public-relations agency that works with start-ups in the Bay area, and Alex is a venture capitalist in Palo Alto."

"I'm working on a magazine piece about the newest wave of Internet companies and whether they're for real or if it's all just another bubble," Hilary explained. "Some of these start-ups seem like nothing but hype."

Caro laughed. "Well, I'm in the business of generating hype, but I like to think there's substance behind some of it."

"There'd better be, since I'm in the business of funding it," said Alex.

"These two know everyone," Peter assured Hilary. "We were all at Stanford together, and a lot of the Silicon Valley entrepreneurs and their financial backers are Stanford alumni."

"Peter and I were even frat brothers," said Alex.

This was also the first I'd heard about Peter being in a fraternity, and it was a hard mental picture to draw—I'd never thought of him as the beer-pong type. "Were there beanies and paddling?" I asked. "Or just making pledges drink until they puked?"

"No, nothing like that," said Peter, smiling and shaking his head. "It was just a bunch of guys hanging out. Not exactly *Animal House*."

Maybe the band caught his words, because a moment later they launched into the Isley Brothers' version of "Shout." The dance floor, sparsely occupied before, started to fill. And that's when Iggie made his move.

"Hey there, homeys," said his reedy voice from behind me. I'd greeted him earlier, but he'd arrived at the same time as a number of other guests, and I hadn't been able to do more than say hello and hastily introduce him to Peter. Now I had the opportunity to better take in his attire, and it was interesting, to say the least. The Google guys, despite their multiple billions, had adopted a spare sartorial uniform that depended heavily on black T-shirts. Iggie, however, was staking out a more fashion-forward look, one that owed more to Versace than Banana Republic and involved a lot of purple velvet. I'd always thought velvet was a no-no in June, but maybe Iggie knew something I didn't. And even if Iggie hadn't been an old friend, he was still a potential client, which went a long way toward helping me overlook any questionable fashion statements.

"Hi, Iggie," I said. "Having a good time?"

"The Igster always has a good time," he said.

I was glad I wasn't taking a sip of my drink, because white wine spurting out of my nose wasn't the image I wanted Peter's friends to take away from the evening. Peter made a choking noise that I knew was his way of trying not to laugh.

"Iggie, have you met Caroline Vail and Alex Cutler?" I asked.

"Sure. We're like this." He held up two fingers to indicate just how close they all were, and Caro and Alex smiled and nodded in agreement, but Iggie clearly wasn't interested in talking to them or to Peter and me—he had a very different agenda. "Ready for that dance, Hilarita?"

When we were in college, Iggie had hit on Hilary with a single-minded perseverance that was staggering when you considered most of the time she didn't pay him enough attention to notice he was hitting on her. But even without the imminent certainty of a billion-dollar bank account, Iggie had been sufficiently self-confident to keep trying. Now he appeared to be picking up where he'd left off, and tonight Hilary had an agenda of her own.

She drained the rest of her martini and handed me the empty glass. "Let's do it," she said, allowing Iggie to lead her onto the dance floor.

"'The Igster'?" Peter said as soon as they were out of earshot. This time I was taking a sip of my drink, but I managed to swallow without incident. "Who does he think he is? Elmo?"

"That's new since college," I said. "He never used to refer to himself in the third-person, and definitely not as 'the Igster.'"

"He's famous for it out here," said Alex, an expression of bemused tolerance on his face. "Or maybe notorious would be a better way to put it."

"I handle public relations for Igobe," said Caro, her own expression equally bemused. "And I've tried to give Iggie some tips on things like wardrobe and assigning nicknames to himself and others, but he likes to do things his way."

"And except for the wardrobe and the nicknames, his way

is usually right," said Alex. "Which is why I put money into his company. My firm is Igobe's biggest outside shareholder. I even helped him with his business plan back when he was just getting started."

"So that's how you two know him?" I asked. "Alex, you invested in his company, and Caro, you do his company's PR?"

They nodded in unison, and I wondered if they were a couple. It was hard to tell from their body language, and there'd been nothing in Peter's introduction to indicate one way or the other, but they shared a similar outdoorsy look, as if they spent a lot of time doing healthy things, like eating trail mix and training for triathlons.

Caro glanced toward the dance floor. "Oh," she said, wincing. "I've tried to give Iggie some tips on dancing, too, but that doesn't seem to have helped much, either."

We all turned to look. The band had reached the slowed-down, writhing-on-the-floor part of "Shout," but only Iggie felt it necessary to actually writhe on the floor. Hilary stood watching, her head cocked to one side and her expression unreadable, a rarity for her.

"The Igster seems to have a thing for Hilary," said Peter. "Is it requited?"

"I hope not, especially since she's supposed to be dating someone else right now," I said. "I think she's just trying to hit him up for an interview for her story. She said she was thinking of making Iggie and Igobe the focus. Although, it could be useful to have a friend who was married to a billionaire."

"I wonder what ever happened to Iggie's first wife," said Alex. "She must be kicking herself for bailing before the payoff."

"Iggie was married?" I asked in disbelief.

Caro smiled at my reaction, revealing perfect white teeth. "There's a lid for every pot."

"Who was his lid? Or pot?" My contact with Iggie had been limited since college, picking up only recently with the discussions about my firm potentially handling his company's IPO, but I was still surprised to have missed an entire marriage, and it was hard to imagine anybody willing to put up with Iggie long enough to marry him.

"Believe it or not, her name was Biggie," said Alex.

"Did she call herself the Bigster?" asked Peter.

Alex chuckled, but Caro shook her head. "It was a nickname—probably left over from not being able to say Elizabeth, or something like that, when she was little."

"Or maybe Iggie made it up. Either way, it fit," said Alex.

Caro leaned forward and lowered her voice as if she were imparting classified information. "Unfortunately, Biggie was a little on the heavy side." She smoothed the pink silk sheath she was wearing over her own trim hips.

"A little?" repeated Alex. "A little on the obese side is more like it." He held his arms out and puffed up his cheeks to indicate that Biggie was a sizable woman. I was still having a hard time adjusting to the idea of Peter in a fraternity, but picturing Alex engaged in raucous male-bonding hijinks was a lot easier.

"She really had a very pretty face underneath all that hair," said Caro. "And she was supposed to be very bright. But the marriage didn't last. I think they met when they were in graduate school at Berkeley, and then they worked together at Iggie's first start-up, the one before Igobe."

"The one that never really got off the ground," said Alex.

"Whatever did happen to Biggie?" Caro mused. "I haven't seen her since the divorce, and that must have been over a year ago. It's as if she fell right off the planet—just disappeared."

"Nothing that big could just disappear," said Alex with another chuckle.

Caro changed the subject then, asking about our plans while we were in town, and I was happy to end the discussion of Iggie's ex-wife before Alex could make any more cracks about the poor woman's weight. As far as I was concerned, anyone who'd had the misfortune to be married to Iggie deserved our full sympathy. We chatted a while longer, but guests of honor were supposed to circulate, so Peter and I eventually excused ourselves and circulated, working our way methodically through the crowd of people outside. Then we headed inside, where he abruptly pulled me down a short passageway and into the small laundry room.

"Hi," he said, wrapping his hands around my waist.

"Hi back," I said, resting my hands on his shoulders.

"You look really pretty."

"Thank you. You look really pretty, too."

"Pretty wasn't what I was going for, but I'll take it. Want to make out?"

"Here?" I asked.

He nodded.

"Now?" I asked.

He nodded again.

"Okay."

★ ★ ★

We emerged from the laundry room a few minutes later, but not before I'd made Peter promise me I didn't look as if I'd just been making out with him in the laundry room. "I want to make a good impression," I said.

"What are you talking about? Everybody already loves you."

"Even your father?" Charles Forrest had a reserved air about him, and it made me nervous. It was hard to tell what he was thinking.

"Especially my father. He was singing your praises just this afternoon."

"Seriously? What did he say?" I could always use an ego boost, regardless of my advanced level of emotional maturity.

"He said—what did he say?" Peter ran a hand through his hair, trying to remember the words, and I reached out to smooth the pieces of hair left standing straight up in the wake of his fingers. "I know. He said you were 'idiosyncractic.'"

My hand dropped to my side. "'Idiosyncractic?'"

"Sure."

"'Idiosyncratic'?" I repeated.

"Uh-huh. Ready to go?"

Idiosyncratic was not normal. In fact, idiosyncratic was pretty much the opposite of normal. It was a blood relative of eccentric, which was practically a euphemism for crazy.

It looked as if I still had a distance to go in convincing the Forrests I could blend gracefully into their normal family.

Back at the party, we ran directly into Ben Lattimer at the bar that had been set up in the living room. He'd exchanged his customary Levi's for a suit in deference to the occasion, but while he looked as handsome as ever, he seemed somehow deflated. "Have either of you seen Hilary?" he asked.

"Um, I think she might be out back," I said, wondering why I felt guilty when it was Hilary who was spending most of her evening with someone who wasn't her boyfriend.

"Thanks. I'll try to track her down."

Peter and I watched Ben walk away. Even his broad shoulders seemed to slump. "I know I shouldn't say this about one of my best friends," I said, "but Hilary can be a menace. She comes on so strong, but then she leaves men hanging. And Ben's a nice guy."

"Ben is a nice guy, but he's also a grown-up. If things with Hil don't work out, he'll get over it. And I know I shouldn't say this about one of your best friends—and I like her, too—but with her track record, he'd probably be better off without her."

Ben was a grown-up, and if he and Hilary were, in fact, headed for the rocks, Peter was right—he would get over it and likely be better off. She didn't seem cut out for long-term relationships, and the longer Ben stayed with her, the more he'd get hurt. But I couldn't help keeping an eye out for him for the rest of the evening. He was clearly in a vulnerable state, gun notwithstanding.

We caught up to him again an hour later, standing on the deck looking out at the tented dance floor. Hilary and Iggie were still dancing—at least, Hilary was dancing, and Iggie was moving with such frenzied energy that he even managed to hit the beat every so often. Ben stared at them as he sipped from a glass that looked and smelled like straight whisky.

"We were going to get some food," Peter told him. "Are you hungry?"

"Come join us," I urged.

"Thanks, but I'm not really in the mood," Ben said, his eyes not moving from the dance floor.

The band wrapped up a spirited interpretation of "Love Shack" then announced that they would be taking a short break, and Hilary and Iggie left the dance floor and started in our direction. His arm was draped over her shoulders, which couldn't have been comfortable given their difference in height, but he kept it there anyway.

"Excuse me," said Ben. I thought he would go to intercept Hilary, but instead he headed back into the house.

"That's not good," said Peter.

"I wonder if I should say something to Hil," I said, watching as she and Iggie made their way through the crowd.

"Have you ever said anything to her that influenced her behavior?"

"No, it's always been a complete waste of time. But maybe if Luisa and I ganged up on her?"

"Has ganging up worked before?"

"It's Hilary. Nothing's worked before. Where is Luisa, anyhow?" I asked. "I haven't seen her in a while."

Hilary and Iggie reached us where we were standing at the top of the steps. "Hey, Raquel, hey, Pedrolino," said Iggie. "We were going to check out the buffet. All of that dancing really builds up an appetite." He patted his velvet shirt where it strained across the beginnings of a pot belly.

"Have you two eaten?" asked Hilary.

"Not yet. We were just trying to find Luisa," I said.

"She's over there," said Hilary, gesturing to the far corner of the tent. Her height gave her an advantage when it came to locating people in crowds. "And it looks like she was right about not needing your help, Rach," she added.

Beyond the dance floor, Luisa was deep in animated conversation with Abigail. And while Abigail bore a significant resemblance to a gazellelike supermodel, if somebody were to make a movie of Luisa's life, the lead role would be played by Salma Hayek. Together, the two were a formidable sight. I made a mental note not to stand next to them in any photographs.

"Whoa," said Iggie, his arm slipping from Hilary's shoulder. "Who's that with LuLu?" Luisa was even less of a LuLu than I was a Raquel or Peter a Pedrolino, but it seemed best to let it pass.

"A coworker of mine," said Peter. "And a friend. Her name is Abigail."

"Abigail," said Iggie thoughtfully. "Babealicious, isn't she?"

Fortunately, he was still gazing at Abigail and Luisa, so he didn't notice Hilary glance over at me and mouth "babealicious" or Peter again making a choking noise as he struggled not to laugh.

I reminded myself of the fees Winslow, Brown would generate if Iggie chose the firm to handle the Igobe IPO and the much-needed momentum those fees would generate on my own path to a Winslow, Brown partnership.

"She certainly is," I said.

The next morning Peter made me go running.

"That's what we always do on Sundays in San Francisco," he said. "A long run along the water and then a big brunch."

"Sounds wonderful," I lied, except about the brunch part. "There's nothing I would rather do this morning. If only I'd remembered to bring my workout clothes. Darn. What a shame."

"I packed your stuff for you."

"You did?"

He smiled in a way that would have been smug if he had been anyone else. "I had a feeling you might forget."

Peter exercised because he enjoyed it. I exercised because I enjoyed fitting into my clothes. "Even my sneakers?" I asked.

"Even your sneakers," he said.

"Oh."

"Come on, it will be fun."

"How are you defining *fun?*"

Ten minutes later, we descended the stairs dressed in shorts, T-shirts and running shoes and found Peter's parents in the kitchen, drinking coffee and reading the paper. Judging by their attire and healthy glow, they'd already been for their own run. I thanked them again for the party, which hadn't wound down until after midnight.

"It was such a treat to finally meet your family, Rachel. I wish they could have stayed longer," Susan said.

The various Benjamins had been among the last to leave the previous evening, and they had gotten along beautifully with the Forrests and their friends, but by my calculations they were now well on their way to the airport, and I considered this excellent timing. While I loved my family, between the joint family dinner on Friday night, a joint family outing yesterday to the Asian Art Museum, and then the party, there had been more than enough opportunities for somebody to dredge up a mortifying tidbit from my past. And since my past was rife with mortifying tidbits, I was amazed to have made it through all of these events safely— prolonging the interaction further would have been courting disaster. But I didn't mention any of that. "They really liked meeting you, too," I said instead.

"Are you two going for a run?" Susan asked.

"Yep," said Peter, reaching into the refrigerator and taking out a couple of bottles of water. He held one out to me, but I shook my head, and he exchanged it for a Diet Coke. I opened the can with pleased anticipation. There was nothing quite like the day's first hit.

"Are you sure you wouldn't rather have some coffee, dear? Or orange juice?" Susan asked me.

"Oh, um, thank you, but I like soda in the morning." In fact, morning was my favorite time to drink soda, although I also enjoyed it in the afternoon and evening.

"Peter, honey, don't you think Rachel might want a glass? Rachel, dear, don't you want a glass?"

"Rachel prefers it out of the can, Mom," said Peter. I did prefer it out of the can. There was something about the way the carbonation and aluminum interacted that made it especially tasty.

"Are you sure, dear?" The perplexed look on Susan's face reminded me that my habits might seem a little strange to the uninitiated.

"You know, I will have a glass. Thanks," I said.

Peter stared at me, the perplexed look on his face an exact replica of his mother's, but he reached into a cupboard and handed me a glass. I poured out the soda and drank it down.

"We'll be back in an hour or so," Peter told his parents.

"An hour?" I said under my breath.

"Have fun," Susan said. "We'll have brunch ready when you get back." Charles raised his coffee cup in our direction without glancing up from the paper.

Peter ushered me out the front door. "Ready?" he asked.

"I don't think so," I said, but he took my hand anyway and began pulling me along the street.

"Is this pace okay?" he called over his shoulder.

"Uh-huh," I said, and it was for a bit, since the first part was all downhill. Peter even trusted me to keep moving once he let go of my hand. The next part along the water was flat and picturesque with the light glinting off the Golden Gate Bridge in the distance, and for a few minutes I felt an inspiring camaraderie with the other runners on the path. But that quickly dissipated.

"Look," said Peter, slowing his pace to accommodate my own, which had started to lag. He pointed to some slippery animals sitting on rocks in the water. They were seals or sea lions, or maybe even walruses, but I was too winded to ask, much less care, nor did he seem to notice I wasn't holding up my end of the conversation as he pointed out other landmarks. By the time we finally turned back I'd been evaluating alternative modes of revenge for a good ten minutes, and when we found ourselves at the bottom of the Lyon Street steps, I had no choice but to draw the line. In truth, there was no conscious decision. My feet simply stopped.

"No," I wheezed.

"No what?" Peter asked, still jogging in place as I rested my hands on my knees and struggled to feed air into my burning lungs.

"No, I'm not running up those."

"We're almost home. You'll feel great afterward." I scowled at his chipper tone.

Two women with legs the size of tree trunks sprinted by us and charged up the steps. "Marathons weren't enough of a challenge, so I started training for an iron man," one was saying to the other.

"My first iron man was a total rush," the other replied.

"I'll meet you at the top," I said to Peter.

He ran up and down the steps several times as I made my way up them just once. "That's obnoxious," I told him as he pranced by me yet again, but he pretended not to hear. He was stretching when I eventually crested the final flight.

"Is this your passive-aggressive way of trying to get me to break up with you?" I asked as we walked the remaining distance to his parents' house. Or, to be more accurate, as Peter walked and I limped.

"You loved every second."

"If that was love, you should have some serious misgivings when I say I love you."

"You know, you'd probably feel better if you hydrated before you ran."

"I did hydrate."

"Rachel. Diet Coke is not hydration."

"You say tomato."

"Maybe you should admit it. You have a problem."

"I don't have a problem. What's my problem?" I asked.

"You're addicted to Diet Coke."

"Yes, but it's not a problem." We'd reached the house, and I contemplated the steps leading up to the front door. They seemed steeper than they had the day before. A bald man passed by walking a Great Dane, and Spot appeared at the bay window and started to bark, but the Great Dane trotted on, oblivious.

"You couldn't last two days without Diet Coke," said Peter.

"Why would I want to?"

"What if I dared you?"

I looked up at him and was alarmed to see he wasn't joking. "That's not fair," I said. Peter knew how I felt about dares—specifically, that you didn't turn them down unless you were comfortable being branded a wuss.

"You mean, you're turning down a dare?"

I considered my options. I didn't really have any, given that I didn't want anyone to think I was a wuss, at least not about something like this. "No," I said reluctantly, "I'm not turning down a dare."

"Forty-eight hours, then. No Diet Coke. In fact, how about no caffeine?"

I gasped. "No caffeine?"

"No caffeine. You wouldn't want to do this halfway, would you?"

"Yes, I would. I absolutely would."

"No caffeine," he repeated firmly.

"Why are you doing this to me?" I asked, forlorn.

"Because I want you to live a long and healthy life." He consulted his watch. "It's ten o'clock. You only need to last until ten on Tuesday. It will be fun."

It was the second time that day Peter had declared something terrible would be fun, and it wasn't even noon.

Little did I know just how much less fun the day would get.

At least Peter had been telling the truth about brunch. I believe strongly in eating frequently and in large quantities, but the Forrests made me feel positively ascetic. There were scrambled eggs and crisp bacon on china platters, warm scones and croissants in a basket, sliced melon and berries in a glass bowl, and a pitcher of fresh-squeezed orange juice.

Of course, nothing goes with bacon quite as well as Diet Coke, but I tried not to think about that. I'd read somewhere that it took smokers three days for their physical addiction to nicotine to pass. Caffeine couldn't be nearly as addictive as smoking. I was starting to feel a little shaky and had the beginning of a headache, but I assured myself the cravings would last only a few hours at the most. When Susan offered me a soda, I politely demurred and asked for herbal tea instead, feeling superlatively normal. But even with a generous dollop of honey, the tea lacked the stimulating kick of Diet Coke. I glanced up at the clock. Only forty-seven hours to go.

We ate in the cozy breakfast room, chatting about the party as we passed around sections of the paper. We were discussing potential outings for the day when I heard my cell phone ringing from up in Peter's bedroom. Years of Winslow, Brown partners phoning at odd hours had instilled a Pavlovian response to that sound, and I jerked up automatically. But, as my mother frequently reminded me, it wasn't polite to take calls during a meal. That never dissuaded me in the presence of my own family, but while it was one thing to be impolite to my mother, it was another thing entirely to be impolite to somebody else's, particularly Peter's. I sat back down.

"Don't you want to get that?" Peter asked.

"It can wait," I said.

"What if it's work?" he asked.

"It can still wait," I said again. Officially, I was on vacation, having taken off the Friday and Monday surrounding the weekend, and I'd put in a superhuman effort before I left to make sure I was fully caught up on the deals and projects I had underway. Nobody from Winslow, Brown should be calling, but that didn't guarantee anything. People in my line of work adhered closely to the saying that time-is-money, and the partners tended to view my time as their money. Not a single one of my vacations had gone uninterrupted since I'd started at the firm.

"Are you sure, dear?" asked Susan.

"I'm sure," I said, resolute.

The ringing finally stopped, but a moment later Peter's own cell phone trilled from upstairs. He twitched. "Do you want to get that, honey?" his mother asked.

"If Rachel can wait, I can wait," he said stolidly.

Peter's phone had barely stopped ringing when mine started ringing again. Then his started ringing again, too.

"Somebody must really want to get a hold of you kids," commented Charles. We were all silent as we listened to the alternating rings from two floors above. I gripped the seat of my chair with both hands to keep myself at the table.

But no sooner had our cell phones stopped than the Forrests' home phone began to ring. "I'll get that," said Susan, just as both Peter's phone and my phone started up again. She reached for the extension on the wall with one hand and started clearing plates from the table with the other, and Charles rose to help her.

I took this as a cue the meal was over and rushed up the stairs to answer my phone, calling over my shoulder for them to leave the dishes to me. Normal future daughters-in-law probably delighted in post-meal cleanup.

I grabbed my BlackBerry a second after it stopped ringing. Peter was more successful, reaching his own phone just in time. He would undoubtedly attribute his success to hydration, even though I'd beaten him up the stairs.

"Hello? Oh, hi, Abigail," he said. "It's Abigail," he

mouthed to me, as if I couldn't figure that out from his greeting. Perhaps he thought caffeine withdrawal was impeding my mental processes. Based on how I was starting to feel, this wasn't entirely out of the question.

I began scrolling through my message log. There were several missed calls, some of which must have come through while we were out on Peter's little adventure in sadism. The most recent were from Luisa.

"Really?" Peter said into his phone. The way he said it, with a combination of curiosity, invitation, and amusement, made me look up. It was the gossipy tone of a morning-after debrief. "I can check with Rachel, but I'm pretty sure Luisa's not dating anyone."

I shook my head to confirm this was true. "Not since she and Isobel broke up last fall. Did something happen?" I asked excitedly, trying to keep my voice low so Abigail couldn't hear me. "With Abigail and Luisa?"

Peter covered the phone's mouthpiece with his hand. "She's not saying anything specific, but she wants the scoop." He took his hand away from the phone and spoke into it. "Luisa was in a relationship for a long time, but they broke up in the fall."

I enjoyed listening to Peter gossip like this—it was a side of him I didn't see often—and it was somehow comforting to know that a woman who looked like Abigail still needed reassurances before embarking on a new relationship. And now I also knew why Luisa had been trying to reach me. She probably wanted the lowdown on Abigail.

My phone rang again, and I consulted the caller ID. Sure enough, it was Luisa. I pressed a button to answer the call.

"Is there something you'd like to tell me, young lady?" I asked with mock severity.

"It's about time," said Luisa, her tone harried. "I've been trying to reach you for ages. It's important."

"Is it?" I asked, still teasing. It was rare for Luisa to be anything but perfectly composed, and I was savoring this unusual role reversal.

But I definitely wasn't expecting what she said next.

"It's Hilary. She's disappeared."

It took a moment for Luisa's words to sink in, but once they did, my response came easily.

"It wouldn't be the first time," I said, which was true. We'd initially been alarmed on those freshman-year mornings when we'd found Hilary's top bunk empty, but we soon grew accustomed to her showing up a day or two later with a satisfied look on her face, and a few days after that there would be yet another guy whose calls she wouldn't take.

"This is serious, Rachel."

"We are talking about Hilary, right?"

"I spoke to Ben. He said she left the party without him, but she's still not back, and he hasn't heard from her. I'm worried."

"Well, we know she was ready to break up with Ben. Maybe this was her way of doing it. Tact has never exactly been one of her strengths, and she and Iggie looked as if they were really hitting it off last night, bizarre as that might seem." Hilary was usually disciplined enough to make sure she was completely finished with one guy before she took up with another, but maybe she was getting less scrupulous about these matters now that we were over thirty. And while I'd thought she had been spending time with Iggie solely for the purposes of her story, perhaps he finally won her over. Stranger things had happened. Hilary had never cared much about money, but a billion dollars could go a long way in making the previously unthinkable thinkable.

"I know that—it was hard to miss them on the dance floor last night. But I tried her mobile, too, and it went right into voice mail, and you know she never lets anything stop her from taking a call, no matter where she is. And there's something else. Do you know if she tried to reach you?"

"I didn't see any calls or messages from her. Why?"

"This is what started me worrying in the first place. I have a strange text on my phone. It was sent shortly after midnight from a number I don't recognize, one with a San Francisco area code. I tried to call the number back, but it only rings and rings before going into an automated voice mail."

"So?" I still wasn't sure what all the fuss was about. "It was probably just somebody's mistake."

"I don't think it was a mistake, Rachel. The message says SOS."

"Oh," I said, the smile fading from my lips.

There are couples who have signals they use to communicate privately with each other in public venues. Fiddling with an earring could mean "I'm ready to leave" while adjusting a shirt cuff could be a warning to stay away from the salmon puffs. My friends and I developed a similar set of signals when we were in college, but SOS was the one we used most frequently. It was easy to form the letters in sign language with one hand by making a fist for the first S, opening the fist into a circle for the O, and then closing it again for the second S. This could be done discreetly, with your hand at your side or even, with enough practice, while holding a drink.

I'd found it to be an especially useful tool at social events when cornered by an ex-boyfriend or someone I would never want to be my boyfriend, ex or otherwise. I would give the signal, and soon one of my friends would arrive at my side, claiming an urgent need to speak to me privately. It might not have been terribly mature, but it was effective. Of course, usually Hilary had been the one doing the rescuing rather than requiring rescue; given her lack of adherence to social norms, she'd never had trouble extricating herself from uncomfortable situations without assistance. For her to use this signal at all was remarkable, and in the context of her unexplained absence, it was definitely cause for alarm.

"Did you check with Jane and Emma?" I asked. "Could one of them have sent it?"

"It would have been three in the morning on the East Coast, but I checked with them anyhow," said Luisa. "And they didn't know anything. So it had to be Hilary. Did you get anything similar?"

"Let me take a closer look at my messages," I told Luisa. I put the call on hold and started scrolling through the log again.

"What's wrong?" Peter asked. He'd ended his own call with Abigail and had picked up on my change in tone.

"I'm not sure yet," I told him, studying the BlackBerry screen. There were the several missed calls from Luisa beginning around nine-thirty. Under those, with a time stamp of twelve-nineteen, was a text message from an unfamiliar number with a San Francisco area code. I clicked it open.

"SO" it read.

That was it. Just the S and the O. As if its sender had been interrupted before she'd had a chance to finish what she wanted to say.

And when Hilary had something to say, she didn't leave it unsaid. At least, not by choice.

I flipped back to Luisa. "We'll be right there," I told her.

On the one hand, there had been some talk about mountain biking, so I was glad to have a valid reason to avoid yet another exercise-based outing. On the other hand, normal people didn't have friends who suddenly went missing, potentially in the company of velvet-clad Internet tycoons. If anything, those were the sort of friends with whom an idiosyncratic person would surround herself.

"It's no problem," Peter assured me. "We can go biking later. We'll just tell my parents we need to track Hilary down first."

"Maybe we shouldn't tell them about Hilary."

"Why not?"

"I wouldn't want them to worry unnecessarily," I said, which he seemed to accept, but mostly I didn't want to confide in him my concerns about not fitting in with his family. After all, normal people don't worry about not being normal.

I insisted we live up to my promise to do the dishes, so we hurriedly loaded the dishwasher before going out on the deck, where we found Susan doing the crossword puzzle and Charles reading a book in the watery sunlight that passed for summer in San Francisco. Spot, curled by Susan's feet, thumped his tail. Peter made our excuses about mountain biking, saying we were sore after the run—which was entirely true in my case—and had decided to catch up with friends instead.

"Is it all right to take the car?" he asked. The simple question made me feel as if we were teenagers up to something illicit, but his parents readily agreed without extracting any promises about not drinking and driving or reminders about curfews. There was some discussion of which hybrid to take, since the Forrests were a two-hybrid family, but that was easily resolved.

Susan turned to me. "Rachel, I think the Tiffany's in Union Square is open this afternoon. It might be fun to swing by later and get started on registering you two. What do you think?"

I thought Peter's family specifically and normal people more generally had peculiar ideas about what constituted fun. While I knew that brides-to-be were supposed to squeal with excitement over china patterns and place settings, I personally didn't see the appeal, nor had I ever been much of a squealer. However, that didn't seem to be the appropriate response. "Tiffany's does sound like fun," I said. Peter gave me yet another perplexed look, but I ignored him.

"How about three o'clock? Will that give you enough time with your friends?" Susan asked.

I certainly hoped so. If anyone was capable of getting herself into a deep fix, I was all too aware it was Hilary—she was uniquely skilled in this area. If we weren't able to find her within a few hours, I couldn't even begin to imagine what sort of trouble she might have encountered.

"That should give us plenty of time," I told Susan, trying to sound more confident than I felt. "We'll see you then."

"Are you sure?" asked Peter as he followed me out the door.

"About registering at Tiffany's or about finding Hilary by three o'clock?"

"Either. Both."

"As sure as I'll ever be," I said. Which turned out to be entirely true.

As Peter steered the Prius up one hill and down another, I tried the number from the text message, letting it ring well after most phones go into voice mail or disconnect. Eventually an automated voice came on, inviting me without enthusiasm to leave a message. I explained I was looking for Hilary and left my own number. Then I replied to the text message for good measure, sending along the same information.

Traffic was light, and we even found parking on Market Street right across from the entrance to the Four Seasons hotel. We took one elevator up to the main lobby and then another elevator up to Luisa's suite. She believed in traveling in style, and she had the wherewithal to support it, which worked out nicely for her. Ben and Hilary were staying in a more modest room at the same hotel, which would have been a stretch for a government employee and a journalist, but Hilary's magazine assignment was covering her travel expenses.

Luisa greeted us at the door, and I remembered belatedly that she wasn't even supposed to be here still. She'd mentioned the day before that her plane home was leaving at an "ungodly" hour, so she should have been gone long before she'd called to alert us to Hilary's missing status. "Didn't you have an early flight this morning?" I asked.

The question had barely left my mouth when something remarkable occurred: Luisa blushed.

I first met Luisa when we were seventeen, and in the years since, I'd seen her smile on occasion, look impassive often, raise one eyebrow frequently and cry just once. But I'd never seen her blush.

"Are you blushing?" I blurted out.

The flush tingeing her olive skin deepened. "Don't be ridiculous."

"I'm not being ridiculous. You're bright red. And you didn't answer my question. Why are you still here?" With Hilary gone, I seemed to have stepped into her role as the blunt one. It might also have had something to do with the increasingly unmistakable onset of caffeine withdrawal.

"I overslept and missed my flight," she said.

Not only did Luisa not blush, she didn't oversleep. Moreover, she hated feeling rushed in airports, so she insisted on arriving no less than two hours before the designated departure time of any flight she took. But she ignored my expression of disbelief and led us into the living room where Ben was already waiting.

Luisa may or may not have overslept, but Ben looked as

if he hadn't slept at all, and based on the way he'd been hitting the Scotch at the party, he probably was hungover, too. He gratefully accepted a bottle of ginger ale from the minibar, and Peter took Luisa up on her offer of a juice. She passed me a Diet Coke without asking, and, exercising tremendous self-control, I passed it back. "No thanks," I said, although my hand tingled where it had briefly touched the coolness of the can.

"What's wrong?" she asked.

"Nothing's wrong. I'm just not in the mood."

"You're never not in the mood."

"Well, you never oversleep," I snapped. Withdrawal was definitely setting in, and not only was it making me blunt, it was making me cranky to boot.

"I dared Rachel to go forty-eight hours without caffeine," Peter explained to Luisa.

"Which hour is it now?" she asked.

"We're in hour three," Peter said. "Only forty-five more to go."

"It's going to be a long forty-five hours," she said.

"I'm just beginning to appreciate that," he said. They shared a hearty chuckle.

"Could everyone stop talking about me like I'm not here and could we instead talk about the reason we're here, which is that Hilary's not?" I said. It was unclear to me why they should find my pain so hilarious.

"A very long forty-five hours," said Luisa to Peter. But she took a seat on the sofa next to Ben, and Peter and I sat down across from them.

We all turned to Ben. After all, not only was he Hilary's

boyfriend, however new and ill-fated that particular relationship might be, he was an FBI agent. We were fortunate to have a trained professional with us at a time like this—surely he would know exactly what to do. We could just sit back and follow his expert direction.

But Ben sat staring into space, absent-mindedly peeling the label from his bottle of ginger ale and apparently unaware of our eyes on him, much less our expectations. If we were waiting for expert direction from him, it looked as if we'd be in for quite a wait.

"So," I said, since Ben didn't, "when did everybody last see Hilary?" I wasn't an FBI agent, but I did watch a lot of crime shows on TV, and this seemed like a reasonable place to start.

"You and I saw her at the buffet around ten with Iggie," said Peter. "And then they sat down at a table with Caro and Alex. But I don't remember running into her after that."

"The last time I saw her was a little after eleven," said Luisa. "She was outside, dancing with Iggie."

"So we have her in the tent with Iggie at eleven. What about you, Ben? When did you last see her?" I asked.

"Huh?" he said, dragging his attention away from his soda label as I repeated the question. "Oh. At about the same time, I guess, dancing with Iggie. I went back inside, and then I looked for her around midnight, when the party was starting to wind down. I couldn't find her anywhere, and she didn't answer her cell. That's when I gave up and assumed she'd left without me."

It seemed undiplomatic to comment on that. "Which means she probably left between eleven, when she was last seen, and midnight, when you couldn't find her," I said instead. Ben nodded.

"When did you start thinking something might be wrong?" Peter asked him in a gentle tone. This had to be awkward for Ben—nobody could enjoy being ditched at a party by his significant other.

He ripped off a long strip of the label. "This morning, when Luisa called."

"You mean, you couldn't find her at the party, then she didn't show up all night, and you didn't think anything was wrong?" I asked. I tried to sound gentle, too, but withdrawal was wreaking havoc with my already limited interpersonal skills.

He shifted uncomfortably in his seat. "We broke up. At the party. Around ten-thirty."

We all tried to look surprised, but only Peter really succeeded. Luisa and I were too familiar with Hilary's history with the opposite sex to imagine much time would elapse before she acted on the feelings she'd expressed to us earlier in the evening. This breakup had been speedy even by Hilary's standards, but it was hardly unexpected, and it certainly explained Ben's passivity this morning.

"So that's why you didn't get too concerned when you couldn't find her," Peter said.

"Or when I didn't see her here. I ended up hitting a bar after the party." Ben gave a sheepish smile. "Drowning my sorrows, I guess. To be honest, I was pretty drunk when I got back, and I probably passed out more than went to sleep. And when I woke up and saw she still hadn't shown up or even left a message, I was pretty pissed."

"But then I called," prompted Luisa.

"I was on my way out the door to head to the airport, but you were so worried that I figured I'd take a later flight and stick around to see how I could help. I know Hilary has the room booked for a few more days."

That was nice of him, I thought. If I were in his shoes, I would have been on the first plane back to the East Coast. "Do you know if she stopped by the room at all?" I asked. "Before you got back, or maybe while you were sleeping? Are her things still there?"

"I took a look around after I spoke to Luisa, and her clothes and toiletries and stuff are where they were when we left for the party. But I did notice that her laptop was missing. And her notebook, too."

"Her laptop and her notebook are both gone?" said Luisa.

"Uh-huh."

Luisa and I exchanged a glance, and I knew we were thinking the same thing. This new piece of information went a long way to clearing everything up, but I wished Ben had mentioned it sooner. It would have saved us a lot of worrying.

"Iggie must have promised Hilary an interview," I said, telling Ben and Peter about her comments the previous night. "We know she was hoping for an exclusive for her article. She probably talked him into it at the party, and then they would have left together and stopped here at the hotel to pick up her gear."

Putting this together was a relief for more reasons than one: if Hilary was with Iggie, then she was unlikely to be in any real danger, and if she'd taken her laptop and notebook with her, then her interest in him had remained professional rather than personal. The notion of a Hilary-Iggie hookup was a hard one to stomach, a billion dollars notwithstanding.

"She likely went with Iggie of her own accord, but then perhaps he wouldn't let her come back, and that's when she texted us," added Luisa. "She's probably stranded at his house or wherever he took her. It wouldn't be easy to overpower her physically, but he might have managed to lock her in somewhere."

"Why wouldn't Iggie have let her come back?" asked Peter. "Would he really do something like that?"

Luisa shrugged, something else I'd seen her do far more than I'd seen her blush. "When Iggie's focused on a goal, he tends to forget about little things like whether or not his actions conform to generally accepted behavior. And remember, he has had a crush on Hilary for well over a decade. Maybe this is his way of acting on it?"

"Or it could be about her article," I said. "Maybe he didn't like whatever angle she was taking on Igobe, and he decided he would hang on to her until he could persuade her to change it. It seems extreme, but Iggie always did have a complicated relationship with reality."

"At least if she's with Iggie we don't have much to worry about," said Luisa. "I know Hilary wouldn't have sent the SOS unless she needed our help, but I can't picture Iggie doing anything particularly dangerous or evil. Can any of you?"

We couldn't, but although being reasonably confident of Iggie's relative harmlessness tempered the urgency we'd initially felt, neither Luisa nor I would be able to completely relax until we'd located Hilary and made sure she was all right.

"Why don't we just give Iggie a call?" Peter asked. "Or drop by his house?"

"I wish it were that easy," I said. "But Iggie's obsessed with privacy. I asked him for his home address when I wanted to send him the invitation for the engagement party, and instead I got a lecture about how he keeps his personal information personal. He wouldn't even give me a phone number or e-mail address. According to him, a guy with as much money as he has—even if most of it's only on paper at this point—has to worry about being a kidnapping target, not to mention the people hoping to hit him up for handouts. The only way I know how to reach him is through his office, but it will be closed for the weekend."

"What about the police?" asked Peter. "Can't they help us?"

Again, we all looked to Ben, and this time he seemed to be paying attention. He shook his head. "We can report Hilary missing, but I don't think it will do much good without proof her disappearance was coerced. She's an adult, and secret codes between old friends aren't likely to be cause for concern to anyone except us."

"And Hilary does have a tendency to strike out on her own without letting anybody know. It would be difficult to convince anyone that this time is different," said Luisa.

"I think we're stuck with trying to find them ourselves. Maybe we can retrace their steps from the party," I said.

"Well, if that's what we need to do, I can call the valet service my parents used last night," said Peter. "If Iggie and Hilary left together, somebody must have seen them—her dress was pretty memorable."

"What there was of it," said Luisa. She gestured to her own laptop resting on a side table. "Meanwhile, I'll log into our online alumni directory. Iggie wasn't the most popular person on campus, but he must have at least one friend left over from our class who would know how to reach him." Luisa cochaired the alumni giving campaign and had proven skilled at persuading our former classmates to cough up donations. I attributed her success, particularly with males, to the lasting impact of her freshman facebook photo combined with her phone voice, which was husky and still bore traces of an exotic accent.

"And while you're doing that, I'll go through Hil's things," I said. I turned to Ben. "We know she was doing research on Iggie and Igobe. She might have left something behind that will give us more information."

The rest of us springing into action seemed to finally energize Ben. "I can make a few calls to some colleagues. Somebody might be able to tap into a database and find out where Iggie lives—there has to be a record of it somewhere. And we could check the hotel's security cameras, too. They would have caught Hilary coming and going last night, and they might also confirm who was with her."

"So we have a plan," I said with satisfaction. I liked plans, and I hoped keeping busy would distract me from my cravings, which were growing more intense with every passing minute. "When should we get back together?"

"It's close to one now," said Luisa. "Three o'clock? But I'll call you if I find somebody who knows how to reach Iggie before then."

"Three sounds good," I started to say before remembering I had a previous engagement. "Actually, could we say four-thirty instead? In Union Square?"

"We can call my mother and postpone," Peter offered.

I considered this for a moment, tempted, but then I decided against it. Susan had seemed sufficiently excited about our planned outing that I wouldn't want to disappoint her, and I doubted ninety minutes one way or another would make much of a difference as far as Hilary was concerned. She was merely being inconvenienced rather than in any real peril—at least, that's what we thought then.

"Postpone what?" Luisa asked.

"We're supposed to meet my mother at Tiffany's to choose things for the wedding registry," Peter told her.

Luisa looked at me, amused. It was yet another expression I'd seen more often than a blush and one that appeared especially frequently when I was the topic of discussion. "You're going to register?" she asked. "You? The woman whose Realtor had to talk her out of buying an apartment without a kitchen? The woman who uses her oven to store her shoes? The woman who can order 'the usual' from every take-out place in Manhattan? The woman who—"

"Yes, me," I interrupted, only a little bit huffy.

"Well," she said. "We wouldn't want to get in the way of that."

Luisa was already online and searching our alumni directory as the rest of us left the suite and took the elevator down to the room where Ben and Hilary were staying. Ben looked up at the paneled ceiling of the elevator and at the mirror on its back wall as we moved between floors. "There's probably a camera hidden in here somewhere," he said, "maybe behind the mirror. The tape from last night should have captured anyone who got off on our floor."

I would never have thought of that on my own, and although I knew there were security cameras in a lot of public facilities, it was creepy to consider just how pervasive they were. I recognized they could be useful in combating crime and thwarting terrorism, and I was all for combating and thwarting such nefarious activities, but I couldn't help but wonder how many times I'd embarrassed myself on camera without realizing someone was watching. It was a reminder of why Iggie's company was so successful—even if you weren't doing anything wrong, there was something comforting in knowing nobody else knew what you were up to.

Ben had left the Do Not Disturb sign dangling from the doorknob. He inserted his keycard into the lock, but he paused before opening the door. "I should warn you. It's sort of chaotic in here."

"I know what to expect," I assured him, "and I know it's not your fault." Hilary never did anything halfway, and that included making a mess. In college, this had been a convenient way for her to ensure she would be awarded the first available single bedroom in any of our living quarters, and apparently she'd seen no reason to change her habits since then. It looked as if her suitcase had exploded over the room's otherwise sleek interior. A neat roller-bag standing in the corner was Ben's, but every other surface was strewn with Hilary's belongings.

Peter's expression upon entering the room combined horror and awe. "Are you sure nobody's ransacked the place?"

"Nope, this is standard. In fact," I said, "it's pretty tame. She clearly hasn't been here long enough to settle in."

"I wouldn't know where to begin," he said, "so maybe I'll just leave you to it."

"Coward," I said.

"Yep," he agreed good-naturedly, picking his way across the cluttered floor. He leaned against the window, took out his cell phone and dialed.

"Can you get reception in here?" asked Ben. "I couldn't."

"It seems to be going through," Peter told him.

"Must be my carrier," said Ben, taking a seat on the bed and picking up the phone on the nightstand. A moment later, Peter was asking his mother about the valet service from the party and Ben was asking to speak to hotel security.

I began sorting through Hilary's things. Unfortunately, the easiest way to do this was to pick each item up and put it away in a more orderly fashion so I could catalog what was there and what wasn't. I examined each piece of clothing before draping it over the back of the desk chair, seeing nothing but the usual assortment of jeans and tops along with a few more formal outfits and finding nothing in her pockets except a jumble of gum wrappers, coins and receipts. There were a couple of books on the desk—an account of the late Nineties' dot-com boom and bust, which was probably background for her article, and a history of jazz which I guessed was Hilary's somewhat disturbing idea of pleasure reading—but, as Ben had said, no laptop and no notebook.

Of course, the dresser drawers were completely empty, as it would never have occurred to Hilary to actually use them for storage when the floor worked so well for her. I opened the closet door, but there I found only a folded luggage rack leaning against one wall, dangling hangers, the plush terry robes provided by the hotel and extra pillows on a high shelf. The only other items in the closet were an iron and an ironing board, but I was confident Hilary wouldn't have thought to even touch either of those—her domestic skills were nearly as limited as my own, and her taste in clothes ran to fabrics of the clinging but nonwrinkling variety.

I moved on to the bathroom. Hilary wore her hair short

and limited her cosmetics regimen to the liberal application of brilliant red lipstick, but she was always experimenting with different skin lotions and creams. I lined up the bottles and tubes on the vanity, but I saw nothing out of the ordinary, although I did sample an absurdly expensive eye cream I'd seen advertised in a magazine. The ad guaranteed an immediate and dramatic reduction in dark under-eye circles, so I patted in the recommended pea-sized dollop below each eye and then stared at my face in the magnifying mirror, waiting for the reduction to begin. After thirty seconds, nothing had happened, and seeing my pores blown up several times their actual size was too troubling to watch any longer. Then I sampled Hilary's lipstick, to see if the bright color would distract from my under-eye circles, but that didn't seem to help, either, and the red clashed miserably with my own red hair.

Sighing, I used a tissue to wipe my lips clean and turned to head back into the bedroom. If there were useful clues to Hilary's whereabouts anywhere to be found, the anywhere didn't seem to be in the hotel room.

But then I spotted Hilary's jewelry pouch, partially buried under a hand towel. It was a flat-bottomed drawstring bag made of patterned silk, gaping open to reveal a tangle of earrings, necklaces, and bracelets. "Aha," I said, to myself, since I could still hear both Peter and Ben talking on their respective phones in the other room.

I had a jewelry pouch that was nearly identical except for the pattern of the silk—Hilary had bought several of them in Thailand years ago and given them to her friends as gifts. The silk was pretty, and the pouches were useful, but she was mostly excited by a special feature each had: a fake bottom that could be pried out to reveal a small secret compartment below. Of course, with the exception of the occasional murder, my life was too dull to have much call for secret compartments, but perhaps Hilary had made use of hers.

I spilled the jewelry out onto the marble counter and tried to work a fingernail into the inner seam where the silk-covered cardboard at the bottom met the edge of the bag. Unfortunately, this was a job for a long tapered fingernail rather than the sort of fingernails I had. I rummaged through the items on the vanity but found nothing suitable until I saw the small sewing kit supplied by the hotel. I would never have used any of its contents to actually sew—such matters were better left in the hands of those less accident-prone than myself—but the kit included a needle that worked perfectly to pry open the false bottom. It lifted out easily to reveal the compartment below, and nestled within was a piece of folded ivory paper. "Aha," I said again, pleased with my success.

"What have you got?" asked a voice behind me.

I nearly screamed but managed to strangle the noise to a muted yelp. I'd been so absorbed in the task and so busy congratulating myself on my cleverness that I hadn't heard Ben come in or even glimpsed his image reflected next to mine in the mirror. "I didn't realize you were here," I said, recovering with an embarrassed laugh. "You scared me."

"Sorry about that."

"No problem," I said, although my heart was still racing. I showed him the jewelry pouch and its false bottom before withdrawing and unfolding the piece of paper.

It was a receipt, on Four Seasons letterhead, dated two days earlier and made out to Hilary for an item she'd left in the hotel safe.

The obvious next step was to retrieve whatever it was Hilary had considered sufficiently important to require such high-security treatment. However, it was unclear whether the hotel would release the safe's contents only to Hilary. I could try to impersonate her, but that wouldn't work if I was asked for identification. Even if we did have her driver's license, and even if a short blond wig and green contact lenses had been readily available, Hilary was more than a half-foot taller than me, and there wasn't any practical way for me to impersonate that.

We discussed calling downstairs to ask about the procedure for redeeming an item from the safe so we could plan accordingly, but we quickly discarded that idea. It would only make the staff think twice when someone actually showed up a few minutes later to redeem something from the safe. Nor, for similar reasons, did we call to ask if the same staff members were on duty as on Friday. Instead we decided to brazen it out and headed for the lobby. If I was asked for ID, we would try to talk our way through any challenge with Ben's identification since he was registered to the same hotel room.

Peter hung back as Ben and I approached the woman behind the front desk. Her hair was pulled into an elegant knot at the nape of her neck, and a tag on her suit jacket lapel told us her name was Natasha. I resisted the urge to make any Rocky and Bullwinkle jokes and rested the hand holding Ben's room key and the receipt on the counter with what I hoped was a proprietary air. "Hi," I said. "We need to pick up something we left in the safe."

"Of course," Natasha said smoothly. "You have the receipt?"

"Of course," I answered, equally smoothly. I handed her the piece of paper and prepared myself to lie about not having any identification with me. But the good news was Natasha didn't ask for it. Instead, she led us to a discreet side door and used a pass to buzz us into an interior room.

At which point we encountered the bad news. Instead of a big vault of the sort you see in movies about bank heists, there were several rows of small safes mounted on a wall. Each of the safes had a digital keypad for a password the guest could set his or herself. And Hilary hadn't bothered to write down her chosen password and leave it with the receipt in the secret compartment, which I considered a serious lapse in planning for the possibility that her friends might need to rescue her from a billionaire with personal-boundary issues.

"Here you are," Natasha said, checking a number on the receipt and indicating one of the safes about halfway down the row second from the top.

"Could we have a moment alone?" I asked her. In the movies, they always left people alone with their safe deposit boxes when they went to retrieve their Nazi artifacts, incriminating documents or unmarked bills from Swiss banks.

Natasha didn't seem to expect that—I guessed most people just entered their passwords, collected their things and left—but she agreed readily enough. The door closed behind her with a soft click.

We looked around the room. The hotel's management

had posted a notice outlining its policy for items left in the safes on the wall to one side. They'd also posted instructions for setting passwords for the safes, advising users to choose a code consisting of between four and six numerals.

"Do you have any idea what her password could be?" I asked Ben.

"No," he said. "I didn't even know she locked anything up in the first place. Why would I know her password?"

Because you're her boyfriend, I started to say, but I managed to catch myself before the words left my head and came out of my mouth.

I turned and contemplated the keypad on the safe Natasha had indicated, wracking my brain for memories of Hilary at the ATM, Hilary at the computer, or Hilary doing anything else that would have required her to enter a personal code, but nothing came immediately to mind. I ran through the usual sorts of considerations that guide people's password choices, but Hilary hadn't lived in the same place for more than a few months at a time since we'd graduated, she didn't have any pets, and she had never cared much about birthdays—in fact, she'd been twenty-nine for several years now. Her twin passions were work and men, and these two interests tended to occupy the majority of her waking hours.

While this line of thinking didn't offer any brilliant insights, thinking about Hilary's passions and her interest in men, specifically, did remind me of last night's conversation about *Party of Five*. Which gave me an idea.

"Okay," I said, taking a deep breath. "Here goes."

I punched in five numbers and pressed the pound key. There was a pause, and I waited for an alarm to blare out and for Natasha to come running, armed with a stun gun or something like that. Instead, a small light flashed green and the word "*OPEN*" appeared on the screen above the keypad.

I breathed out with surprise and relief. I really hadn't expected that to work.

"What was the password?" Ben asked.

"It's 9-0-2-1-0," I said.

"What's that?"

"Dylan's zip code." Ben looked confused, but this was no time to explain Hilary's long-standing crush on Luke Perry in his career-defining role—he probably wouldn't appreciate that the only guy ever to hold her interest on a sustained basis was a figment of Darren Star's imagination. I twisted the latch and opened the door to the safe.

Inside, zipped into a clear plastic bag, were two items: a pen and a photograph.

"Everything all right in here?" asked Natasha, poking her head through the door.

"Everything's great," I said. I withdrew the bag and slipped it into my purse, and we followed her out of the room.

Peter, Ben, and I huddled on one of the sofas in the lobby, studying the photograph. It was of three people in their mid-to-late twenties, two men and a woman, standing on steps that led up to the columned portico of a stone building. The man in the center we all recognized easily—it was Iggie, back in the days when he still wore thick glasses, cut his own hair, and dressed without the assistance of an overly adventurous stylist.

The Lasik and the professional haircut were definitely an improvement, but I was less sanguine about his updated wardrobe.

"That's probably Biggie on the left," I said, then explained to Ben about Iggie's ex-wife and Caro's and Alex's comments the previous night. The image in the photo matched their description perfectly: a heavyset woman with big brown eyes and masses of brown hair shielding much of her face.

"The building behind them looks sort of familiar, too," said Peter. "I can't quite place it, but I think I've seen it before."

But none of us recognized the person standing to the right of Iggie, a bulky but relatively nondescript guy with nearly as much hair as Biggie, and there were no helpful names or dates written on the back of the picture to indicate who he might be.

"So what does this mean?" asked Ben.

For an FBI agent—essentially a professional investigator—sometimes he seemed a little slow to connect the dots, I thought. But then I admonished myself. My withdrawal was making me uncharitable, as well as blunt and cranky, and Ben was not only hungover, he had just gotten dumped. I reminded myself again that a lesser person would have washed his hands of the matter and hightailed it home.

"That Hilary put an old picture of Iggie and his ex-wife in a safe?" I said. "Probably that she thought there was a juicy story about them. And maybe it involved the other guy in the picture, too. And maybe she started asking Iggie about whatever she thought the story was, and he was happier letting sleeping dogs lie. At least, that's my theory." I slipped the photo back into the plastic bag for safekeeping and started to return the bag to my purse.

"Wait," said Peter. "What about the pen?"

"What about it? It's just a pen." It was a metallic color and a bit thicker than usual, but without a brand name or any other markings. While it was a step up from a disposable ballpoint, it was hardly a Mont Blanc, or even a Sharpie. I'd removed the cap and even checked that it wrote with ink and not some sort of magic clue-revealing substance, but as far as I could tell that was the extent of its usefulness.

"Then why would Hilary put it in the safe, Columbo?" he asked, reaching over and taking it out of the bag.

"Did you really just call me Columbo?"

But Peter didn't respond. He weighed the pen's heft in one hand and examined each end. Then he smiled. "I think it's more than a pen," he said. He pulled at its non-writing end, and it came off in his hand, revealing a short metal prong. "Voilà."

"What is it?" I asked. "A weapon? Does it shoot darts or squirt poison or something?"

"No, but sometimes it scares me to think about how your mind works. This is even better than a poison-squirting pen. It's a memory stick," he said.

"How is that better?" I asked, disappointed.

"There could be anything on it," Peter said. He pointed to the prong. "See, this is where it plugs into a USB port. Hilary could have copied the entire hard drive of her laptop onto here, practically. Documents, pictures, videos—anything. And whatever's on here, Hilary clearly felt it was important enough to make sure she kept it locked up."

"Oh," I said, considering the possibilities with growing

enthusiasm. "Could we attach it to Luisa's computer and see what's on it?"

"That should work," said Peter.

"Perfect," I said. "Let's go back upstairs."

"Um, it's already two-thirty," said Ben.

"So?" I said.

"So?" echoed Peter.

And then I remembered. "So we're supposed to meet your mother in half an hour," I said, glancing at my watch. My heart sank. Finding out what was on the memory stick sounded a lot more interesting than shopping for place settings, not that that was such a high bar. Just about anything had to be more interesting than shopping for place settings.

"Are you sure you don't want to reschedule?" Peter asked me again. "My mom will understand."

"She's not going to have to," I said. Even if I'd been willing to tell Susan about Hilary's disappearance, it didn't seem justified. After all, we still didn't have any reason to think she wasn't with Iggie, or that Iggie could pose a serious threat. The interruption wouldn't take that long, and now that I was normal, I had to make the normal choice, which was to meet my future mother-in-law, as promised, at Tiffany's.

With admirable restraint, I took the pen-memory stick from Peter and handed it to Ben. "Will you give this to Luisa to check out on her computer?"

"Okay," he said. "And I'll see if I can take a look at the tape from the surveillance cameras, too. I told the security guys I'd stop by their control center."

"Thanks," I said, although I almost wished he hadn't

mentioned the tape, because it only reminded me of something else that would be far more interesting than shopping for place settings. "We'll meet you at four-thirty."

I took Peter's arm and steered him toward the elevator before my willpower could run out.

Union Square was close enough that we walked the few short blocks, leaving the Prius on Market Street. In fact, we arrived at Tiffany's early, which only added to my frustration. We probably would have had plenty of time to check out whatever was on the memory stick ourselves instead of leaving it to Ben and Luisa.

At least I had the opportunity to impress Susan with my punctuality, as she was early, too. We found her in the crystal department with a saleswoman named Marge who introduced herself as our "registry consultant." They were deep in discussion of the relative merits of different stemware brands and designs. I'd never actually used the word *stemware* before, nor had it occurred to me to have opinions about it, but looking at the array of goblets and tumblers mostly just made me think how much nicer they'd look if they were filled with Diet Coke.

"Rachel, dear, how would you describe your taste?" asked Susan.

"Traditional?" asked Marge. "Contemporary?

Usually I just trusted the bartender to choose the glass he or she thought most appropriate for whatever drink I ordered—I never specified traditional or contemporary. "Um, well, uh, gee," I said, searching for words. I turned to Peter, who was the person who actually cooked and poured beverages on those isolated occasions when cooking and pouring beverages occurred in our apartment. "What do you think?"

He shrugged. "Whatever you want is fine by me." Then his phone rang and he pulled it from his pocket and checked the screen. "It's the valet service calling me back—I should take this." He wandered off with the phone, leaving me alone with his mother, Marge and several-hundred stemware options, which seemed horribly unfair, at best.

It quickly became clear I wasn't ready to make firm decisions about stemware just yet, nor was I ready to make firm decisions about casual china, fine china, flatware or even table linens. However, I did learn that my tastes defied conventional description. I was pretty sure I overheard Marge describing them as "all over the map" to one of her colleagues, and it didn't sound as if she meant it as a compliment. Apparently most brides-to-be came into the store better prepared than I, having already studied these matters extensively.

Susan seemed to take my indecision in stride. In fact, she seemed to misinterpret it as my savoring the process. "You're right, dear," she said. "This is too much fun to rush through on our first trip." There was something ominous about hearing this outing described as if it were merely the beginning of a long series of similar outings, but I tried not to think about that. We left the store loaded down with catalogs, Peter trailing behind us, still on his phone.

I was relieved to note that not choosing anything for the registry hadn't taken very long—it was barely four o'clock. Peter and I would be well ahead of schedule to meet up with Luisa and Ben. I was opening my mouth to thank Susan for her help when she opened her own mouth. "Saks is right here," she said. "What do you think, Rachel? Do you want to take a quick spin inside and see what they have? I could use a few fresh things for summer."

Given that summer in San Francisco seemed to call for the sort of clothing most people wore on Arctic expeditions, I had difficulty seeing how Saks would be the best place to find what she needed, but she was eager to continue shopping. I looked to Peter for help, but he didn't even notice, intent on his ongoing cell-phone conversation. "Sure," I said, summoning up a smile that I hoped appeared as eager as Susan's.

She linked her arm through mine. "This is such fun. I can't tell you how many times I've wished I had a daughter to do girlie stuff with." Peter had two older brothers, and they were both married, but one lived in London and one lived in Hong Kong—I guessed their wives didn't afford Susan much in the way of regular daughterly companionship. Nor did I have the heart to warn her just how unfulfilling I was likely to be on the girlie front. I might not be able to describe my tastes in stemware, but I was fairly confident my tastes in apparel did not run to the girlie.

When Susan had said she could use a few fresh things for summer, she apparently had meant I could use a few fresh things for summer. Fifteen minutes later I was in a dressing room with an assortment of items she believed would look adorable on me. One would expect that someone like her, a respected attorney with a thriving local practice, would favor the tailored and professional, but everything she'd picked was either pastel or flowered, and several of her choices were both. I personally preferred black—it went with everything, which meant I never had to worry about my outfit clashing with the scenery, much less my hair, but I hadn't wanted to rain on Susan's shopping parade.

Unable to decide which pastel-flowered item to try on first, I closed my eyes, spun around once, and selected the first thing my hand touched, which turned out to be the pair of jeans I'd worn into the store. This was clearly an omen, but suppressing that thought I repeated the eyes-closed, spinning-around selection process. This time my hand landed on a pink sheath, nearly identical to the dress Caro Vail had worn the previous night and perfect for a tennis-playing blonde. I sighed and shimmied into it, all too aware that I wasn't blond and that I sucked at tennis and all other activities requiring eye-hand coordination. Then I opened the dressing room door so Susan could see.

"I love it!" she cried, clapping her hands together. "Do you love it?"

I looked around for Peter. He was near the center escalators, still on his phone, but he saw me trying to catch his eye and gave a distracted smile and wave.

"See? Peter loves it, too," said Susan.

She insisted on paying for the dress, signing the credit-card slip with a happy flourish that gave me a bad feeling about what would surely come next. "Now, we need to get you some shoes you can wear with that dress, dear," she said. A pink dress was bad enough, but pink shoes were more than I could have dreaded. However, within twenty minutes a sales clerk was busily wrapping up my very own pair. All of my efforts to act like the perfect future daughter-in-law had resulted in my future mother-in-law dressing me up like a bridesmaid.

This was probably ironic on some level, but I was too conscious of being late to meet Ben and Luisa and too badly in need of a Diet Coke to figure out how. My head was pounding and my hands had started to twitch. I was rooting through my purse, hoping in vain that I'd stashed some Advil in there, when the photo of Iggie, Biggie and person-unknown fell out onto the sales counter.

Susan got to it before I did. "Here you go, dear," she said, handing it to me, but then she paused, looking at the picture. "What a small world," she said. "How do you know Leo?"

"Leo?"

"Leo. Here." She pointed to the guy standing to the right of Iggie.

"I don't know him, actually. The person in the middle is someone I know from college, Iggie Berhrenz. He was at the party last night."

Fortunately, Susan didn't ask why I was carrying around a picture of Iggie, as that would have been hard to explain, nor did she think it strange when I asked if she knew Leo's last name.

"Now, what was it?" she mused. "I may have forgotten, but I'm not sure if I ever knew it. He was always just Leo."

"Then how did you know his first name?" asked Peter, who had reappeared at my side far too late to intercede in Susan's purchases on my behalf.

"From Berkeley," she said, pointing at the building in the background. "That's Sproul Hall, on the U.C. Berkeley campus. Remember when I taught a seminar at the law school there, a few years back? Leo was one of the graduate students who worked in tech support. You know, helping faculty when they had computer problems. He could fix anything, and he was always so nice about it. Once, he stayed up all night helping me recover a lost file, and he refused to let me pay him anything extra for his time. And he's a friend of your friend. What a small world," she repeated in wonder.

It wasn't that small. After all, Iggie and his ex-wife had gone to graduate school at Berkeley, as well. But at least we now could put part of a name to the unidentified face, and it shouldn't prove too hard to find out the rest of the name, or, I hoped, to track down its owner and ask him why he thought Hilary had felt it necessary to stash the picture in such a top-secret locale. He might even know where we could find Iggie. All we had to do was check with the university and ask them about former graduate students named Leo who had worked in tech support and helped visiting law-school instructors. With a name like Leo, it would be easy, I thought, pleased.

My pleasure was almost enough to blot out any concerns about just where Peter's mother thought I'd be wearing my pink dress and matching shoes.

We said goodbye to Susan outside Saks after agreeing to meet for an early dinner in Chinatown. She offered to take the shopping bags home, which was nice of her, but it also meant I wouldn't have the opportunity to accidentally allow my new outfit to be crushed under a passing cable car.

"Thank you for standing idly by while your mother dressed me up like Bridesmaid Barbie," I said to Peter as we waited to cross Post Street.

"I thought you looked cute," he said, putting his arm around my shoulders. "The pink is amazing with your hair."

I found his utter cluelessness about such matters to be part of his charm, so I didn't bother to debate this with him. "What were all those phone calls?" I asked.

"The valet service tracked down the guys who parked cars at the party last night and had them get in touch with me.

There were three in total—high-school kids who work for the service on weekends."

"Did any of them remember Hilary?"

"Did I mention they were in high school? They all remembered Hilary. She's the living incarnation of adolescent male fantasy."

"I'm sure there were posters of women just like her decorating the walls at your frat house," I said.

"It wasn't that sort of fraternity," he protested. "In fact, we were pretty nerdy. And why are you so surprised I was in a fraternity?" The light finally changed, and we hurried across the street.

Because fraternities are so normal, I thought but didn't say, nor did I say I shouldn't be surprised given how normal everything else was about him and his family. "Was there a matching sorority?" I asked instead. "Where people wore a lot of pink?"

"Caro's sorority was sort of like a sister sorority. And Caro likes to wear pink. So, yes, I guess there was a matching sorority where people wore a lot of pink."

A mental picture of a sorority house filled with pastel-clad triathletes flashed before my eyes. I gave silent thanks that I'd lacked the spirit of adventure applying to a college in California would have required before returning to the matter at hand. "So what did the male adolescents have to say?"

"Ben and Luisa are right over there," Peter said, pointing them out in line at a coffee cart. "Why don't I wait and tell you all at the same time?"

The four of us purchased beverages and found a table on the plaza. It was a pleasant spot, especially during those fleeting moments when the sun managed to break through the clouds, and a breeze carried the faint notes of a saxophone accompanied by the occasional clang of a cable car's bell or a barking dog. My seat faced directly onto the statue at the plaza's center, a woman doing an arabesque atop a Corinthian column. She looked energetic and healthful, as if she hadn't been deprived of vital carbonated and artificially sweetened cola refreshment. I, on the other hand, had the Rice-a-Roni theme song running through my head, courtesy of the cable cars, and was trying to make do with seltzer, which was doing nothing to relieve my withdrawal symptoms.

"This is a useless drink," I said, jabbing at the ice in my plastic cup with a straw.

"Only forty-one hours left," said Peter, his tone encouraging.

"You forfeited your right to comment when you let your mother trick me out like a prom queen," I said to him.

"I thought it was Bridesmaid Barbie," he said.

"The two are hardly mutually exclusive," I said.

Luisa giggled.

I looked up, startled. Giggling was as unprecedented as blushing. "Did you just giggle?" I asked her.

"What can I say? It's funny." She pulled her cigarette case and lighter out of her handbag.

"I'm glad you're taking such pleasure in my suffering," I said.

"Who wants to debrief first?" asked Peter, wisely steering the conversation onto a more productive path. "Luisa, how about you? Did you find a way to reach Iggie?"

She shook her head. "I had no idea he was such a man of mystery. First I left messages at Igobe, and I even tried to send a couple of e-mails to obvious addresses like Iggie@Igobe.com and TheIgster@Igobe.com, but they bounced right back. Then I must have made calls to two dozen of our classmates, including everyone who lived on our hallway sophomore year, but even his old roommates didn't know how to find him. They haven't heard from him since college, and one of them is still harboring quite the grudge—I got an earful about how Iggie borrowed his autographed picture of Bill Gates and never returned it."

"Bill Gates? As in the guy who founded Microsoft? That Bill Gates?" asked Ben, who had been silently sipping his latte up until now.

I nodded. "Iggie always used to wonder if he should bother sticking around until graduation. He said he already knew more than most of the professors and Bill Gates dropped out of college and did just fine without a degree. If you haven't gathered as much by now, Iggie was never the sort to be paralyzed by self-doubt."

"He was absolutely confident that he would eventually be as successful—if not more so—as Bill Gates or Steve Jobs or any of the other technology moguls," added Luisa. "And this was even before the Google guys or any of the other more recent Internet billionaires."

"So was that it?" Peter asked her. "Nobody knows where he is or how to reach him, but his old roommate wants his Bill Gates picture back?"

"I do have one potential lead," Luisa said, taking a cigarette out of her engraved case and tapping its end on the table. "Somebody mentioned she may know a way to get in touch with him. I'm going to follow up with her later."

"Who's that?" I asked. "Someone from college?"

"No, just a friend." She busied herself with her silver lighter.

"Which friend?" I asked. I'd seen Luisa light cigarettes on countless occasions, and it had never required such concentration.

"Just a friend," she repeated, finally releasing a lick of flame from the lighter and touching it to the tip of the cigarette.

It was unlike her to be evasive, but perhaps being evasive went with the blushing and giggling. And my withdrawal hadn't completely compromised my powers of deductive reasoning. Putting together the blushing and giggling with the phone call Peter had fielded that morning indicated with abundant clarity that the "friend" in question was almost certainly Abigail—not that I had any idea as to why Abigail thought she could locate Iggie when nobody else could. It was also abundantly clear that Luisa hadn't "overslept" on her own.

I was about to ask her who she thought she was fooling with her coy references when her phone rang. She dug hastily into her bag to retrieve it and checked the caller ID. "I'll just be a minute," she said, jumping up. "Hi," she said into the phone, her voice practically giddy. She walked toward the far side of the statue, but even at a distance I could see her cheeks redden.

I didn't know what to think of anybody anymore. Fearsome, fearless Hilary was sending out distress signals and cynical, self-contained Luisa was behaving like a love-struck teenager. And I was supposed to make sense of it all without caffeine. It didn't seem fair, but it did prove to me how far I'd come. I was definitely normal compared to the two of them.

I turned to Ben. "What about you, Ben? Did you get a chance to check out the security tapes?"

He nodded. "I spent the last couple of hours reviewing the footage from the different cameras."

"How did you convince hotel security to give you access?" asked Peter. "Did you show them your FBI identification?"

Ben took another sip of his latte. "Uh, well, yeah. But I guess they took pity on me, too."

"Why's that?" I asked.

"I told them my girlfriend was cheating on me and I needed to prove it."

That excuse must have been close enough to the truth to be embarrassing. Ben might be a bit slow sometimes, but he was really taking one for the team, I thought with growing respect. It was too bad Hilary couldn't see how he was coming through for her. Maybe she'd rethink the potential for their relationship.

Luisa rejoined us, lowering herself into her seat and stowing her phone in her purse. Her cheeks were still flushed. "Where were we?" she asked with a bright smile.

"Ben was telling us about the security tape," Peter told her.

"How's your *friend?*" I asked.

"Did you see Hilary with Iggie?" Luisa asked Ben, ignoring my question and busying herself with lighting another cigarette.

"No, just Hilary," Ben said. "She came in on her own a little before midnight. One of the cameras caught her at the lower lobby entrance. Another caught her going up in the elevator from the main lobby and getting off on our floor, and then another caught her getting into a different elevator a minute or two later with her laptop and notebook.

And then the camera for the lower lobby showed her leaving. But I didn't see Iggie in any of the footage."

"Well, she definitely left the party with him," said Peter. "One of the kids who works for the valet service remembered them leaving, and not just because of Hilary's dress. Iggie's driving a Lamborghini these days."

Luisa whistled, which I assumed meant a Lamborghini was impressive. She felt about cars the way Hilary felt about Luke Perry.

"The crazy thing is, Iggie wasn't the only one—somebody else at the party was driving the exact same make and model," said Peter. "The kid couldn't remember who. He only remembered Iggie because he was with Hilary, and he couldn't understand what someone like her would be doing with a guy like him. He also said Iggie tipped him with a hundred-dollar bill and told him to buy Igobe stock when it goes public."

"So we've confirmed that Hilary left with Iggie and then went to the hotel to get her laptop and notebook, just like we thought. Did you see anything else of interest on the security tape?" I asked Ben.

"A couple of things, but I don't know if they're relevant. Somebody else from the party came and went about fifteen minutes after Hilary—going up to the same floor and then leaving a few minutes after that. I didn't actually meet him at the party, but I have a good memory for faces, and I'm pretty sure it was the same guy."

"What did he look like?" I asked.

"About our age. Medium height, brown hair, wire-rimmed glasses. Sort of an average-looking preppie in a blazer and khakis."

Ben's words were almost exactly the same as those I'd used to describe Alex Cutler to myself. "That sounds like your friend Alex," I said to Peter.

"True," he said. "But it also sounds like half the guys in the Bay area. And what would Alex be doing going in and out of the Four Seasons at midnight?"

"What else did you see?" Luisa asked Ben. "You said there were a couple of interesting things."

Ben grinned, the first full-on smile I'd seen from him this weekend. "I'm not sure you want me to say."

"What do you mean?" asked Luisa.

"Well, I saw you."

"Oh," she said, with dawning realization. Her blush had begun to subside, but Ben's words seemed to reignite it.

"The security guards were pretty psyched," said Ben. "They wanted to rewind the tape and watch it again."

"Oh," repeated Luisa, her cheeks reddening even more.

"Oh?" I asked.

"Who wants to know what was on the memory stick?" she said.

"Who wants to change the subject?" I asked.

"What was on the memory stick?" asked Peter, coming to Luisa's rescue.

Luisa flashed him a grateful look. "Two files," she said. "I think the first is encrypted somehow—no matter which program I used to open it, all I ended up with was a bunch of ones and zeros."

"I can check that out later," said Peter. "I might be able to figure out how to decrypt it. What was the other file?"

"That one's text—a beginning draft of Hilary's article,"

she said. "And it looks as if she definitely intended to focus on Iggie's company. There was only the title and an opening paragraph, but what little she'd written is all about him and Igobe, and it's quite provocative."

"Provocative?" asked Peter. "How?"

"Does she say anything about Iggie's wardrobe? Or about how he calls himself the Igster?" I asked.

"I think the working title says it all. Ready for this?" We waited expectantly as she exhaled a stream of smoke. "'Igobe: Naked Emperor 2.0?'"

"Question mark included?" I asked. She nodded.

"'Naked Emperor 2.0?' What's that supposed to mean?" asked Ben.

"I would guess it's a reference to 'the emperor has no clothes,'" said Luisa, omitting the "obviously" with which I would have started my own response to that question.

"And it's a play on Web 2.0, which is how people are referring to the most recent wave of Internet companies," I added. "What does the rest of it say?"

"As I said, it's only the first paragraph, but it makes clear from the outset that she thinks there's more spin than substance where Iggie and Igobe are concerned," said Luisa.

"He won't like that," I said.

"No, he won't like that at all," she said.

"If his ego is everything you two have said," added Peter, "he especially won't like that being printed in a national magazine."

"It's not just his ego," I pointed out. "Negative press could make it difficult for Igobe to sell shares to the public at the high prices people are talking about. Which means Iggie won't be a billionaire, and his investors won't be able to recoup their investments with astronomical profits. The markets are still skittish about Internet companies after the dot-com bust—investors tend to flee from anything even the slightest bit questionable." And getting Winslow, Brown involved in an unsuccessful IPO could be a career-limiting move, but I kept that thought to myself.

Ben started to say something then, but his words were drowned out by an exhilarated whoop from behind us.

We all turned to look as a girl on a skateboard launched herself off the top of the granite steps on the north side of the plaza. Her feet separated from the board as she soared into space, tucking her body into a ball and somersaulting in midair. I watched with a mixture of wonder and horror, certain we were a split second away from seeing her smash headfirst onto the pavement.

But the board landed with a clatter at the bottom of the steps, and she landed lightly on top of it, and together they hurtled our way at maximum velocity. Just when I thought she would collide with our table, she flipped the skateboard out from under her feet and caught it neatly with one hand, alighting right next to my chair.

"Are you Rachel Benjamin?" she asked me, not the least bit winded.

I nodded, too stunned to speak.

"Some old dude gave me twenty bucks to give you this." She tossed a small package onto the table.

And then she sped off, across the square and out of sight.

While the rest of us were still gawking after Skater Girl, Peter sprang to his feet and sprinted in the direction from which she'd come, bounding up the stone steps as if he hadn't already done more of a workout today than most people did over the course of any given month. He paused at the top, scanning first one side of the square and then the other, but after a minute he shrugged and rejoined us at the table.

"I thought the guy who paid her might have been watching to make sure she gave it to the right person," he explained. "But I didn't see anyone. At least, not anyone familiar or anyone who seemed to be taking any notice of us." It was a good thought, and I appreciated how quickly he'd both had it and acted on it even if it hadn't yielded any insight.

There would be plenty of time later to comment on the death wish a person must have to make a habit out of skateboarding in a city like San Francisco, with its steep down-hills, impossible uphills and pedestrian and vehicular traffic, much less debate whether or not skateboarding was hopelessly passé. Instead, we turned our attention to the package Skater Girl had left behind. It was the sort of generic, padded brown-paper envelope that could be found in any drugstore, about the same size as a paperback book. My name was printed on the front in black felt-tip pen—large block letters in a hand none of us recognized.

"Open it," urged Luisa.

"What if it's a bomb?" I said

"Don't be absurd. Why would it be a bomb?" she asked.

"Why would somebody drop a padded envelope in my lap in the middle of Union Square?" I countered.

"I don't think it's a bomb," said Ben.

"Me, neither," Peter agreed. "Especially not given the way she chucked it onto the table."

I gingerly held the package up to one ear. It wasn't very heavy, and I couldn't hear anything ticking, but I was fairly certain bomb science had advanced beyond the point where an alarm clock was required to detonate an explosive. I'd learned the hard way that airport security believed a simple lip gloss could take down a plane.

Luisa heaved a sigh of impatience, grabbed the envelope from my hand, ripped it open, and dumped the contents on the table. "See," she said, when we weren't all blown to bits. "It's not a bomb. Although," she said, checking inside the envelope to make sure she hadn't missed anything, "a bomb might have made more sense."

We all looked at the item that had fallen out of the envelope. It was a model of the Lincoln Memorial, roughly two inches long and an inch high, molded out of plastic and with a handy ring attached to the top so it could be used as a keychain. A tiny Abraham Lincoln looked out from behind the front colonnade, his expression grave.

"This just might be the most random thing that has ever happened to me," I said.

"Even more random than what happened over spring break our senior year?" asked Luisa.

"I thought we'd agreed not to discuss that," I said.

"No," said Luisa. "*You* agreed not to discuss that. The rest of us have been saving it for the right moment." Peter and Ben looked from Luisa to me, clearly wondering what long-ago impropriety could trump this anonymous gift on the randomness scale.

"Well, now isn't the right moment," I said, making a mental note to forbid toasts of any sort at my wedding. That spring break was just one of several things Peter would be better off not knowing anything about. "We should be focusing on the keychain."

Luisa looked bemused, but at least she didn't giggle.

We took turns examining the model, passing it around the table. Peter was last, and I watched as he turned it over in his hands. "Is it secretly a gadget of some sort?" I asked hopefully. The molded plastic didn't weigh more than a few ounces, but perhaps the top opened up into another memory stick somehow.

But he shook his head. "I don't think so. What we see seems to be what we've got. Does the Lincoln Memorial have any special meaning for you?"

"Not that I'm aware of," I said.

"Why don't we all free-associate?" suggested Luisa. "Just say the first thing that comes to mind when we think of the Lincoln Memorial."

It was a strange idea, but nobody had any better ones, so we agreed it was worth a try.

"'Four score and seven years ago,'" said Peter, who'd done a double major in history and engineering.

"Ford's Theatre and John Wilkes Booth," said Ben, the federal agent.

"President's Day weekend, white sales and hot tubs," said Luisa. She was trained as a corporate lawyer, but shopping and skiing, particularly the après-ski lounging part of skiing, were two of her favorite pastimes, and she'd always appreciated Washington and Lincoln for the role they played in making these activities possible.

"The penny. And the five-dollar bill," I said. I did work in finance, after all. "Oh, and mustard."

They stared at me. "Mustard?" asked Luisa.

"We went to Washington, D.C., on a school trip when I was in high school. I bought a soft pretzel from one of the snack carts just before we went to see the Lincoln Memorial, and by accident I got mustard on my shirt," I explained. "But then it made it easy for me to remember that Daniel Chester French was the sculptor who did the Lincoln statue. Because of French's Mustard. Which was good, because that was a question on the pop quiz our teacher gave us on the bus ride home." They continued to stare at me. "We are free-associating, right?"

"I hadn't realized just how dependent you were on

Diet Coke to think clearly," said Luisa, lighting yet another cigarette.

This was more of a simple observation than anything else, and there was more than a grain of truth in it, but in my delicate state I found it hard not to be provoked by her words, especially given the direction in which her own free associating had led her. "Listen, Little Miss Hot Tub, I've now gone—" I checked my watch "—eight full hours without caffeine. I may be a little bit grumpy, but I think I'm holding up well, all things considered."

"Of course you are, Rachel," she said, her tone soothing, as if she were speaking to a small child. "And we're very proud of you."

Maybe if I hadn't been in withdrawal, I wouldn't have taken offense. As it was, I took her tone as the verbal equivalent of throwing down the gauntlet. "I'd like to see how you'd do without cigarettes for eight full hours."

"I'd do fine, thank you," she said.

"Then I dare you," I said.

"Dare me what?" she inquired, simultaneously arching one eyebrow and breathing out smoke.

"No cigarettes for eight hours." Then I had an even better idea. "No—wait—how about no cigarettes until ten on Tuesday morning?"

"Tuesday?" she said. "Why Tuesday?"

"That's when my dare runs out. It's only forty hours away."

"You're really daring me?" she asked, a note of trepidation creeping into her voice.

"You can turn it down, of course. I mean, that would be the wussy thing to do, but you have the option."

She glared at me. "I'm not a wuss."

"Prove it," I said.

"Why should I have to?"

"Why should *I* have to?"

"This is a very unattractive side of you, Rachel."

I couldn't disagree. Withdrawal was definitely not bringing out the "attractive" in me. But I'd backed her into a corner and she knew there was only one way to escape with her dignity intact. "Do you accept the dare?"

"Fine," she said eventually, but she didn't sound like she thought it was.

"Good," I said. "So no more cigarettes until Tuesday morning at ten. Starting now." I held out the cup with the remains of my seltzer.

She glared at me some more, but then she closed her eyes, took a final deep drag and exhaled a final stream of smoke. Wistfully, she dropped the half-smoked cigarette into the cup. There was a soft sizzle as it hit the liquid and went out.

I smiled at her. "This will be fun."

"How, precisely, are you defining *fun?*" she asked.

The four of us cleared our table and headed back toward the hotel, and along the way we summarized what we thought we knew: Hilary had gone off with Iggie to interview him for her article, with Iggie potentially misinterpreting her overtures as a chance to realize his long-unfulfilled romantic aspirations. But once he found out what she was actually planning on writing, he must have flipped and decided to hold on to her until she changed her mind, at which point Hilary had managed to send out the SOS signals. So we still needed to track down Iggie if we hoped to find Hilary.

This all would have sounded bizarre to the casual listener, but its bizarreness had been nearly eclipsed by the appearance of my new Lincoln Memorial keychain—the Iggie-Hilary scenario now seemed almost dull in contrast. It was possible that bestowing keychains of national monuments on unsuspecting people was part of some exercise in avant-garde street theater, but as it was I had no idea why "some old dude" would have paid twenty bucks to give me something so peculiar and in such a peculiar manner, much less whether it had anything to do with my missing friend.

Luisa and Ben had decided to postpone their respective trips home until we'd extricated Hilary from Iggie's grasp, which was an especially generous gesture for Ben to make given his role as recent dumpee. I suspected he saw rescuing Hilary as an opportunity to win her back, which was likely doomed as a strategy—she had strict rules about treading the same ground twice when it came to relationships. Regardless, he'd already proven himself useful, and I was glad we had his help. I was also confident that Luisa had her own reasons for sticking around, reasons only partially related to any concern for Hilary's safety.

Peter and I were due to meet his parents in Chinatown shortly, but Luisa and Ben said they would check with the hotel doormen to see if they could confirm it was indeed Iggie who had chauffeured Hilary to and from the hotel the previous evening and ask if by any chance they'd mentioned where they were going when they left. They would also contact the tech-support center at Berkeley to attempt to identify the mysterious Leo—from the comments Caro and Alex had made the previous evening, it seemed as if it would be easier to find him than to find Iggie's disappeared-from-the-planet ex-wife, and perhaps Leo would know how to reach Iggie. He might even know why Hilary had thought it necessary to stash that photo in the hotel safe.

"Is there a way to get a picture of the other man you saw on the tape?" I asked Ben as we reached the hotel entrance on Market Street. "The one from the party?" I was curious as to whether it was, in fact, Alex Cutler or if it had been someone else entirely.

He shook his head. "I tried to freeze the recording and print some still shots, but they came out really grainy. I could probably convince the security guys to let you take a look at the tape, though."

"If you really want to know, I'll just call Alex and ask," said Peter. "I doubt it was him, but I'm sure he'll tell us, one way or the other, and if he was there, he'll tell us why. And once I get to my computer, I can try to figure out how to decrypt the other file on the memory stick."

"What about your 'friend,' Luisa?" I asked, knowing full well who her "friend" was. "The one who thought she might know how to track down Iggie?"

"Oh, I'm supposed to catch up with her in a bit," Luisa said breezily.

"Good," said Peter, before I could comment on Luisa's breeziness. "We'll call you when we're finished with my parents."

"Sounds like a plan," Ben agreed.

Chinatown was just far enough away to be a longer walk than I was up for since I was still feeling the aftereffects of the half-marathon Peter had bullied me into that morning. I gave him the choice of either carrying me or driving, and he opted to drive.

Once in the car, Peter put in a call to Alex Cutler, but his number went right into voice mail. He waited for a long moment, listening to the recording before leaving a message. "Alex, it's Peter. This is going to sound like a strange question, and I'll explain when I talk to you, but did you happen to swing by the Four Seasons after the party last night? Give me a call when you get a chance. Thanks."

I checked my own messages while Peter was on the phone. I'd been monitoring my BlackBerry throughout the day to make sure there were no further communications from Hilary, but I hadn't paid too much attention to the other e-mails and voice mails that had accumulated. Most were from work colleagues, and none required an immediate response. The exception was a message from Laura Taylor, the junior-most person on the team that had worked on the materials for Tuesday's presentation to Igobe.

"Hi, Rachel, it's Laura. Something came up on the Igobe pitch, and I wanted to run it by you." Her tone was apologetic and slightly nervous—she was only a year out of college, and difficult as it was for me to accept, in her eyes I probably appeared senior enough to be intimidating. But I couldn't help but wonder if the nervousness had something to do with the deal itself. It wouldn't be surprising, given what I now knew about Hilary's article. Perhaps I'd been a bit hasty in concluding it would be just the thing to put me firmly back on the partner track.

I dialed Laura's number. "What's up?" I asked in my most friendly and least intimidating voice.

"This is going to sound sort of strange," she said, and then she hesitated, as if she were wondering if whatever she had to tell me was too strange to share. She had no way of knowing that strange was well on its way to being the theme of the day, and I told her as much.

"I was doing some final preparations for the Igobe meeting on Tuesday, making sure I had all of the background information," she said. "And I'd gone through the file of press clippings on the company when it occurred to me it might be a good idea to check out what people are saying about Igobe online, too."

This made perfect sense—some of the most informed commentary on tech businesses came from bloggers, not mainstream journalists. I complimented Laura on her thoroughness and initiative, two qualities the firm appreciated in its junior bankers, along with the willingness to obey all orders, work hundred-hour weeks and otherwise uncomplainingly relinquish one's personal life to further enrich the partners of Winslow, Brown.

"Did you learn anything interesting?"

"I'm not sure," she said. "Most of the well-known bloggers agree with everything the mainstream press has been saying—that Igobe's technology is revolutionary and breaking new ground and everything. But then I found some blogs written by hackers—it's like they have their own online subculture—and they're circulating an odd rumor."

"What kind of rumor?"

"They're saying Igobe's technology can be hacked."

"Oh," I said. "That's not good."

Igobe's entire value was in the promise of its technology to protect people's privacy, to wrap their online identities in an impenetrable layer of security. That value went away completely if the technology wasn't hack-proof; its users would be left exposed—just like the allegorical emperor in his imaginary new clothes. I wondered if this was the direction in which Hilary had been headed with her article—perhaps she'd come across a similar rumor. It would definitely explain her working title. I'd been worried about Iggie not liking the angle Hilary was taking, but I hadn't realized just what her angle was or how much he wouldn't like it.

"Do any of the blogs say who's managed to do the hacking?" I asked Laura.

"The rumor is there's only one person who knows how to breach the security protocols, and he's very secretive. That's not uncommon for hackers, probably because a lot of what they do is illegal. But here's the strange part—the hacker claims to have an elaborate plan to bring Iggie Behrenz down and Igobe with it. The guy is waging some sort of personal vendetta—the blogs are saying he used to be a close friend of Iggie's but now he's out for revenge."

As soon as she said this I thought of Leo, Iggie's last-nameless computer-savvy Berkeley pal. They had looked pretty cozy in Hilary's photo, but that picture had been taken years ago. There was plenty of time for Leo and Iggie to have had a falling-out since then, and it wasn't hard to imagine the Igster alienating someone so thoroughly. "I don't suppose anybody has a name for the guy, do they?"

"In a way, I guess. I mean, he seems to have an online code name of sorts. But I don't see how it could be his real name. In fact, it could be a her. That's sort of what the name implies." She hesitated again.

"What is it?" I asked, expecting something with a lion theme, a variation of Leo.

"Petite Fleur."

"Petite Fleur?"

"Petite Fleur."

"Oh," I said again, momentarily at a loss. Who knew my Lincoln Memorial keychain would find itself competing for the day's most random prize so soon?

"It's French for Little Flower," added Laura.

"Can it mean anything else?" I'd taken a few years of French in high school, but it had been a long time since Madame Weber's lessons had occupied any space in my head. Something had to be jettisoned to make room for Madonna lyrics, and French had really only been useful for ensuring I didn't accidentally order tripe or something equally disturbing in fancy restaurants.

"I don't think so," she said. "I even double-checked in a French-English dictionary. So that's when I called you. Since you know Igor Behrenz personally, I thought you might know who this old-friend-turned-enemy could be and what the story is."

Not only did she have no way of knowing just how strange something had to be for me to consider it strange, she had no way of knowing just how clueless I was when it came to Iggie. I couldn't even locate him, let alone explain anything about his personal history. And my initial idea about the hacker being Leo now seemed misguided—for the bulky man in the picture with that shaggy mane of hair to call himself Petite Fleur would be an enormous stretch, even online, where people regularly give free rein to their alter egos. It would be like me calling myself Rambo.

But I promised Laura I'd find out what I could and thanked her for the heads-up. It was important for Winslow, Brown to know what it was getting into. If Igobe's technology was compromised, then so were its business prospects, which meant that underwriting its IPO could leave our firm financially vulnerable and even cause serious damage to its white-shoe reputation.

And it wasn't just Winslow, Brown's reputation I was worried about—my own reputation was on the line, as well. I was the one who'd urged the firm to go after the Igobe business, trading on my personal relationship with Iggie. If there were questions about Iggie, I'd be found guilty by association.

I felt a chill pass over me that had nothing to do with the climate. All the glory I'd hoped for could just as easily morph into something far less appealing should I unwittingly lead the firm into disaster.

It took us a while to find parking, but eventually Peter squeezed the Prius into a spot on a side street, and we passed on foot through the pagoda-roofed arch marking the official entry to Chinatown. Stores catering to the tourist trade lined Grant Avenue's sloping sidewalk, offering cheap porcelains and knock-off designer handbags, and there was no shortage of tourists shopping for souvenirs on this June evening. Personally, I'd had enough shopping for one day.

I filled Peter in on my conversation with Laura Taylor as he led me up the street and then down a small alley. "Petite Fleur?" he asked. "Are you making that up?"

"I'm not that creative."

"*Au contraire, mon chère.* You are *très* creative."

"You sound like Pepé Le Pew."

"Who's Pepé Le Pew?"

I froze in place, aghast. "You really don't know?" I asked. It was one thing not to have watched *Party of Five*—Peter had never been in its targeted demographic—but classic cartoon characters were the building blocks of cultural literacy. "Didn't they have Saturday-morning cartoons here when you were growing up?"

"I don't know. We were always doing stuff on Saturday mornings."

"Kids aren't supposed to do stuff on Saturday mornings except watch cartoons and eat sugar cereals while their parents sleep late. What could you possibly have done instead?"

"We'd go hiking or sailing or biking. That sort of thing."

"I didn't realize you were abused as a child."

He laughed and took my arm. "I liked it."

"Did you at least get to eat Cap'n Crunch before you were dragged off to the wilderness? Or Fruit Loops? Please tell me you got to eat Fruit Loops."

"Oh, look—we're here."

"You're changing the subject."

"True. But we're still here."

Despite its Chinatown location, the restaurant was an intimate and relatively untouristed establishment the Forrests had been patronizing on a weekly basis for as long as Peter could remember. Based on how he described their usual weekend schedule, I guessed they were all too exhausted even to consider cooking by the time Sunday night rolled around. They probably would have had more stamina if they'd included more sugar and caffeine in their diet.

The elderly hostess greeted Peter as if he were her long-lost grandchild, scolding him for his prolonged absence and seemingly unsatisfied with his explanation that he now lived on the opposite coast. Then her gaze landed on me. "Who is this?"

"This is my fiancée," Peter said. "May, this is Rachel. Rachel, this is May."

"Hi," I said.

She looked at me, and then at Peter, and then at me again. "Fiancée?" she asked, surprised. In fact, she sounded vaguely accusatory. Given that she'd been seeing Peter regularly for more than three decades, I guessed she had expected to be among the first to know when Peter got engaged, but anything else she had to say was cut short by Susan waving us over from where she and Charles were already seated.

We reached the table at the same time as a waiter with a chilled bottle of white wine, which he uncorked and poured as we discussed the menu. After some debate, we placed an order for enough food to feed a professional football team and its entourage and the waiter departed just as Peter's phone rang. He showed me the caller ID—it was Alex Cutler—and excused himself to take the call outside. I watched as he crossed the restaurant, neatly sidestepping another waiter with a soda-laden tray. Even from a distance, the sight of the tall glasses of bubbling dark liquid nearly brought tears to my eyes. The wine felt smooth and refreshing on my tongue, but Chinese food, like bacon, tastes best with Diet Coke.

Plates of spring rolls and dumplings began arriving almost immediately, and Peter's parents didn't feel the need to wait for his return before digging in, which was fortunate because I was hungry and Peter had been waylaid by May on his return. She seemed to be talking his ear off, and from where we sat across the room it looked as if it would be a while before he'd be able to extricate himself.

"Did you have a good time catching up with your friends, dear?" Susan asked me as I took a big bite of scallion pancake. "Your college roommates seem very interesting. You must have been a colorful group when you were all at school."

Since my mouth was full, I couldn't do more than smile and nod, which was convenient, because I wasn't sure how I would have responded otherwise. *Colorful* was not the word I had hoped Peter's mother would use to describe either me or my friends. As adjectives went, it wasn't quite as bad as *idiosyncratic,* but it was still closer to *wacky* or *peculiar* than I would have liked.

"And it must have been nice for you to meet Peter's college friends, too," Susan added. "I was worried it would be awkward to have Caro there, but Peter didn't think it would be a problem."

"Why would it have been awkward?" I asked, spearing a dumpling with my chopsticks and preparing to dip it in the dish of Hoisin sauce. Caro struck me as one of the least awkward people I'd ever met—she'd been all smiles and congeniality the previous evening. Good social skills were probably a prerequisite for a successful career in PR. Needless to say, I would have been hopeless in that line of work.

"Oh, I know she and Peter ended everything on a friendly note, but after all that time together, to then attend his engagement party—well, it just seemed like it could be awkward."

"All that time?" I asked.

"All what time?" asked Peter, sliding into his seat.

"All that time you were seeing Caro, honey. I mean, you two started dating freshman year and then you were together off and on until last summer—why, that's longer than a lot of marriages. She was practically a member of the family. I was just telling Rachel how glad I was it wasn't awkward for her to be at the party last night."

The dumpling slipped from my chopsticks and splashed into the Hoisin sauce. Drops of liquid splattered the table-cloth, my sleeve, and, improbably, Charles' glasses. Word-lessly, he removed them and wiped the lenses with his napkin before returning them to his face and picking up his own chopsticks again.

I might not have had Caro's social skills, but I was pretty good at math. And by my calculations, Peter had dated someone else for nearly half his life. Which would have been fine.

If, that is, he had ever mentioned it to me before.

"Rachel, try one of the spring rolls," urged Susan. "These are Caro's favorite."

The rest of the meal passed in a blur. I temporarily forgot about Hilary and Iggie, Leo, Biggie, memory sticks, security cameras, the Lincoln Memorial and Petite Fleur. All of the insecurities I thought I'd safely vanquished were back in res-idence, and apparently they'd used their hibernation period to multiply.

Peter had made the occasional oblique reference to an ex-girlfriend, but I'd never asked for specifics, much less statis-tics about the duration of his average relationship. I didn't want concrete names or anecdotes to feed my neuroses, nor did I want to invite any questions about my own gory romantic past. Still, it seemed as if he could have told me he'd been all but married to someone, and that that someone had been Caro Vail.

Meanwhile, I'd been so proud of my normal relationship and of the progress I'd made in proving to Peter's normal family what a normal daughter-in-law I would be. But now I knew I'd only been deluding myself. Charles was a man of exceedingly few words, but what words he did use were thoughtfully chosen—he hadn't pulled *idiosyncratic* out of a hat. And I could now see Susan's shopping expedition for what it was: a pathetically desperate attempt to make me over into the sort of woman she'd want as a daughter-in-law, one who had opinions about stemware, looked fetching in pink and couldn't wait to have children she could take on nature-intensive Saturday-morning outings and deprive of sugar cereals.

And knowing that woman already existed, that for all intents and purposes she'd already been a member of Peter's family, just made the obvious question all the more glaring: what was Peter doing with me? For fifteen years he'd made a choice to be with Caro—a woman who probably would name her own dog Spot, given the chance—and fifteen years couldn't be written off as a mistake. Fifteen days or fifteen weeks, definitely. Even fifteen months. But fifteen *years?*

It was conceivable that after his decade and a half with Caro, Peter had needed a relationship vacation, an idyll of sorts with her polar opposite. And, if the ring on my finger was anything to go by, he'd managed to convince himself I was more than that. But now I had to wonder all over again whether I was anything more than a passing fancy, a temporary blip of insanity that he'd shake his head over once he came to his senses and returned to his normal life.

While these unsettling thoughts were racing through my head, Peter didn't seem to have noticed anything was amiss. In fact, his behavior pretty much fit the dictionary definition of *oblivious* as we progressed from appetizers to entrées and then passed around the plate of fortune cookies that arrived with the check. I broke open my cookie, hoping for some sort of prophetic intervention, or at least something that could be interpreted as releasing me from my promise to forgo caffeine.

But the message was all too clearly meant for me: it was completely blank. I didn't even have any lucky numbers. Just a clean strip of white paper.

I almost put my head down on the table and wept.

"What do you kids have on tap for tomorrow?" I heard Charles ask as we prepared to leave, but the words could barely penetrate my fog of miserable confusion.

"Rachel hasn't spent much time in San Francisco," said Peter. "And since we're both taking a vacation day, I thought we could do some sightseeing."

He really *was* oblivious. We didn't have time for sightseeing. Had he completely forgotten about finding Hilary? But, I thought to myself, if he could forget to tell me about dating another woman for fifteen years, forgetting about our rescue mission would hardly be a challenge.

"Did you have anywhere special in mind?" asked Susan.

"Just the usual. You know, Fisherman's Wharf, Alcatraz,

that sort of thing," Peter said. "Maybe even take a ride on a cable car if Rachel doesn't think it's too much of a cliché."

"That's a wonderful idea," said Susan. Of course, she hadn't had the Rice-a-Roni jingle stuck in her head all day. She turned to me. "You might want to go to SF MoMA, too. I know that it can't compare to MoMA in New York, dear, but they usually have some interesting exhibits. And if the weather cooperates, you can take a picnic to the park across the street. You know, where the Martin Luther King memorial is."

I perked up, and not just because picnics and soda were inextricably linked in my mind. I could sense Peter perking up in the same way next to me.

"The Martin Luther King memorial?" he asked.

"In the Yerba Buena Gardens. You know, right next to the Moscone Center. You must have been there before," said Susan.

"As in the 'I Have a Dream' Martin Luther King?" I asked. "That Martin Luther King?"

"Actually, Martin Luther King, Jr.," said Charles, pushing his chair back and helping Susan up from her seat.

"It would be a nice stop on your itinerary for tomorrow," suggested Susan.

"Are you thinking what I'm thinking?" Peter asked me as his parents led the way out of the restaurant.

"I'm thinking a lot of things right now," I told him, somehow managing to keep my tone even. "But one of them is that we might want to start our sightseeing tonight."

12

Charles and Susan were parked near us, so they walked us to our car. This meant I didn't get a chance really to say anything to Peter until I was belted into the passenger seat, but once there the first item on my agenda was to call Luisa and tell her to grab Ben and meet us at the Martin Luther King memorial.

"We're in the middle of dinner. We haven't even had dessert. Why do we need to come meet you?" she demanded. "Are you in the mood for a soft pretzel? Do they sell soft pretzels at all American monuments? Do you expect me to rush through dinner and traipse all over town just because you need a soft pretzel? And then do you expect me to clean up after you when you spill mustard everywhere?" Judging by her tone, she was rapidly sinking into her own pit of withdrawal-triggered despair, and her pit sounded even deeper and darker than my pit.

"Martin Luther King, Jr., gave his 'I Have a Dream' speech at the Lincoln Memorial during a Civil Rights march in the sixties. So it's possible the keychain of the Lincoln Memorial was meant to lead us to his own memorial," I explained patiently. My withdrawal symptoms had only intensified during the course of the day, but I'd had more time than Luisa to adjust to feeling lousy. I also had a little thing like finding out about Peter's fifteen-year relationship with his perfect match to distract me from any physical discomfort.

"What does that have to do with Hilary?" she asked.

"I don't know. Probably nothing. But we might as well check it out."

"I guess we don't have anything better to do," she agreed after extensive coaxing on my part. "And we can catch you up on what we've learned once we see you."

I hung up the phone and looked over at Peter, who was doing his best not to run over any jaywalking pedestrians.

"They're going to meet us there?" he asked.

"Yes, although Luisa sounded a bit grumpy about it."

"Withdrawal?"

"I hope so. Otherwise she's in the worst mood of her life for no good reason."

He laughed, seemingly unaware that we were about to have a very serious discussion.

"Is there something you forgot to tell me?" I asked sweetly, opting for the passive-aggressive approach.

"What?" he said, swerving to avoid a group of tourists in matching orange visors. "Oh, right—my call from Alex. He says he wasn't at the Four Seasons, and he's pretty sure he doesn't have any identical twins from which he was separated at birth. We also talked about a game of doubles tomorrow, around lunchtime."

"Doubles?"

"Caro left a message earlier suggesting the same thing—they both thought it would be fun for us all to get together."

"Doubles as in tennis doubles? At lunch?" People were supposed to eat during lunch, not dress up in silly outfits to whack at things with glorified butterfly nets.

"Caro can lend you a racket and something to wear. I told them I'd get back to them. I wanted to make sure you were up for it and that we had the entire Hilary thing resolved. By the way, did you like how I covered with my parents? I figured you'd rather they thought we were sightseeing tomorrow than doing what we'll probably be doing."

"That was good," I acknowledged, but mostly I was amazed at the easy way he bandied Caro's name about, as if their relationship was something we'd discussed thoroughly and laid to rest long ago, and as if there was nothing I'd rather do than borrow her clothes to play a sport I'd been officially declared incapable of learning by more than one professional instructor. A mental image of Caro in tennis whites, blond, tan and radiating athletic prowess, next to me in tennis whites, not blond, not tan and radiating athletic incompetence, flashed before my eyes, and my half of the picture wasn't pretty.

Since passive-aggressive hadn't worked, I discarded the passive part and switched over to just plain aggressive. "When I asked if you'd forgotten to tell me something, I was referring to how you'd forgotten to tell me you and Caro dated."

"I didn't tell you that?" The surprise in his voice sounded genuine, at least.

"No, you didn't."

"Oh. I thought I had."

"It must have slipped your mind. It also must have slipped your mind to tell me that this dating lasted for a decade and a half."

"A decade and a half? It couldn't have been that long," said Peter, braking for a red light. Then he thought about it for a moment. "Actually, maybe that is right. We met when I was eighteen, and we broke up when I was thirty-three. So it was a decade and a half, off and on. Wow—it sounds like a really long time when you put it like that, doesn't it?"

"Especially when you're hearing about it for the first time."

"The first time? But I told you I'd dated people before. Wouldn't it have been sort of weird if I hadn't?"

"You told me you dated *people*. Not one person. And not for fifteen years."

"You never seemed to have wanted details. In fact, you usually changed the subject when anything came up about people either of us have dated."

"Well, now I want details," I said, steeling myself. "I want the list."

"The list?"

"Of women you've dated." Perhaps there was more off than on in the "off and on" of his relationship with Caro. That would go a long way toward making me feel better. Many meaningless ex-girlfriends were infinitely preferable to a single meaningful one.

"It's a pretty short list. There was my high-school girlfriend, Ashley, from the cross-country team. I wonder what ever happened to her?"

"I don't think high school counts."

"No high school? Okay, then scratch Ashley. After high school, there was Caro. And there were a few women I went out with once or twice when Caro and I were taking breaks. Do a couple of dates count?" His tone was distracted, and he was scanning the streets for a parking space as he spoke. "Mostly it was just Caro."

"You told me you hadn't dated anyone seriously."

"I hadn't," he said. "I didn't."

"Fifteen years' worth of not serious?" I asked, incredulous. "How can fifteen years not be serious?"

"It wasn't like that."

"Then how was it?"

"We just fell into it. You know how it is. We got along really well, and we liked to do a lot of the same things. It was almost the path of least resistance. I don't think either of us ever intended for it to last as long as it did. It just sort of happened. Aha," he said, pulling the Prius into a space on Fourth Street. "Perfect."

"Fifteen years?" I repeated.

He shifted the car into Park and turned to face me. The sun had only recently set, but his chocolate-colored eyes looked black in the dusk. "Rachel. I promise you. It wasn't serious. I would have told you if it was. You're the only person I've ever been serious about."

"Who broke up with who?" I asked. "Or whom?"

"Is that really important?"

"I'd like to know."

He looked away, pushing the ignition button to turn off the car and unbuckling his seat belt. "Technically, I guess she broke up with me."

This was most definitely not the answer I'd been hoping to hear.

It was past nine, and there were a few people scattered across the grass of the Esplanade, listening to a lone musician playing a saxophone, but otherwise the park was empty, and Luisa and Ben hadn't yet arrived. We found the memorial easily, a waterfall of Sierra granite facing onto the Esplanade and lit by floodlights. Water gushed over its fifty-foot wall of rock to splash into a pool below, from which a cloud of mist rose into the cool night air. The waterfall was pretty, but we couldn't see how it was particularly relevant, so we followed the walkway that led behind it to a series of glass panels displaying photographs of the assassinated civil-rights leader and excerpts from his writings and speeches.

We moved from panel to panel, studying the quotes and the faces captured in black-and-white. "Through our scientific genius, we have made this world a neighborhood; now, through our moral and spiritual development, we must make of it a brotherhood," read one panel. "I would rather die in abject poverty with my convictions than live in inordinate riches with the lack of self-respect," read another. "When machines and computers, profit motives and property rights are considered more important than people, the giant triplets of racism, materialism, and militarism are incapable of being conquered," read a third.

"The guy had a way with words," said Peter in admiration.

"But I have a feeling he wasn't much in demand as a speaker at his local Young Republicans club," I said.

"Or at his local Old Republicans club," said Peter.

"I wonder what Iggie would make of all this?" I asked, still trying to figure out if we were in the right place and if the reason we were here had anything to do with Hilary. It was better than thinking about Peter's list, assuming anything with less than two items on it could accurately be called a list. "He's all about inordinate riches and computers and profit motives."

"You're an investment banker," Peter reminded me. "And I run a start-up. And we both hope to profit inordinately from our work one day. It's not like we're so much purer than Iggie."

"But we do have better fashion sense."

"I won't argue with that."

Studying the panels further didn't yield any startling insights into the mysterious keychain, or even any insights that weren't startling. I was getting frustrated when we heard footsteps on the walkway and first Ben and then Luisa appeared around the corner.

"This had better be worth it," said Luisa.

"Find anything?" asked Ben.

"No, unfort—" I started to say before I realized there was someone else with them.

"Hey, Abigail," said Peter.

"Hey," said Abigail. A slight breeze ruffled her silky brown hair. "I hope you don't mind that Luisa invited me along—we were having dinner when you called."

"Of course not," I said.

I would have given anything at that moment to be able

to raise one eyebrow, and to raise it in Luisa's direction. As it was, I had to make do with smirking, which was nowhere near as satisfying. She ignored me anyhow. Withdrawal, in addition to making us both blunt and cranky, was doing nothing for our respective levels of maturity.

"Did you find anything?" asked Ben again.

"No, we seem to be on a wild goose chase," I admitted.

"I keep waiting for another skateboarder to show up," added Peter.

"So we didn't have to rush through our meal to meet you here?" asked Luisa. "We could have ordered dessert like civilized people? They had crème brûlée. I could be eating crème brûlée right now. You know how I feel about crème brûlée." I didn't know how she felt about crème brûlée, and I couldn't remember her ever having a sweet tooth before, but I guessed her withdrawal symptoms were taking the form of an insatiable need for sugar. They were clearly strong enough to offset any desire to show Abigail the sunnier side of her personality.

"Well, this is still a nice place, and it's educational, too," I said.

"I'm sufficiently educated already," said Luisa. "Let's go."

"What's that?" asked Abigail, pointing at a spot near my right foot.

"What's what—" I started to say.

Then I looked down at the spot she'd indicated. "Oh."

A small rock rested in the shadows of the walkway, sitting at the base of the panel with the quote about machines and computers. And there was something propped between the rock and the panel.

I crouched to get a better look. A small padded envelope had been wedged into the space, but one corner protruded from behind the rock, as if whoever had left it there wanted to ensure it would be seen only by someone searching the area with care. I took hold of the protruding corner with my thumb and index finger and delicately slid the envelope from its hiding space.

Even in the dim light, it wasn't hard to see that the envelope was a twin of the one Skater Girl had delivered that afternoon or to make out the now-familiar block letters spelling my name.

Peter took off immediately, disappearing around the other side of the waterfall. He returned a few minutes later, just as disappointed as he'd been earlier that day. "Nobody's out there," he said. "The people who were on the Esplanade before have gone."

Ben, meanwhile, had been looking for cameras. Checking for surveillance tape must have been a standard part of FBI training, or perhaps it was the part Ben remembered best. But even if there were cameras, I doubted they'd be helpful. Hundreds of people must have come through here today, maybe even thousands—it was tourist season, after all. Assuming we'd be able to talk whatever security personnel there were into letting us view any footage, what were the odds that there was a camera pointed at just the right angle to provide a clear view of whoever had tucked the package into its hiding place? Ben must have been thinking along the same lines, because he gave up his search with a shrug when Peter returned. "I don't see anything," he said.

Which left us with the package itself. The five of us stood in a circle on the walkway, looking at the padded envelope resting in my hands.

"This had better not be another keychain," I said, testing its weight. The envelope and the handwriting on it were identical to the envelope from Union Square, but this one had a bit more heft to it.

"Maybe it's a bomb," suggested Luisa, but she was mocking me. I was beginning to wonder whether our friendship would be able to withstand another thirty-six hours of withdrawal.

"Do you want me to open it?" asked Peter.

"No, I can do it." I pulled on the little tab that peeled back to slice open the top of the envelope and peered inside. Light glinted off something metallic.

"What is it?" asked Ben.

"Strange," I said. "That's what it is. Very, very strange."

I reached into the envelope and withdrew a shiny new iPod, complete with headphones.

"Nice," said Peter appreciatively. "I was thinking of getting you one just like that to take to the gym."

I didn't know when, exactly, he thought I'd be going to the gym, but I could disabuse him of that particular fantasy later. "I guess Christmas came early this year. But why would somebody give me an iPod?"

"Perhaps to help you expand your cultural horizons beyond national monuments and television shows meant for teenagers," said Luisa. "You could download operas and symphonies. Or subscribe to podcasts from the BBC and NPR."

"I don't think whoever left this intended for me to bore myself to death."

"Maybe there's something already on the iPod that's a clue of some sort," offered Abigail. "A song or photograph. Something like that."

This, in contrast to Luisa's suggestion, was a good idea. I wondered if it was possible to trade in Luisa for Abigail, at least until Tuesday morning at ten. "How do I turn it on?" I asked. It's possible I was the last American under the age of eighty who had never used an iPod.

"Here," said Peter. He took the device from my hand and pressed the track wheel. A second later, the small screen lit up. We huddled around him, watching as the Apple icon gave way to a menu of options.

"Try Photos first," I said, thinking about the picture we'd found in the safe, but clicking on Photos led only to an empty screen. He clicked on Music next, but this also produced nothing. Then he clicked on the Videos option in the menu.

"Jackpot," he said, tilting the screen up so we could all get a better look. There was only one item listed, but it was clearly meant for me: it was titled "Play Me, Rachel."

It was a simple enough request, and it had worked for Lewis Carroll. "Okay," I said, "Let's play it." Peter handed me the headphones, and I inserted the buds into my ears.

"Ready?" he asked.

I nodded, and he pressed Play. The screen went dark for

a moment, and I belatedly started worrying that I was about to see something I wouldn't want to see. But before I could even think of any examples of things I wouldn't want to see, images began appearing on the screen and a staticky audio track filled my ears.

The video was a montage of sorts, a series of black-and-white clips of the same man in a variety of settings: behind a speaker's podium, striding through a crowd, shaking hands with other men, bending to pick up a child. Each clip morphed into the next as someone spoke passionately in a foreign language over the footage. I thought it sounded like Spanish, but, as I mentioned before, I'd taken French, and I remembered precious little of that. The man himself didn't look unfamiliar, but I couldn't place him. He had the same shaggy bulk Leo had in the picture in my purse, but these clips were clearly much older, and this guy's favorite outfit seemed to consist of a beret and fatigues, whereas Leo had been wearing a T-shirt and jeans.

Luisa had pressed her head in close to my own to see the screen, and she said something beside me, but I couldn't hear her. I removed one of the earbuds. "What?" I asked. "I'm trying to listen."

"Give me that," she demanded.

"Why?"

"Just give it to me." She grabbed the earbud from my hand and stuck it into her own ear. I'd never seen her quite this testy before, and we watched the rest of the clip together in silence.

"Do you know who that was?" she said when the montage had drawn to a close a half-minute later. "Could you understand the Spanish?"

"Well, no."

"I didn't think so," she said with satisfaction. "You may know everything there is to know about TV and American tourist attractions, but I spent my youth studying important subjects, like political history and foreign languages."

I didn't see what political history had to do with understanding Spanish. It also wasn't a fair comparison given that Spanish was hardly a foreign language to Luisa, but we could debate that when she wasn't nicotine-deprived. "Are you going to share with us your knowledge of political history and foreign languages? Or are we supposed to guess?" I asked.

"It's Che Guevara."

"Who?"

"Ernesto Guevara de la Serna. El Che. Born in Argentina in 1928 and executed as a revolutionary in Bolivia in 1967."

"Oh," I said. I'd heard of him. In fact, I'd seen the movie, feeling virtuous since it had subtitles. "You mean, the guy from *The Motorcycle Diaries?*"

"The movie was based on the actual diaries Che Guevara kept during a trip he made by motorcycle to a leper colony in Peru. The experience played a critical role in shaping his radical philosophy."

"The guy in the movie was better looking," I said.

"Che Guevara was a Marxist, right?" said Ben.

"Right," said Luisa. "And the audio's from a speech he gave in the sixties, talking about the importance of using technology to further socialism."

"Well, whoever's leading us on this scavenger hunt either knows a lot about leftists or he is one. Or maybe both," said

Peter. "But where does he want us to go next? I'm pretty sure there isn't a Che Guevara monument in San Francisco."

My earlier frustration was turning to annoyance. "And we're not any closer to knowing why he's leading us on a scavenger hunt in the first place, or if any of this will help us find Hilary."

We were all silent for a moment, thinking. The ambient noises of the city—traffic, a dog's bark, the clang of a cable car's bell—competed with the rush of the waterfall to fill the quiet. I wondered if I was ever going to be able to get the Rice-a-Roni theme song out of my head. Every cable car I heard only exacerbated the problem.

Abigail was the first to speak. "You know," she began, almost hesitantly, "Luisa had started to tell me about everything that's happened over dinner. About Hilary's disappearance, and the article she was working on and the picture in the safe. And then the keychain, and now this video. It's all been reminding me of someone I used to know. Especially when you called it a scavenger hunt, Peter. The person I knew loved scavenger hunts—he loved any sort of puzzle. But it can't be him."

"Why not?" I asked.

"The person I'm thinking of—well, he's dead."

"Leo?" asked Luisa.

Abigail looked at her in surprise. "Who told you about Leo?"

"He was the other man in the picture Hilary stored in the safe. Peter's mother identified him—she remembered him from when she used to teach at Berkeley. Then I called the university's technical-support hotline, right before we met up for dinner, and I asked if a graduate student named Leo had ever worked there. The woman who answered had overlapped with him, and she told me about the fire. I was getting to that part of the story when Rachel called and we had to rush over here." This last was delivered with yet another pointed look at me. If this kept up, I might have to release Luisa from the dare purely out of self-defense.

"How did you know Leo?" Peter asked Abigail.

"And you still haven't explained why you think you can get in touch with Iggie," said Luisa.

I'd been watching Abigail's face, and maybe it was a trick of the light, but she was starting to look familiar in a whole new way, a way that had nothing to do with her resemblance to Christie Turlington.

"You're Biggie, aren't you?" I said.

She turned to me, her brown eyes wide. "How did you know?"

14

I'd first met Abigail only six months earlier, just after she started working at Peter's company. At the time, Peter couldn't stop talking about how pleased he was with his new hire's business acumen and technical savvy, and, unaware of her current sexual orientation, I'd been far more concerned about what she and Peter might be up to together in the present than what she might have been up to on her own in the past. Nor had it occurred to me then to worry about what Peter might have been up to in *his* past.

She had changed dramatically from the woman in the picture with Iggie and Leo, and it was more than the differences in shape and hairstyle that made her so unrecognizable. There was a self-possessed confidence to her now, a confidence the woman in the picture, hiding behind her veil of hair, had lacked. I could only guess as to how much of the change had to do with the physical transformation and how much of it had to do with extricating herself from a bad marriage. Either way, her caution in entering new relationships suddenly made sense in a way it hadn't before—who wouldn't be cautious after having been married to Iggie?

A security guard came by just then and informed us the park was closing, so we returned to the Four Seasons, settling around a table in the lounge off the lobby. I held my tongue when Luisa ordered a rum and Diet Coke, a drink I'd never seen her order before, her or anyone legally old enough to order drinks, but clearly she felt it necessary to torment me. I was feeling less than one-hundred percent myself—in fact, I was feeling about three percent—but judging from Luisa's behavior, caffeine withdrawal was a mere drop in the withdrawal bucket compared to nicotine withdrawal, and she blamed me for everything she was feeling. I also didn't give it much thought when Ben ordered a cheeseburger along with his beer. I'd assumed he'd had dinner with Luisa and Abigail, but apparently not. Still, I didn't wonder what he'd been doing instead—I was too curious about what Abigail had to say.

"We all met in graduate school at Berkeley," Abigail told us. "That was about four years ago. I was earning my M.B.A., and Iggie and Leo were both finishing up their doctorates in computer science, but we ended up taking the same class on entrepreneurship and technology. It was a popular class for business students, because so many of us wanted to find jobs at tech start-ups after graduation, but it was also a sort of crash course in business for people in the sciences. Iggie and Leo had already been kicking around an idea for a software venture, and they wanted to learn how to finance and build a new company."

"Was that Iggie's first business, the one that never got off the ground?" I asked, remembering Alex Cutler's comment the previous evening. It was hard to believe that conversation had taken place barely twenty-four hours ago.

"Who told you that?" she asked, shaking her head. "If anything, their original idea was exactly what Igobe's become. They first called the company Igleo, a combination of both their names, but after Leo died Iggie stripped out his name. But the concept was always to create software to help people maintain their anonymity on the Internet. They hadn't yet begun development when I first met them, but they knew what they wanted to do, and they'd mapped out how it would all work technically. What they hadn't figured out was whether they'd make money off it."

"Why couldn't they just sell or license the software to people?" asked Luisa. "That's how Microsoft and other software companies do it, right? And isn't that how Igobe's doing it now?"

"That's how the software business has worked traditionally, but more and more Internet businesses are making their money from advertising instead. All of the major portals like AOL and Yahoo! are supported by ads, and so are the big search engines and social networks," said Peter. His own company was working on ways to speed the flow of data across the Internet, but it didn't deal with consumers directly. Instead, his customers were the cable and phone companies that provided consumers with Internet access.

"So Iggie and Leo couldn't decide whether to sell the software to people or to let advertisers support it—was that the crux of the matter?" asked Luisa.

"No. It was a lot more basic than that," said Abigail. "What they couldn't agree on was whether to make any money from the software at all."

We all stared at her, collectively perplexed.

"Not make money?" asked Ben.

"What do you mean?" asked Peter.

"Then why bother?" asked Luisa.

I was relieved the concept was just as shocking to them as it was to me—I sometimes worried that working in finance had so steeped me in avarice I no longer had a firm grip on how regular people felt about these things. "How could Iggie not want to make money?" I asked. "Iggie's been obsessed with making money for as long as we've all known him. The guy had an autographed picture of Bill Gates in his dorm room, and it wasn't because Bill was such a babe."

Abigail smiled at our reaction. "I know it's hard to process. But it wasn't Iggie—he was all for making money, and for making as much of it as he possibly could. It was Leo. He was pretty left-wing to start with, even by Berkeley standards. And then his father died while we were in school, from cancer. I don't remember what his father did—some sort of middle-management job at a big corporation, I think—but Leo was convinced if he hadn't been working so hard his entire life he wouldn't have gotten sick. The experience made him even more radical. I went to the memorial service, and Leo did a reading from *Das Kapital* and then went on a rant about how his father had been alienated from the fruits of his labor."

"And that's why all of the leftist clues made you think of him?" Peter asked.

"That's part of it. But only a part—it was more than the politics that reminded me of Leo. I mentioned before that he loved puzzles, and not just solving them, creating them, too. I could practically picture how much fun he'd have coming up with the clues you've been getting. A lot of developers hide surprises in the computer code they create—they call them Easter eggs—but Leo took almost more pleasure from burying Easter eggs in his code than in writing the code itself. In fact, the only thing he liked better was hacking into other developers' code and finding *their* Easter eggs."

I was already paying close attention, but this made me lean forward in my seat. "Leo was a hacker?"

"A lot of software developers are. It's like a game to them, and there's a certain amount of ego involved, too. They're all trying to one-up each other by showing they can hack each other's code. Some companies even pay hackers to try to get into their systems, to help them identify weak spots by seeing if they can break through firewalls and find flaws in security protocols."

At this point, only Peter knew about my conversation with Laura Taylor. He looked at me. "Sound familiar?"

I nodded. "Abigail, have you ever heard of a hacker named Petite Fleur?" It was hard to ask this with a straight face, but somehow I pulled it off.

"Excuse me?"

"Petite Fleur is the online pseudonym—at least, I think it's a pseudonym—of someone who says he can hack Igobe's technology." I filled them all in on what Laura had told me.

"It sounds so much like everything you've told us about Leo. An old friend of Iggie's who's now an enemy but has the technical know-how to compromise Igobe's security. Who better to do that than Iggie's partner in developing the technology in the first place?"

"Leo was more than a partner," said Abigail. "Iggie's talented and he has great commercial sense, but Leo was the true technical genius. Leo was responsible for the most sophisticated parts of the software's design. But this hacker, and the person who's been sending you these clues, can't be Leo. Leo's dead."

"Are you absolutely sure about that?" asked Peter, taking the words from my mouth.

"He's dead. I wish he weren't, but there's no way he could have survived the fire that killed him."

"What happened, exactly?" asked Luisa. "The woman at Berkeley mentioned a fire, but she didn't give me any other details, and it didn't seem appropriate to ask."

Abigail took a sip from the glass of red wine she'd been nursing. "Leo had a cabin in the hills above Silicon Valley, off Skyline Boulevard. It was just a small place compared to some of the mansions people have built in the area with Internet money, but it was in a beautiful spot. On a clear day you could see all the way to the Pacific from one side of the house and to San Francisco Bay from the other. Leo thought of the cabin as his private retreat. He'd usually go up there alone, shut himself in, light a fire in the fireplace, put on some music and lose himself in work for days at a time. The report was that he must have fallen asleep one night with a fire going. The fire got out of control, and the cabin burned down with him in it."

"Are you positive he was in it?" I asked. After all, Abigail had just described a classic way to fake one's own death, not that I had any idea why Leo would want to do such a thing. All of the other signs pointed at Leo and in such a definitive way as to smooth over any disconnect between his picture and the delicate femininity of the hacker's online alias. I was reluctant to let a small thing like people thinking he was dead get in the way.

"The cabin was so isolated it took a while for the fire trucks to arrive, and by then there wasn't much left but ashes. Nobody inside could have survived, and nobody did. Once the fire was out, all they recovered were some bone fragments and teeth." Abigail gave a small shudder, remembering. "That's how they ended up identifying both Leo and Scat."

"Scat?" asked Ben.

"Leo's dog," she explained. Scat seemed like a strange thing to name a dog—it was more like the sort of thing you'd say to a cat—but not everyone came from the Forrest school of pet-naming. "He really loved that dog."

"When did all of this happen?" I asked, disappointed. It was hard to argue with bones and dental records.

"About eighteen months ago. Leo and Iggie were fighting all the time by then, and things were getting really bitter between them. All of the initial development was done on the software, and the preliminary testing was complete. They were ready for a broad commercial launch, but they still hadn't resolved their disagreement about money, and Leo would complain that he never had time to get any work done, because Iggie was constantly scheduling meetings with venture capitalists to talk about business plans and deal terms. Leo wanted to start small and make some of the software available for free, but Iggie thought from the beginning that the technology could be worth billions, and he wanted the venture-capital firms to invest in the company so they could finance a big splashy marketing campaign and grow the business quickly."

"I guess we know which path he took," I said. Now you couldn't browse the Web, turn on the TV or pick up a magazine without encountering an Igobe ad. They were even plastered on buses and taxis. It seemed wrong that a product whose key selling point was its ability to protect one's privacy was advertised in such an invasive way.

"Iggie did exactly what he wanted once Leo wasn't around to argue with him."

"Then what happened? With you and Iggie?" Luisa asked, her tone gentle. She had plenty of gentleness to spare for people she didn't hold responsible for her nicotine-deprived state, and she also had her own reasons to be interested in Abigail's personal history.

Abigail looked down at her glass of wine. "I didn't have a lot of experience romantically, and Iggie really swept me off my feet when we were in school. It never felt right to me, but I didn't know how it was supposed to feel. The marriage started going south pretty much right after the wedding, but Leo's death was the catalyst. It sounds like a cliché, but it drove home that I only had one life to live. I left Iggie a few weeks after Leo died, and I made a lot of other changes." She lifted her eyes to meet Luisa's. "And here I am."

This was as good an opportunity for a tender moment as I'd ever seen, and if I'd been less impatient or if Luisa had been nicer to me that day I would have let it take its course. "And there's Iggie, about to become a billionaire," I said instead. "That's awfully convenient."

Abigail managed to tear her gaze from Luisa, and I could tell I'd struck a chord. "It was convenient, wasn't it? This is going to sound crazy, but part of me always wondered whether Iggie had anything to do with the fire. The timing of everything couldn't have been better for him. Once Leo was dead, Iggie could take the business in the direction he wanted, without any obstacles. He's already made a bundle since then, and once Igobe goes public, he's going to be seriously rich."

"Was there any suspicion of arson?" asked Ben.

"No. At least, not officially. The investigators said it looked as if a spark had landed on the rug in front of the hearth. The fire spread quickly from there, and Leo didn't manage to get out. But they didn't find any evidence of foul play. Iggie kept telling people he thought it was suicide, that Leo was still depressed about his father's death and set the fire himself. He said Leo wanted to die in a fire because his father had been cremated. But Iggie saying all that just made me wonder if he was trying to deflect suspicion from himself."

"Did Leo have any other close friends or relatives?" I asked. Perhaps somebody else had suspected Iggie of foul play, too, somebody who knew enough about Igobe's software to hack it and who cared enough about Leo to avenge his death. Maybe a commie computer-whiz girlfriend who called herself Petite Fleur?

But Abigail shook her head. "Leo was a loner, especially after his father died. All he cared about was his work, and music and Scat. He was a big fan of the masses, but only from a distance."

"Did Iggie know you suspected him?" asked Peter.

"Maybe. Probably. But it didn't worry him. There wasn't much I could do about it. It wasn't like I had any proof. He was home the night of the fire, working in his home office, but he might have sneaked out for an hour or two without my noticing, especially since we were barely speaking at that point. He could have gone up to the cabin, incapacitated Leo in some way and then started the fire to cover his tracks. I never would have thought he had it in him, but he's always been so ambitious, and everything fell into place for him once Leo was out of the way. He didn't even pretend to be upset when Leo died. Two days later he'd renamed the company and cashed a big check from a venture-capital firm. Two weeks after that, ads for Igobe were everywhere. And now Igobe's about to sell shares to the public for more money than I think even Iggie ever dreamed of."

A silence fell over the table; each of us was thinking through the implications of what Abigail had told us, and I don't think I was the only one feeling a newly heightened sense of alarm, and it wasn't just because my hopes for the career-redeeming prospects of the Igobe IPO were fading fast. While we'd been concerned that Iggie wouldn't be pleased if Hilary wrote an article claiming Igobe's technology could be hacked, we'd dismissed the idea that he presented a real threat.

But that was before we knew what had happened to the last person to get in Iggie's way. We had a lot more to be concerned about if Iggie was capable of murder.

15

Peter seemed as shocked as any of us about Abigail's secret history, but I guessed she hadn't included details about her personal life on her résumé. "Can you get in touch with Iggie?" He asked her now. "Or do you know where he lives?"

"We used to rent a house in Los Altos, but he's moved since then, and I don't have the new address or even a phone number. He's paranoid about people knowing his personal information. And we handled all of the correspondence for the divorce through our lawyers. Iggie wasn't very happy about the split, to put it mildly, and it was easier not to deal with him directly." She hesitated. "I'd mentioned to Luisa that there's someone I can call who always knows how to reach him. It won't be easy—it's a last-resort type of option—but I can do it if you're desperate."

"We're pretty desperate," I said.

"We might even be very desperate," said Luisa. "Given what you've told us about Iggie, it sounds as if Hilary could be in serious trouble."

Abigail seemed to be taking our measure, weighing just how desperate we really were against making a call she was reluctant to make. Apparently we came across as sufficiently pathetic, or maybe she was just trying to please Luisa or even Peter, who was not only her friend but her boss, as well, although this sort of thing certainly wasn't covered in her job description. "Okay. If it's that important to you, I'll give it a shot."

She'd had only a few sips of her wine while we'd been talking, but now she lifted the glass to her lips and took a big gulp, as if to fortify her for what she was about to do next. Then she took her cell phone from her bag. "I'll be back in a minute."

But a full twenty minutes elapsed before Abigail returned, and when she did she looked as if she could use another glass of wine, or perhaps several Valium with a bottle of tequila as a chaser.

"Victory?" asked Luisa hopefully.

Abigail waved a slip of paper with a phone number scrawled across it. "I wouldn't call it that, but I did get a phone number. It's a six-five-zero area code, so it's somewhere near Palo Alto, but I couldn't get an address."

"Who did you call?" I asked. "Or whom?"

"Even The Igster has a mother," she said with a wry smile. "And let's just say that the apple didn't fall far from the tree. A tree who thought naming her first-born Igor was a fabulous idea."

Abigail felt it would be best for her to make the call to Iggie, but the rest of us wanted to listen in, and after some persuasion, she agreed. "In fact, it would probably be good to have other people witness how impossible a conversation with him can be—otherwise you'd think I was making it up. But we should hurry," she said with a glance at her watch. "Iggie goes to bed exactly at midnight when he has work the next day, and he never answers the phone once he's started his prebed routine."

I didn't particularly want to know what Iggie's bedtime routine might entail, and I was glad when nobody else asked. We decided to go up to Luisa's room, where there was a speakerphone. Now that we knew we were being watched, we were all on our best behavior in the elevator, although it seemed unfriendly not to wave at the cameras hidden behind the mirrors. Once in the suite, Luisa took the phone from the desk and set it on the glass coffee table in the living room so we would all be able to hear.

Peter and I took the sofa as Ben leaned against the window and Luisa settled into an armchair. Abigail pushed one button to activate the phone's speaker and another to secure an outside line before punching in the digits on the scrap of paper. "This could get ugly," she warned as she dialed. "It's been a while since I've spoken to him."

"We all know how difficult conversations with former partners can be," said Luisa reassuringly. I couldn't help but sneak a look at Peter when she said this, wondering whether he found conversations with Caro difficult. None of my previous relationships had lasted long enough even to merit the term *partner.*

Iggie had given so few people his contact information he had no reservations about answering his phone practically before it rang. "Who wants the Igster?" piped his reedy voice.

"Iggie, it's me."

There was a long moment of silence on the other end. "Biggie?"

Abigail winced, and I had the feeling she was already regretting her decision to let us listen in. "How many times have I asked you not to call me that?"

"You haven't asked me anything for more than a year, remember? That's how long it's been since I've heard from you. One year, twenty-three weeks, four days, three hours, and six minutes. And you didn't send a Christmas card." Even over the speaker the sulkiness in his tone was grating and unmistakable.

"I didn't send anyone a Christmas card. I'm Jewish."

"Dr. Grout says your behavior has been very hostile."

"I didn't call to discuss your therapy, or Dr. Grout."

"Dr. Grout thinks your unwillingness to discuss my therapy is indicative of deeply rooted neuroses. He could help you with that."

Abigail rolled her eyes and put the phone on mute as Iggie continued to talk. "I'm sorry," she said to the rest of us. "This is even worse than I thought it would be." We all tried to look encouraging as she unmuted the speaker. "That's very generous of Dr. Grout, but he's got plenty on his plate already without worrying about me."

"But we are worried, Biggie. I told Dr. Grout about seeing you at the party last night, and we're very concerned."

"Why's that?" she asked.

"We think you may be anorexic, or at least anemic. But

don't worry, we can help you. And we know why you're calling, too. We were expecting your call, and we're willing to consider it. But first we think you owe me an apology."

"I'm assuming that by *we* you're still talking about you and Dr. Grout?" asked Abigail. I personally hoped so; the royal *we* was strange enough when royalty used it.

"Of course I'm talking about Dr. Grout," said Iggie. "You know I tell him everything. And we knew you'd be back, and we know why. But you're going to have to get in line, Bigs. Everyone wants a piece of me now."

Abigail took a deep breath in and exhaled slowly. When she spoke next, it was with restrained precision. "Iggie, as I made abundantly clear one year, twenty-three weeks, and however many days and hours ago, there is not a single piece of you or Dr. Grout I will ever want. Which is why I explicitly relinquished any claims to your assets in the divorce settlement."

Iggie chortled. "Dr. Grout told me you'd try to play it cool. That's why you were avoiding me last night."

Exasperated, she ran both hands through her hair. "Yes, that's exactly it. You and Dr. Grout know me better than I know myself. I'm playing it cool. But that's still not why I'm calling."

"Okay, I'll play your game. Why are you calling, then?"

"I'm with some of your old college friends, and they're trying to find Hilary Banks. She seems to have disappeared."

"What? Disappeared? Hilarita?" The sulkiness had been replaced by hammy, overemoted surprise. Drama classes obviously hadn't been part of his Ph.D program.

"Nobody's seen her since she left the party with you last night."

"Left the party with me? What are you talking about?"

"Don't act like you don't know what I'm talking about. The parking attendants remembered you. Unless someone else is driving a Lamborghini, tipping the valet with hundred-dollar bills, and telling him to buy Igobe stock. Does that sound like someone else to you?"

I could practically hear Iggie's mind working as he tried to figure out how to wiggle out of this one. "Maybe," he said, his tone back to sulky. Given the mood swings we'd witnessed during a single phone call, perhaps it was a good thing he had such a close relationship with his mental-health professional.

"Come on, Iggie. Just tell me what happened after you left the party," said Abigail.

"Nothing happened. Zippo. Nada. Zilch."

"Then where is Hilary?"

"How would I know? I dropped her off at her hotel, and then I went home. That's all there is. End of story. Finito. Elvis left the building and the fat lady sang."

"Are you lying to me?"

Sulky now gave way to a silky persuasiveness that wasn't even partially successful. "I'd never lie to you, Big— I mean, Abigail."

"Sure you would, if it served your purpose. You tried to lie to me thirty seconds ago—you just didn't get away with it. I need you to promise you're telling the truth."

"Okay, I promise."

"That's not good enough, Iggie. I want you to swear to me you don't know where she is."

"Fine. I swear."

"That's still not good enough. Swear on something important. Swear to me on Phyllis."

There was another long moment of silence on the other end of the phone. "That's low, Biggie."

"I need to know for sure you're telling the truth."

"All right, then," he said grudgingly. "I swear on my mother's honor. I haven't seen Hilary since I left her at the Four Seasons, and I don't know where she is. There. Are you happy now?"

Abigail put the speakerphone on mute again. "I have to admit, I sort of believe him," she said to us. "Iggie has a love-hate relationship with his mother, but he takes her honor very seriously. But I also don't think he's telling us everything he knows—he sounds sort of cagey, like he's holding something back. It's hard to tell without being able to look him in the eye."

"Let's get together, Bigs," suggested Iggie, as if he'd heard what she said. "It's been too long, and I've got to say, I'm completely digging the new you. I never realized you could be so feisty."

"Feisty?" asked Abigail, taking the phone off mute. Her expression was pained, and I made a mental note not to tell her about the "babealicious" comment the previous evening.

"Like a wildcat." Then he growled.

Fortunately, Abigail had muted the phone again, because Peter was doing his trying-not-to-laugh choke, and I wasn't even trying not to laugh. The corners of Luisa's lips were twitching, and Ben let out a muffled guffaw.

Abigail looked around the room. "This is a really good friend of yours?" she asked, her eyes moving from Ben to me to Luisa. She seemed to be hoping we'd changed our mind about Hilary in the last hour, but we all nodded. Then she looked at Peter. "And she's important to you, too?"

"She's important to Rachel, so that makes her important to me," he said.

She pointed a finger at him. "You may owe me a promotion after this, or at least a raise." She unmuted the phone, interrupting Iggie as he continued to make what I guessed he considered to be the noises of a feisty wildcat. I was glad we weren't privy to any visuals that might have been accompanying the sound effects. "What about tomorrow, Iggie?"

He stopped growling. "Tomorrow? Really?"

"Really."

"We could have lunch. You like lunch, right? I have a personal chef at the office. He'll make whatever you want. What do you want? You looked like you could use a good meal." His tone had brightened considerably.

"I'll have lunch with you tomorrow at your office," she confirmed. "See you then."

Iggie was still eagerly ticking off a list of potential menu items when Abigail hung up. "Well, that was excruciating," she said to us.

"I may owe you a raise *and* a promotion," Peter said.

She shrugged and flashed the same wry smile. "I wouldn't turn anything down, but the occasional reminder of just how happy I am not to be married to him is probably a reward in itself."

We all owed Abigail, but we also felt as if we knew even less now than we did before. If she was right, and if Iggie was telling the truth, then we had no idea what had happened to Hilary once he'd dropped her off at the hotel. We might not have to worry about what Iggie might be up to, but we did have to worry about what person or persons unknown might be up to.

This new level of uncertainty was more than a little discomfiting, especially since we had no additional evidence which would merit calling in the police and practically no leads left to explore except for the lone encrypted file from Hilary's memory stick. The Che Guevara video might as well be encrypted, too, for all the sense it made, and we still didn't know if it was linked in any way to Hilary's disappearance. I liked focus and structure, but there was nothing around which we could organize, no obvious steps to take. It didn't help that we were all exhausted—none of us had gone to sleep until late the previous evening, and it would have been a long and stressful day even without excessive exercise and the sudden elimination of important stimulants from my diet.

Then I remembered something that had been on Ben's and Luisa's to-do list. "What about the doormen? Did either of you get a chance to ask if they saw Hilary leaving last night?" That was one way to check if Iggie was telling the truth, and it might also provide us with some ideas as to what we should do next.

"We spoke to the guys on duty earlier," said Ben. "None of them was working last night, so they couldn't help us, but the shift changes at midnight, and they said a couple of guys who worked the late shift last night may be on again tonight."

Luisa checked her watch. "It's ten of twelve now. Why

don't we go downstairs and catch them as they change shifts?"

"You can walk us out," said Peter. "We can hear what they have to say, but after that we should probably call it a night. I can also check out the other file on the memory stick once Rachel and I get back to my parents' house. I have some programs on my laptop that might help me decrypt it."

Otherwise we were fresh out of inspiration, even after a nostalgic but unproductive round of Che Guevara free-association.

It's not easy to make a quick getaway from the San Francisco Four Seasons, because the lobby's on the fifth floor. Separate elevator banks lead from the guestrooms to the lobby and then from the lobby to the street, and changing elevator banks requires a trip from one corner of the lobby to another. But as trips go, it's a relatively painless one, a short stroll in a tasteful setting, and it shouldn't be particularly dangerous.

Unless, that is, it's late on a Sunday night. The hotel is a favorite of Wall Street types, and while a day trip to the West Coast isn't out of the question for those accustomed to traveling in first class when a private jet is unavailable, morning meetings can make an overnight stay inevitable. And there must have been a lot of meetings scheduled for Monday morning, because the lobby was thick with bankers just arrived from the last flight from New York. It was probably inevitable I'd run into someone I knew, and sure enough, I did.

I was following everyone out of the first set of elevators when I spotted Clay Finch, an acquaintance from a prep course I'd taken years ago for the Series Seven exam, a securities-industry accreditation. Clay was an enormously tall and extremely serious guy with a nonexistent sense of humor, although its absence might have been less noticeable if he hadn't insisted on wearing bow ties. I thought a sense of humor was a prerequisite for wearing bow ties, both generally and about the bow ties, but either Clay felt differently or he mistakenly believed his sense of humor was present and intact.

I hardly came up to his waist, so it was possible I could slip by unseen, and I briefly toyed with the idea of pretending I hadn't noticed him. But subterfuge always backfired, at least when I practiced it, and networking was supposed to be important in my line of work. I told my friends I'd meet them downstairs and stopped to say hello.

"Rachel. How nice to see you." Coming from most people, Clay's formal greeting and professional handshake would have seemed icy, but from him it was the equivalent of a kiss on the mouth, albeit without tongue.

"What brings you to town?" I asked.

"I could tell you, but I'd have to kill you," said Clay. Investment bankers were supposed to keep their clients' business confidential, and his was the standard reply to questions like mine, but it was usually delivered with a smile and a chuckle. Clay didn't smile much, and he never chuckled.

The conversation quickly dried up from there, and, having satisfied any networking obligations, I started on my goodbyes. "Well, Clay, it was great to run into you—" I was saying when I noticed a familiar-looking envelope tucked into the crook of his elbow, right at my eye level, and my words froze in my mouth.

His arm hid most of the address, but I could see all I needed to see: the tail end of Clay's last name, INCH, written in large block letters.

I considered accidentally bumping into him in the hope he'd drop the envelope, but that would be like trying to fell a redwood by poking it with a Q-tip. Instead I simply pulled it out from under his arm. Fortunately, Clay was Clay, so if this bothered him it was impossible to tell.

"Where did you get this?" I asked, turning the small package over in my hands. It was another twin to the one in which I'd received my iPod, which I guessed made it the triplet to the one in which my Lincoln Memorial keychain had been delivered, and the handwriting spelling out Clay's name was unmistakably the same.

"It was waiting for me when I checked in."

"Do you know what it is or who it's from?"

"I have no idea. I wasn't expecting anything, and, as you can see, there's no return address. The people at the front desk said it arrived this afternoon, but nobody could remember who made the delivery."

"Let's open it," I suggested, as if opening other people's mail was the most natural thing in the world.

"Uh—"

"Allow me." And before Clay could protest, I pulled on the little tab, ripped open the top, and tipped the contents into my hand.

I wasn't sure if I was hoping for a surprise, but I didn't get one. Clay's envelope held a Lincoln Memorial keychain, just like mine. The anonymous mastermind behind this particular scavenger hunt must have gotten a good deal at whichever novelty store he frequented, or perhaps he always bought in bulk.

"Isn't that strange?" asked Clay, peering down at the keychain. Of course, he hadn't even received the special Skater Girl treatment. "What do you think I'm supposed to do with this?"

I didn't known what to tell him, but I didn't get the chance to say anything anyway, because we were interrupted by someone calling our names at full volume from across the lobby. The shrill voice sounded as if it belonged to a particularly articulate and peppy macaw, but I would have known it anywhere and Clay probably would, too. We'd sat in the same classroom as its owner, Camilla Gergen, during our prep course, and nothing could make a room seem smaller than being trapped in it with Camilla Gergen's voice.

She joined us with a level of excitement I found excessive given the occasion and the flimsy nature of our prior acquaintance. "Get OUT! I don't BELIEVE it! What are you two DOING here?"

"Hello, Camilla," said Clay. He had no "how nice to see you" to spare for her, but he bent stiffly when it became clear she intended to air kiss him on not one but both cheeks, whether he liked it or not.

"MUH!" she said to one cheek. "And MUH!" she said to the other.

"Hi," I said, submitting to my own set of air kisses.

"This is SO weird. It's the weirdest! All of us together again. It's just like our Series Seven class!"

"Just like it," I agreed amiably. The class had taken place eight years ago in an office building with thirty other people, an instructor and an overhead projector, but debating its resemblance to this encounter would only prolong it, and I now very much wanted to talk to Clay alone.

"Let's grab a drink!" said Camilla. "It's been way too long since I've seen you both. I think the lounge is still open."

I fumbled for an excuse that would involve Camilla shutting up and going away. "Wow, does that sound like incredible fun, but—"

"Oh, my GOD! Did you get one of those, too?" She was pointing at the keychain resting in my palm.

"Too?"

Camilla held up her own padded envelope. CAMILLA GERGEN was printed on the front in the same distinctive handwriting. "I got one when I checked in. I thought it was a gift or something from the hotel, since I stay here so often. But it's not from the hotel. I don't know who it's from. Isn't that just the weirdest coincidence that you got one, too? What are you going to do with yours? I don't know what I'm going to do with mine. I have the cutest little keychain already, with my initials on it and a little picture of my pug and me. See? Do you like pugs? Isn't he just the cutest? Now, how about that drink? They have the yummiest olives in the lounge here. And pistachios. I love pistachios, don't you?"

Her voice would make fingernails on a chalkboard sound like Chopin, and it didn't help that she used it so liberally.

But one word—*coincidence*—screeched into my ears and kept ricocheting off the walls of my skull.

It couldn't be a coincidence that we'd all received the keychains. There had to be a connection, but that didn't mean I knew what the connection was. My brain would have kicked into overdrive if it had been sufficiently nourished, trying to figure out what the three of us had in common besides our prep course and our profession more broadly. I scanned the lobby, checking to see if any other yuppies were holding padded envelopes or Lincoln Memorial keychains, but we seemed to be the lucky few.

Then Camilla unwittingly made up for the hours I'd spent in that classroom and the handfuls of aspirin I'd downed trying to remedy the headaches she'd caused.

"I bet you're both here to pitch the Igobe IPO!" she squealed. "My firm's scheduled for nine tomorrow morning. When are you two up?"

"I could tell you, but I'd have to kill you," said Clay, stone-faced, but a muscle in his jaw twitched, and I knew Camilla had guessed it in one.

That Iggie had promised me that Winslow, Brown would be the first firm to make its presentation to Igobe was the least of my concerns. I could postpone getting angry about his scheduling at least two other firms ahead of mine once we'd found Hilary and straightened everything else out.

I said a hurried goodbye to Clay and Camilla, leaving Clay to extricate himself from Camilla's grasp and without telling them about my own keychain, much less about the iPod video. Neither seemed particularly eager to figure out what their keychains meant, and I doubted they would be rushing over to the Martin Luther King memorial tonight, so if this was a contest I felt confident I'd maintain my lead.

The elevator took only a few seconds to descend from the lobby to the street, but that was all the time required for a couple of things to make themselves nice and clear. I still had more questions than answers, but I did know now that the keychains, and the scavenger hunt for which they were the first clue, had nothing to do with Hilary's disappearance. They were messages from somebody not just to me, but to all of the investment bankers competing for the golden prize of handling Igobe's IPO, and the messages seemed intended to make us think twice about the role we would play in making Iggie obscenely rich. Of course, the messenger had overlooked a critical factor: investment bankers, by definition, weren't exactly fertile ground either for second thoughts or planting the seeds of social revolution. We were all about capitalism in its purest and least fettered form.

I now also knew that the messenger had to be related to Igobe in some way. How else could he—or she—know which firms would be pitching the Igobe IPO, who the contact person was for each firm, and where each could be found today? That was hardly public information. My whereabouts must have been especially challenging, since I wasn't staying at a hotel, but somebody in Iggie's office could probably have accessed his calendar and address book, tracked me down at the Forrests' house, and even trailed me from there. It wouldn't have been easy—in fact, it would have involved a lot of work—but this person seemed to be a man—or a woman—with a mission: specifically, to derail Igobe and its IPO.

I dashed through the elevator doors as they opened, eager to tell everyone else what I'd just learned, but when I raced out to Market Street, the only person there was a lone uniformed doorman. I looked up and down the nearly deserted street in confusion.

"May I help you, miss?" asked the doorman. His nametag read Dmitri.

"What?" I asked, distracted. Had they ditched me? Given Luisa's current state of mind, it wouldn't surprise me, and I couldn't speak for Ben or Abigail, but it was hard to imagine Peter doing such a thing.

"May I help you?" Dmitri asked again.

"Oh. Sorry. Sure. By any chance were you on duty last night around this same time?"

He smiled and chuckled. He could have given Clay Finch some pointers. "Some people were here just a few minutes ago, asking me the same question."

"Where did they go?"

He gestured back inside. "I sent them to the other entrance, on Stevenson Street. The guys there were on last night. I have Saturdays off."

"Great, thanks." It was a relief to know I hadn't been abandoned, but I did have to wonder what Dr. Grout would make of the speed with which I'd entertained the possibility.

I hurried back inside and across the marble floors of the lower lobby to a rear entrance I'd never used before, although it was officially the main entrance to the hotel. A circular drive served as a drop-off and loading point for passengers, and I found my friends standing at the curb, talking to another doorman and the bell captain.

"What took you so long?" Luisa asked me, but she didn't wait for my response. "You won't believe it. These men say there were *two* Lamborghinis here last night, both black."

"Just like the two at the party," added Peter.

"They were both already parked here when we came on at twelve," said this doorman, whose nametag read Gustav. "We see some nice cars around here, but two Lamborghinis together are pretty hard to miss."

"Did you see the drivers?" asked Ben. "Or anyone getting in or out?"

"The cars had tinted windows, so there might have been other people inside I didn't see, but both of the drivers got out," said the bell captain. His name, according to his nametag, was Ray, which squashed my budding theory that the Four Seasons didn't hire people with boring names. "One regular-looking guy, sort of preppie, and then a guy dressed head-to-toe in purple velvet."

"That must have been Iggie," said Luisa. "Unless there's a purple-velvet trend of which I'm unaware, which would be disturbing."

"On so many levels," I agreed.

"Iggie sounds right," said Gustav. "One of the cars had a vanity plate: IGSTER1. And now that I think about it, the other car had a vanity plate, too, but I can't remember what it said."

"Was it Alex something?" I suggested helpfully. Peter glanced at me, his expression unreadable.

"I don't think so," said Gustav, thinking. "I'd know it if I saw it, but I can't remember it offhand. And the two guys seemed to know each other already. It wasn't like they were meeting for the first time and bonding over their cars. They talked for a minute or two, and then they both got back into their cars and one drove away."

"Which one?" Ben asked.

"I don't remember," said Gustav.

"Me, either," said Ray. "But a blond lady came out a few minutes later and got into the car that was still there, and then that one drove away, too."

"Was the blonde really tall? And wearing a really small dress?" I asked.

This elicited a smile from them both. "It was like something out of a ZZ Top video," admitted Ray.

"Could you hear what the men said? When they got out of their cars?" asked Luisa.

They shook their heads. "And we couldn't really tell where they were headed, either, if that's what you're going to ask next," said Gustav. "The only way out of here is down Stevenson Street, and that dead-ends on Third, which is one-way. But once they were back on Market, they could have gone anywhere."

A Town Car drew up to disgorge some more banker types, so we thanked them for their help and let them get back to work.

"Well, either Iggie was lying or Hilary got into the other Lamborghini," said Abigail.

"Maybe we should ask your friend Alex what he's driving these days," I said to Peter. "He may not have been the preppie guy in the footage from Hilary's floor, but he could be the preppie guy with the Lamborghini. We know there were two Lamborghinis at the party, and we know Alex knows Iggie. And that he's preppie."

Peter looked uncomfortable. "Listen, I know Alex about as well as you know Iggie. It's not like he's my best friend, but he already said he wasn't here last night."

Ben cleared his throat. "You know, I forgot to mention this before—it must have slipped my mind with everything else that's happened, and at the time I didn't think it was important—but I got a call from a friend of mine at the Bureau a couple of hours ago. He didn't have any luck finding an address or phone number for Iggie, but he did manage to trace the number of the phone that sent the text messages. It's registered to a company of some sort, but it just has letters for a name, no words at all."

"What are the letters?" I asked.

"*A—C—V—L—L—C.*"

"That's it!" It was Gustav, who had rejoined us after attending to the occupants of the Town Car. "That was the other plate! *A—C—V—L—L—C!*"

I turned to Peter. "The *A* and the *C* could be for Alex Cutler. And the *V* could be for Ventures, right? ACV, LLC. Is that the name of his firm?"

Peter shifted his weight from one foot to the other and stuck his hands in his pockets. "I think it's something like that."

"And he said his firm invested in Igobe, which means he's looking at a big payoff from the IPO. So he's probably as interested as Iggie in making sure there's no bad news about the company."

"Probably," Peter agreed, but with reluctance. I guessed he didn't like the idea of his former fraternity brother being on the side of evil, and I could understand that sort of loyalty.

But there were too many little clues leading to Alex to ignore. A quick phone call to directory assistance taught us that Alex was nearly as protective of his privacy as Iggie, and just as hard to locate. We thought about asking him directly, via phone or text, where he lived, whether he knew where Hilary was, or, at the very least, what kind of car he drove, but if he was a bad guy, these questions would tip our hand even more than we'd already tipped it by asking him if he'd been at the Four Seasons in the first place.

Which was why I said the words I thought I'd never hear myself say, although I probably didn't get the inflection quite right. If anything, my tone was grim.

"Tennis, anyone?"

We took another few minutes to regroup in the lower lobby. Abigail tried Iggie again on her cell phone, hoping to ask him about Alex, but he was no longer answering since it was past his bedtime. An image of Iggie in purple satin pajamas and an eyeshade, clutching a stuffed elephant, appeared before my eyes, and I hoped it would go away soon. Meanwhile, Peter texted Alex and Caro to let them know we'd meet them for doubles at twelve-thirty at their tennis club in Palo Alto. If all went well, Alex would pull up to the club in his Lamborghini, and then we could pummel Hilary's whereabouts out of him with our rackets, rescue her and get on with our lives. This was assuming, of course, that it wasn't too late to rescue Hilary, an alternative none of us wanted to consider.

"We could carpool down there in the morning," suggested

Abigail. "I've been thinking it might make sense to try to catch Iggie off guard by dropping in earlier rather than waiting until lunch, and it would catch him even more off guard if I brought you all along. Which would have the added benefit of helping me to avoid any one-on-one time with him. Igobe's headquarters aren't far from the club, and there's a mall nearby where we can hang out while you're at tennis."

The opportunity to confront Iggie in person was tempting, and, after the phone call we'd witnessed, we could all appreciate why Abigail would want to trade her intimate lunch with Iggie for a group event. And after I'd finished telling everyone about Clay and Camilla and their matching keychains, everyone agreed it made sense for more reasons than one to try to talk to Iggie directly, although Luisa's decision probably had more to do with Abigail and the mention of a mall than anything else.

"If Iggie has any shame, he'll be embarrassed he lied to me about meeting with other banks first," I said. "That might give us some leverage when we ask about Alex. We can also ask him if he has any ideas as to who might want to spoil his IPO. Maybe the keychain guy is a disgruntled employee."

"I suspect Iggie's surrounded by disgruntled employees," observed Luisa.

"And he doesn't have much shame," said Abigail. "But it can't hurt to ask."

Ben offered to try to pull a few more strings to procure a list of Lamborghini owners in the area, and Peter volunteered to pick everyone up at the hotel in the morning, assuming his parents could spare a hybrid.

"Unless it would be more convenient for Abigail if we

picked her up at home," I said. "Abigail, would that be more convenient for you?"

Luisa shot me a murderous look. What she and Abigail planned to do after we left was none of my business, especially if it involved Abigail not waking up in her own bed, but I couldn't resist the opportunity to get back at Luisa just the tiniest bit. I'd been insufferable, as well, but it was important to keep the score even on the insufferability front.

"That's all right," said Abigail easily. "I'll meet up with you here. Thanks, though."

"Yes, Rachel. Thank you," said Luisa, but there was a menacing edge to her voice that made me glad we weren't alone.

It was fortunate that Peter remembered where he'd parked the car, because I didn't. A few minutes later we were buckled in and heading back across the city to Pacific Heights. He gave up trying to find anything of interest on the radio once it became clear nothing could be heard over my yawning.

"We'll be there soon," he assured me. "There shouldn't be any traffic at this time of night."

"Good," I said, but it came out muffled by yet another enormous yawn. "Ouch."

"What's wrong?" he asked.

"My jaw cracked."

He laughed. "Life with you is always an adventure."

He said it affectionately, and I knew he meant well, but the words reminded me of what I'd been too busy to think about for the past few hours—namely, that I was merely his way of getting over Caro after she'd broken up with him, a sort of palate-cleansing interlude of oddity that would last until she either took him back or he found someone else comparably normal. And thinking about this only made me more anxious than I'd been already, between trying to track down Hilary, ingratiating myself to Peter's parents and making sure I didn't completely screw up my career.

I could feel myself being sucked into the preliminary loops of a doom spiral. I really needed someone to talk to, but my usual confidantes were either long asleep on the East Coast, missing, or too gripped by nicotine withdrawal to be of any use. Luisa's specific brand of calm rationality would have been particularly comforting, but she was too scary right now even to contemplate seeking her out for emotional support.

Since nobody appropriate was available to discuss my relationship with Peter, I decided I might as well use this time productively and ask Peter about another relationship. He might have been in denial about Caro and whether fifteen years together could be interpreted as serious, but perhaps I could figure out what was going on between him and the fourth member of our little tennis klatch. Assuming tennis had klatches.

"What's with you and Alex Cutler?" I asked.

"What do you mean?"

"Why do you keep defending him? Is it because you're brothers?"

"Brothers?"

"Frat brothers. Like Bluto and Otter."

He laughed. "How many times have you seen *Animal*

House, anyway? Trust me, Bluto and Otter wouldn't have had anything to do with us. Even the Kevin Bacon character would have stayed away."

"Then is it just because you've known Alex for such a long time?" We were stopped at a traffic signal, and red light spilled through the windshield. It was a good color for Peter, but it probably wasn't the best look for me. The light turned green, and the car moved forward.

"No. I mean, we were friendly, and he always seemed like a nice enough guy, but he wasn't one of my closest friends."

"Then why did you invite him to the party?"

He glanced over at me. "Do you really want to know?"

"Sure."

"It's sort of silly. You promise you won't laugh?"

"Why would I laugh?" If Peter laughed at every silly thing I did, he'd be in perpetual hysterics.

"Well," he said, sounding unusually awkward, "I was hoping I could set him up with Caro."

"Set him up with Caro?"

"I thought they might make a good couple. Do you think they'd make a good couple? That is, if he ends up not being the sort of guy who goes around abducting your friends?"

"That's a pretty big if," I said, and it was, but inwardly I was trying to figure out why Peter would want to play matchmaker in this particular situation.

What kind of man cares enough about the woman who broke up with him—after fifteen years, no less—to set her up with someone else? Either Peter really was too good to be true, or he was so in denial about what a perfect couple *he* and Caro made that he'd gotten himself completely turned around mentally and was trying to sidestep the obvious by fixing her up with Alex. The poor guy had definitely been spending too much time with me: it was exactly the sort of convoluted combination of suppressing certain emotions while misdirecting others into self-defeating action for which I was famous among my friends.

"Caro hasn't really dated anyone since we— I mean, since she broke up with me. And she and Alex seem to have a lot in common," Peter was saying. "They've known each other for a long time, but maybe it just hasn't occurred to either of them to think of each other in a relationship sort of way. I thought that maybe if I gave them a little push, something might take."

"Uh-huh," I said noncommittally. Of course, if I had even half of a functioning brain, I should have been urging him on. Surely Caro would be less of a threat if she was safely involved with someone else, regardless of whether that someone else was potentially a kidnapper? But even if Alex was innocent, and even if he and Caro did get together, I knew it would only be a temporary fix.

One day, and probably sooner rather than later given the pace at which "adventures" seemed to pile up in my wake, Peter would remember how normal his life was with Caro and realize that was the sort of life he was meant to live.

By the time we let ourselves in through the Forrests' front door it was after one. I was hoping Peter's parents would be asleep rather than awake and wondering why their son's idiosyncratic fiancée was dragging him around the city with her colorful friends until all hours, but my hopes were only half-met. Susan was in bed but Charles was still up, reading in the den as jazz played in the background and Spot dozed at his feet. However, neither Charles nor Spot appeared even mildly curious as to where we'd been since dinner. Charles glanced up only briefly enough to wish us a good night before returning to his book. Spot glanced up equally briefly, thumped his tail once and went back to sleep.

Upstairs, I handed Peter the pen with the memory stick we'd retrieved from the safe, and he booted up his laptop while I went into the bathroom to do my own bedtime routine. The bright light over the sink only emphasized my pallor and lack of muscle tone, reminding me that another reason it would be convenient for Alex Cutler to drive up in a Lamborghini tomorrow and confess was that I would then be able to skip the tennis game. I flexed my biceps in the mirror, but I saw nothing remotely resembling definition, so I finished brushing my teeth and returned to the bedroom.

Peter was seated at the desk with his laptop open before him, typing as rapidly as was possible using only his index fingers and occasionally a pinkie. For reasons I'd never understood, he'd always resisted learning how to type. His old textbooks and childhood mementos still filled the shelves above the desk, including a framed picture of his high-school cross-country team along with their female counterparts. I'd glanced at it quickly before, but now I didn't want to know which of the coltlike girls, each bathed in the sort of rosy, endorphin-fueled glow that only a ten-mile romp across rugged terrain can deliver, was Ashley.

"Any luck?" I asked.

"I'm getting there," he said distractedly. "Give me a few more minutes."

"Okay," I said, opening the closet door to put my jacket away. Then I recoiled in horror.

I'd managed to forget completely about the afternoon's shopping expedition, and I hadn't thought to prepare myself for the sight before me now. The pink dress was hanging in the closet, clashing with my other clothes almost as badly as it clashed with my hair, and the matching pink shoes were lined up neatly on the floor underneath.

Then I noticed something else. Maybe Susan had been confident I'd want to keep the dress forever, or maybe she'd already guessed at my plans for my new ensemble and wanted to nip them in the bud. Either way, she'd taken it upon herself to remove the tags. I stared at the dress, utterly foiled. What could I possibly do with it now? Auction it off on eBay? With my luck, Susan would bid on it for herself so we could have matching outfits.

"Here we go," said Peter, just in time to stop me from descending a loop further down the spiral of doom.

"You got it?"

"Yep," he said with satisfaction.

Well, at least something had gone right this evening. I let the dress swing back in line with the other hangers and crossed over to the desk, carefully averting my gaze from the cross-country team photo and bending to look at the screen.

In an open window was what appeared to be the text of an e-mail sent to Hilary. The date was from Friday, but the sender's e-mail address was blank.

"It was encrypted with a fairly common program you can

download free off the Internet," Peter told me. "You need a password to run the decryption function, so I tried Dylan's zip code again, and it worked."

"You're very talented," I said.

"You're easily impressed," he said, pulling me down onto his lap for a better view of the screen. "I still couldn't figure out how to unblock the sender's address, and I don't know if this tells us much otherwise. But what do you think?"

I read the text. It was short and simple, and it probably would have made perfect sense to Hilary. I found it a bit less enlightening.

Monday night. Same time, same place. I'm promising you the story of the century. Take the precautions we discussed.
P.S. This e-mail will self-encrypt when you close it.

That was it. Or almost it.

At the bottom of the e-mail the sender had included a quote. And I might not have had Luisa's extensive grounding in political history, but I recognized it anyhow.

Workers of the world unite.

Perhaps I'd been a bit hasty in concluding that Hilary and my Marxist Santa Claus had nothing to do with each other.

18

It was only a few minutes after seven when I opened my eyes, but I was alone when I did, which didn't surprise me. I'd never been the sort of person who leaped out of bed in the morning. In fact, I was more the sort of person who swatted blindly at the snooze button with one hand while the rest of me slept on, relishing the happy warmth and comfort under the covers. Peter, on the other hand, woke before the alarm had a chance to go off, literally bounding out of bed and into his day. Caro probably did, too, I thought, grumpy.

I was feeling extra sluggish this morning, undoubtedly as a result of the combined effects of caffeine deprivation and whatever was the opposite of a runner's high. I rolled over a few times, giving my body the opportunity to sink back into sleep, but nothing happened, so I slowly propelled myself into a sitting position and just as slowly into a standing one. Then I extended a foot in the direction of the bathroom.

At which point I fell over.

I lay on the floor like a defective Weeble, cursing Richard Simmons, Jane Fonda, and everybody else who could be blamed for making it seem as if fitness should be a goal for anyone but elite athletes. Peter had said yesterday's run would be "fun," but not only was it not fun, the muscles in my legs were now so tight they couldn't do the flexing they needed to do to walk. I was descended from a long line of wise, if pale, people who fastidiously avoided breaking a sweat, along with eating any vegetable that didn't come out of a can, and most of them had lived well past the average life expectancy. It seemed as if we could all benefit from emulating their habits. There might even be a best-selling lifestyle manual in it.

I spent a few more minutes on the floor, fantasizing about my new life as a best-selling author of lifestyle manuals while trying to knead the stiffness from my calves. Then I dragged myself up into a standing position again and attempted forward movement. The massage had helped a bit, and if I walked only on my toes, taking mincing baby steps, I was marginally mobile.

The Forrests weren't the kind of family that expected everyone to be fully dressed at all times, so I minced down the stairs in my robe and pajamas, which were actually an ancient pair of Peter's pajamas I'd snagged from one of his dresser drawers. There was something cozy about their well-worn oversizedness, and I made a mental note to snag the remaining pairs to take back with me to New York. For all I knew, this trip would be my last chance to raid his adolescent wardrobe and I should make the most of it.

Peter and his parents were sitting in the breakfast room, looking chipper and with plates of traditional breakfast-type food in front of them, just like in a television commercial. I hadn't realized real people ever ate breakfasts like this on a weekday.

"Is everything okay?" asked Peter after I'd safely lowered my body onto a chair. "We heard a crash. I was about to go up and check on you."

"I—I just dropped something." That something was myself, but there was no need for them to know that.

"Rachel, dear, would you like a soda?" asked Susan, proud to have remembered my preferred morning beverage. She probably found mine such a strange choice that remembering it wasn't much of a challenge.

I wanted a soda so desperately I could chew off my own arm, but I managed to smile and shake my head. "I'll just have some herbal tea again, thank you."

Not only did Peter's family eat breakfast as if they were in a commercial, they made conversation in the morning as if they didn't feel it was necessary to be fully caffeinated before diving into personal interactions. At least, Peter and Susan made conversation while Charles read the paper. Peter told her about our changed itinerary and the planned field trip to Silicon Valley, although he fibbed and said it was because he wanted to show me around Stanford.

"And we're going to meet up with Caro and Alex Cutler for tennis," he added, neglecting to mention that Alex Cutler was most probably a criminal. He was still operating in innocent-until-proven-guilty mode on that front, which only validated my theory that he was exceptionally skilled at deluding himself about his personal relationships. "They both work near Palo Alto and said they could get away for a lunchtime game."

"That will be fun," said Susan with enthusiasm, but experience was teaching me that anything a Forrest thought would be fun was likely to be painful and potentially dangerous. She turned to me. "Be careful, dear. Caro has a killer serve. And her backhand is deadly, too."

"Good to know," I said, hoping even more intensely we would be able to unmask Alex Cutler as an evildoer before Caro could kill me with either her serve or her backhand. Neither seemed a particularly appealing way to die.

"Is Alex a good player, Peter?" asked Susan.

"I think so. I've never played with him before, but he said he plays a lot." He took a sip of coffee. "I have to admit, I'm hoping it will be good for Alex and Caro to spend some more time together. Maybe they'll hit it off."

"Hit it off? You mean romantically?" asked Susan.

Peter nodded. "Sure."

"Hmm," said Susan, taking a sip of her own coffee. "I don't know if I see them together, honey. Do you see them together, Rachel?"

Yet again, she'd caught me with my mouth full. All I could do was give a noncommittal murmur, though that's all I would have produced even if my mouth had been empty.

"I just don't know if I see them together," she repeated.

"It can't hurt to try, can it?" asked Peter.

"Of course not," she said, but she sounded doubtful.

I thought I knew why she sounded that way, and it wasn't because she suspected Alex of abducting my friend. How could she possibly see Caro with Alex when she still hoped Caro would end up with her own normal son?

Peter and I managed to get ourselves washed and dressed and into a hybrid by half past eight. Fighting traffic across the city was almost as difficult as it had been to fight off Susan's offers of juice, cereal, toast, English muffins, scrambled eggs, fried eggs, poached eggs and sausage, but it was less stressful because it wasn't necessary to be polite to the traffic. Of course, Peter being Peter, he was polite anyway. Except he couldn't stop humming.

"What are you humming?" I asked.

"I'm not sure. Whatever my dad had on the stereo last night. I can't get it out of my head."

We made a pathetic pair: I still had "Rice-a-Roni, the San Francisco treat," playing on in an endless mental loop and Peter was humming jazz. Caro probably loved jazz, I thought—all normal people did. To me it was the musical equivalent of Camilla Gergen's voice but less pleasant. And neither Peter's humming nor Rice-a-Roni were doing much for my mental state. My crankiness had not abated since yesterday; if anything, it was gathering force, and it didn't help that to my various withdrawal and fitness-induced woes was added a fierce craving for pilaf.

It took more than half an hour to get from Pacific Heights to the hotel, a drive that had taken less than fifteen minutes when we'd made it in the opposite direction at one that morning. Gustav and Ray were gone, replaced by the day-shift staff, but Luisa and Abigail were waiting for us.

"Where's Ben?" I asked as they slid into the backseat.

"Do I look like Ben's keeper?" snapped Luisa, quickly putting to rest any hopes that her mood had improved overnight. At least I could be confident she was keeping up her end of the dare. This was the only reason I refrained from remarking on Abigail's clothes, which were different than what she'd been wearing the previous night but also looked suspiciously like an outfit I'd recently seen on Luisa.

"Ben said he had a few things he wanted to follow up on here in the city," supplied Abigail before embarking on a detailed discussion with Peter of which route to take. Apparently the 101 was more direct but the 280 more scenic.

My brain was still working too slowly to wonder what, exactly, Ben was following up on or if it was related in any way to what he'd been doing while Luisa and Abigail had been dining *à deux* the previous evening. Nor did I pay attention to the route Peter ultimately decided upon, as I never paid attention to directions when I wasn't driving. Whichever highway we ended up on was choked with cars in both directions, including an astonishing number of hybrids. I'd seen a handful of them in Manhattan, and even a few hybrid taxis, but here we were surrounded.

As we meandered south in stop-and-go traffic, Peter and I filled in Luisa and Abigail on the text of the file he'd decrypted, showing them a printout of the e-mail, and together we discussed the ways in which the various dots might connect.

"Let me make sure I understand," said Luisa in a way that

really suggested she was having difficulty understanding how she'd found herself involved in this whole mess in the first place. "To start with, there's Marxist Santa, who's trying to throw a wrench into the Igobe IPO by leading all of the investment bankers who might handle the IPO on a scavenger hunt."

"It's not the most direct way to go about things, but I can't figure out why else he'd be targeting the people he's been targeting," I said.

"And we're sure that Marxist Santa has inside access to Igobe?" asked Abigail.

"How else would he know which bankers to target?" I said.

"And then there's the hacker, Petite Fleur, who also wants to bring Igobe down by compromising its technology," said Peter.

"So Petite Fleur is second. And then there's the third person we know Hilary's met with at least once, presumably about her Igobe article, and who also has a soft spot for Karl Marx," Luisa said.

"Which suggests that the third person from Hilary's e-mail could be the same as the first person, Marxist Santa," I concluded. "And maybe Marxist Santa knows what Petite Fleur is up to, and that's what he's promising Hilary will be the 'story of the century.' Or maybe Marxist Santa and Petite Fleur are one and the same."

"Obviously," said Luisa dryly. I had to admit, I was pretty confused myself.

"Is it possible that this person—or persons—kidnapped Hilary?" asked Abigail.

I thought about that. "I guess it's not impossible, but Hilary's on his side. Or their side."

"And which side is that?" asked Luisa.

"The side that's standing in the way of the people who would benefit from an Igobe IPO. Namely, Iggie and Alex Cutler," I said, trying to sound less confused than I felt.

"It would be good to know when and where 'same time' and 'same place' are supposed to be," mused Abigail. "Did Hilary tell any of you where she'd been in the days leading up to the party?"

She might have, I thought guiltily, but I'd been so wrapped up in proving my normality I hadn't paid much attention.

"I only remember her mentioning she'd been doing research," said Luisa. "I don't think she told me where, and I didn't ask."

"Ben might know," suggested Peter.

Ben hadn't seemed to know much of anything thus far, but maybe he'd come through on this. "We should call him. Do you know if he's still at the hotel—" I started to ask.

But then I had another idea, and it was nothing short of brilliant. "I think I may be a genius."

"Rachel, you are many things, but you are not a genius," said Luisa.

I chalked this up to nicotine withdrawal and let it go. "Hilary left a pile of receipts in her room. Maybe one of the receipts is from where she met the person from the e-mail."

"So we could put together where Hilary was and when she was there from the receipts?" asked Peter.

"Exactly. Then *we* can meet up at the same time and same place with the person who sent the e-mail, and he might be able to help us locate Hilary. And maybe we can also find out if he is, in fact, Marxist Santa and what he thinks the story of the century is."

"That's a great idea," he said. Of course, Peter would be enthusiastic about anything that didn't incriminate his old frat buddy, but even Abigail, who hadn't spent the better part of a year convincing herself she was in love with me, agreed it was a great idea, and she chimed in to say so. To my credit, I did not turn around to say "so there" to Luisa in the backseat.

"Let's call Ben right now," I said. "Maybe he can start piecing together Hilary's trail, and if we don't have any luck with Iggie or Alex, we can pick up from there."

"Fine," said Luisa, "I'll call Ben and run it by him." This was as close as I was going to get to an admission from her that my idea was a good one. She reached Ben on his cell phone and spoke to him briefly, explaining about the e-mail and the receipts.

"Well?" I asked when she'd completed her call.

"He says he'll get on it in a bit," she replied.

"Did he think it was brilliant?" I asked. "I bet he thought it was brilliant."

"Stop fishing for compliments."

"How was that fishing for compliments?"

"Please."

"I wasn't fishing. I was simply asking what Ben said." She harrumphed in response.

"Did you just harrumph at me?"

"Don't be ridiculous."

"I'm not being ridiculous. You're being ridiculous."

"I'm not being ridiculous. And you started it."

"I did not start it. You started it."

"What precisely did I start, Rachel?"

"You know what you started—"

"AARGHH!" This was from Peter, not Luisa. Horns blared as he cut across three lanes of traffic and pulled onto the highway's shoulder.

"What's wrong?" asked Luisa, alarmed.

"Are you okay?" I asked as he jammed the car into Park.

"*I* am fine," he said between clenched teeth. "The two of you, however, are not. You've been at each other's throats since we got in the car. In fact, you've been at each other's throats since yesterday. Either stop the bickering now, or you're going to get out and walk, and I won't care if you go through a case of soda and a carton of cigarettes on the way."

"We can't do that," I pointed out. "We were dared, and we don't want to be wusses."

"Then don't be wusses. But the choice is the same. Which is it going to be? Ride and behave, or walk and bicker?"

"We weren't bickering," said Luisa. "Do you think we were bickering, Rachel?"

"Of course not," I said. "But who knew that putting Peter behind the wheel would turn him into such a dad?"

19

Only Abigail's calm mediation, Luisa's and my promises that we'd try to act like reasonable adults and the suggestion that we make a quick detour to pick up some nicotine gum convinced Peter it would be safe to get back on the road. I'd never seen him throw a tantrum before, even one as relatively mild as his had been. A perverse part of me enjoyed learning what it to took to push him over the edge, but I knew better than to tell him that.

Fortunately, we didn't have much farther to go. Signs started popping up for Redwood City and Atherton, followed by Menlo Park and Palo Alto. We were going a couple of towns south of Palo Alto to Santa Clara, just past the "Googleplex" in Mountain View and Yahoo!'s Sunnyvale headquarters. Sunnyvale was part of Silicon Valley, so the vale was legitimate, and the weather here was definitely sunnier than in San Francisco, but it seemed to me that only a person who either had something to hide or a reckless need to tempt fate would name a place Sunnyvale.

We pulled off the highway just before ten, letting Abigail guide us the few remaining miles. The buildings we passed looked like those in any recently built American office park, but the signs out front bore the sort of playful names specific to start-ups run by people barely out of their teens, and the cars in the parking lots indicated which buildings' inhabitants had already struck Internet gold and which were still toiling away in the hopes of a future payoff. Igobe's pre-IPO parking lot held more of the latter type, but there was a gleaming black Lamborghini parked in a reserved space in the first row.

"Looks like the Igster's in the house," said Peter, pointing out its vanity plate, IGSTER1, as he steered into a nearby slot reserved for visitors.

"And it looks like his employees are being alienated from the fruits of their labors," said Luisa, observing the lesser cars in the lot and chewing furiously on a wad of Nicorette. As a general rule, she considered gum tacky, but she'd been willing to make an exception for the sake of Peter's nerves, and her mood had made a dramatic turn for the better once she unwrapped the first piece. It was too bad there wasn't a gum replacement for Diet Coke.

"Iggie's been having a hard time holding on to talent," Abigail told us as we left the car and headed toward the entrance. "A lot of start-ups around here don't pay much, but they are generous with stock options, so if the company does well and goes public, the options can be worth a lot. There are more than a few janitors and mail clerks who've made millions that way. Iggie's tightfisted with everyone but himself, and he's been stingy not only with salaries but with the options, too. It's making it difficult for him to hire the best people, which is one reason why Igobe's still using Leo's original software designs, but it's going to be a problem when he needs to start work on the next generation's software release and updates."

Yet another thing it was good to know before I committed my firm to handling the Igobe IPO. The more I heard, the more I wondered if it would make sense to cancel tomorrow's meeting altogether, whether Iggie was a kidnaper or not.

In front of the building, purple flowers planted in a circle of green grass spelled out Igobe's name in its trademark bubble letters. It was hard to imagine Winslow, Brown with such a logo, much less spelling it out in tulips—the firm generally stuck to a dignified sans serif font that didn't require watering—but Silicon Valley culture had little in common with that of a white-shoe New York investment bank, save a fascination with money. Once the automatic glass doors of the entranceway slid apart with a muted swoosh, the differences became all the more striking. We stepped right into a vast open-plan work space that looked as if it had been lifted whole from a satire of dot-com era excesses. Twentysomethings dressed in geek-hipster chic zipped around on scooters, while others flopped on brightly colored beanbag chairs or chatted in front of glass-fronted refrigerators stocked with an array of designer beverages. The decorator who had outfitted Winslow, Brown's headquarters in dark paneling, Persian rugs, and wing chairs would have fled, shrieking in terror, if the scene hadn't given him a coronary first.

Only one other person besides us didn't seem to fit right in, but she wouldn't have fit in at Winslow, Brown, either. Across the expanse of carefully distressed polished concrete sat a reception desk made from molded purple plastic, and behind the desk and its collection of lava lamps sat an older woman with frizzy gray hair, red-framed glasses and a purple visor stitched with the Igobe logo. Even though she was of average weight, she was wearing a muumuu patterned in a neon-shaded floral print that made me think with newly discovered affection of the pink dress hanging in the closet back at the Forrests' house.

"Just shoot me now," said Abigail, freezing inside the entrance.

"What's wrong?" asked Peter.

"I can't believe it. She's still here."

"Who's still where?" asked Luisa.

But before she could respond, the woman behind the desk emitted a noise that sounded like a curdled yodel and would have put Camilla Gergen to shame. "Yoo-hoo! Biggie!"

Abigail blanched, something I'd thought only happened in books. "Twice in twelve hours," she muttered, and for a moment I thought she was going to retreat back through the sliding-glass doors. But then she squared her shoulders and strode forward.

"Hello, Phyllis," she said politely. "I didn't realize you were still working here."

So this was the tree from which Iggie had fallen.

"Of course I'm working here. My baby needs me! But we weren't expecting you for another couple of hours, Biggie," said Phyllis in a tone that managed to grate, scold and condescend in one fell swoop. "Igor's scheduled in back-to-back meetings until noon. You know how busy he is. And we thought you were coming alone. Who are your little friends?"

I hadn't been called anyone's "little friend" since the third grade. "This is my boss, Peter, and his fiancée, Rachel," Abigail said. "And this is my friend, Luisa."

Judging from the way Phyllis set her lips, outlined in coral pencil a shade darker than her lipstick, she wasn't even remotely pleased to see us, which seemed unfair. We were clean and neatly dressed, and we'd all managed to plaster amiable meeting-someone's-mother expressions on our faces. I might not be looking my best, but Luisa was beautiful even when cranky and chewing gum, and Peter had the sort of unassuming good looks that always made me worry people thought he could do better when they saw us together.

But it was Luisa, standing closest to Abigail, who was the source of her displeasure, notwithstanding her resemblance to Salma Hayek. Phyllis gave her the once-over and sniffed before turning back to Abigail. "Dr. Grout is right. This is just a phase you're going through, Biggie. You've probably been watching too much of that Ellen DeGeneres person. I know it's all the rage right now, but you and Igor are so well matched. You really shouldn't let fashion dictate your choice of life partner."

"Yes. I blame it all on Ellen," said Abigail in the mild tone I was learning she reserved for sarcasm.

But sarcasm was lost on Phyllis. "Igor needs someone to

be the woman behind the man. You were perfectly suited for that, Biggie. And it's so much healthier when people play their proper roles in a relationship. Even Dr. Grout thinks so. There's nothing as fulfilling as maintaining a happy household. Taking care of others is really the very best work a woman can do."

Abigail opened her mouth, probably to debate her proper role and just how happy her household with Iggie had been, but then she closed it, apparently recognizing how futile any attempt at debate would be. "Could you let Igg— I mean, Igor know I'm here?" she asked instead.

"I told you already. He's in a meeting, and he's much too important to be disturbed." Phyllis didn't comment explicitly on our relative unimportance, but it didn't take much imagination to guess what she was thinking. The Igster's ego had clearly had some help from his mother in reaching its current size.

We seemed to have arrived at an impasse, but then Iggie himself appeared around a distant corner, herding Camilla Gergen and a small flock of other banker types, presumably her colleagues, toward the exit. I ducked behind Peter—I'd seen enough of Camilla the previous evening to last for another eight years—but the space was sufficiently large that the group could pass at a safe distance with only snatches of their conversation echoing in our direction. We heard *billion* more than once, which probably explained why Iggie had shown them the courtesy of accompanying them to the door rather than letting them find their own way out.

Once Camilla and her companions were safely on the other side of the sliding-glass panels, Phyllis, who had apparently accepted that Iggie was bound to see us waiting for him and decided to take control of the situation, gave another yodel. "Yoo-hoo!" she called. "Igor! Look who's here, baby!"

While Phyllis may have played an important role in developing Iggie's ego, she had less control over other parts of his psyche and had been unable to extinguish the torch he still carried for his ex-wife. Once his eyes landed on Abigail he practically skipped over to the reception area. He was again dressed all in purple, from his shoes up to his shirt, although today he'd opted for silk instead of velvet. I wondered if Prince was aware someone was raiding his wardrobe.

"She came early, and she brought some people with her, which is very inconvenient. I told her you were busy and that she'd just have to wait," Phyllis said. "Your next appointment will be here any second, and you don't have time for her now. Your calendar will get all backed up."

"That's okay, Ma," said Iggie. "I can always make time for Biggie."

He seemed about as thrilled as Phyllis had been to see that Abigail wasn't alone, but he still welcomed us all graciously and offered a tour of the premises, eager to show off the scale of his company's operations.

"Thanks, Iggie, maybe later. There are some things we wanted to discuss with you first," I said.

"In private," added Abigail, with a pointed look in Phyllis's direction. It was possible giving pointed looks was a skill she came by naturally, but it was so well done I suspected Luisa had been coaching her.

"Whatever you want, Biggie. We'll just be a few minutes, Ma."

I could feel Phyllis's glare on our backs as Iggie led us through the maze of low-walled cubicles, waving cheerily at the geek-hipster minions we passed before showing us into a glass-walled conference room. "Check it," he said, flipping a switch. Instantly, the glass panes seemed to fill with smoke, and what had been clear was now opaque. "Is that cool or what?"

We all agreed it was cool, although simple Venetian blinds or even some tasteful drapes would have been just as effective, but we couldn't waste valuable minutes admiring the office decor, especially with Phyllis likely to interrupt at any moment.

"So, Iggie, was that Camilla Gergen from Ryan Brothers we saw just now?" I asked. We'd agreed on the drive down to start by putting him on the defensive, assuming such a thing was possible where Iggie was concerned.

"Who?" he said, with the same hammy overemoted surprise he'd tried on the phone last night. It was no more convincing in person.

"It's all right, Iggie," I said. "I know you're talking to other banks about the IPO. Anyone in your shoes would do the same thing." This was true, although I doubted many people would want to wear his purple Doc Martens. "Did you tell them all they'd be first up to pitch, too?"

"No, Rachel, your firm is going first. Really. The Ryan Brothers people were just here to give me some advice about—uh, about—"

"Don't worry, Iggie. I understand. In fact, it's probably a good thing you're talking to so many different firms, because the more I hear about Igobe, the less sure I am that my own firm would want to represent you. We prefer to work with companies with stronger prospects, and it sounds as if the future here might be less rosy than you'd like everyone to believe."

"What are you talking about?" he asked, his tone growing as defensive as we'd hoped.

"We know that there are rumors that your technology can be hacked, and we know that Hilary was writing an article that was critical of Igobe," said Abigail. "And we also know there's a fifty-percent chance you were lying about whether you did more than drop her off at the hotel."

"How did you get to fifty percent?" asked Iggie, ever the math prodigy. I noticed he didn't question what she had said about either the hacker or Hilary's article.

"There were two Lamborghinis at the Four Seasons that night, and we know one of them belonged to you. We also know one drove off without Hilary and one drove off with her," said Luisa.

"Which means she was either with you or she was in the other car," concluded Peter.

"Oh," said Iggie with relief. "That's easy. She must have been in the other car, because she wasn't with me. I just dropped her off, like I told you." He rubbed his hands together. "Now, are you guys staying for lunch, too? Because I was hoping to have some private time with Big— I mean, Abigail."

"Not so fast, Iggie," said Abigail. "Who was driving the other Lamborghini?"

"How should I know?"

"You should know because the guys working the door at

the hotel saw you both get out of your cars and talk to each other," she said.

"Wow, Biggie. You really have been following my every move, haven't you?" Iggie sounded touched, as if he was interpreting the legwork we'd done as a sign that Abigail cared about him rather than distrusted him.

"Not at all," I said. "We're just trying to find Hilary. We know from eyewitnesses and from the hotel's security cameras that you took her to the Four Seasons, we know she went upstairs for her laptop and notebook, and we know she came back downstairs and got into one of two Lamborghinis that were there that night. If you were just dropping her off, why did you stick around and talk to the other driver? And who was he?"

"I told you, we were just talking about our cars. There aren't a lot of Lamborghinis around. Not many people can afford to drop that much green on a set of wheels, if you know what I mean." He looked around, as if to make sure that we did, in fact, know what he meant and to see if anyone appreciated his impromptu rhyming skills. "We talked about our cars, and then I skedaddled. Sans Hilarita."

"Why did you leave without her?" Peter asked.

"And why didn't you go forward with the interview you promised her?" added Luisa. She asked this as if we knew about the interview for sure, but she was bluffing, something at which she excelled, although she'd scoffed at my repeated suggestions that she pursue a career in professional poker. "Did something make you change your mind while you were waiting for her?"

Iggie didn't say anything for a moment, and I could almost

see the wheels spinning in his brain as he tried to calculate which excuse we might find most credible. "Okay," he said eventually, his tone resigned. "Do you really want to know what happened? The whole truth and nothing but the truth?"

"That's why we're here," said Abigail. "That and to spend quality time with you."

But sarcasm was lost on Iggie, too. "I ditched her on purpose. I told her I'd give her an interview for her story, and then I took off while she was getting her things from her room."

"Why would you do that?" I asked, indignant on Hilary's behalf.

"Because the Igster doesn't get mad, Raquel. He gets even."

"What's that supposed to mean?" asked Luisa, equally indignant.

"It means I spent years going after Hilary in college, and she acted like I was invisible unless she was having problems with her computer or needed help with her science requirements. But now I'm a success, and suddenly she can't get enough of me."

"So you ditched her?" Peter asked, incredulous. "That was your way of getting even?"

"I thought she could use a taste of her own medicine. Let her see how it feels to be on the receiving end of rejection for once."

"How mature," said Abigail in her mild tone.

"Hey, it felt good. We got to the hotel, and I told Hilary I'd wait for her to get her notebook and stuff. She went inside, and I was about to take off when I saw the second Lamborghini. I stopped to talk to the other driver for a minute, but then I hit the road. Put the pedal to the metal. Left her high and dry. Slipped out the back, Jack. Made a new plan, Stan. Hopped on the bus, Gu—"

"All right," Luisa interrupted. She'd never been much of a Paul Simon fan. "We understand. You left her there to avenge her ignoring you in college."

"Which was more than ten years ago," I couldn't help but point out. I was a big believer in holding long-term grudges, but this was excessive even by my statute of limitations.

"I just wish I could have seen her face when she came back downstairs and realized I was gone." He couldn't contain the smug smile that had spread over his own face as he told us what he'd done.

"You must be very proud of yourself," said Abigail.

The sarcasm sailed over his head yet again. "Dr. Grout thought it was a critical breakthrough. An important step on the journey to self-actualization. He's even thinking about writing a paper on it."

"Is Dr. Grout a real doctor?" I asked. "With a degree and a license and everything?"

"Of course he is," said Iggie. "Why do you ask?"

20

We spent a few more minutes pressing Iggie about the driver of the other Lamborghini, but he steadfastly maintained that all they'd spoken about was their shared passion for cars that cost more than the gross national product of certain developing countries.

Then Phyllis's voice cackled out from a hidden intercom. "Igor? Igor, baby, your ten-thirty appointment is waiting in the lobby. And there's a call holding for you, too. Don't you think it's time your little friends were leaving?" For Iggie's sake, I hoped the intercom was audible only in the conference room, as this wasn't the sort of communication to inspire trust and confidence in one's employee base.

After the tag-team browbeating we'd delivered, Iggie was so thrilled to be rid of us he barely protested when Abigail told him she wouldn't be able to stay for lunch, after all, and

I was fairly certain he didn't see her crossing her fingers behind her back when she assured him she'd be in touch to reschedule. He escorted us through the sea of cubicles to the exit, following the same return path he'd used with Camilla Gergen and her team and steering a wide berth around his mother's station.

As the front doors slid apart, I turned to glance back, curious as to whether my hunch about Iggie's next appointment was right.

Sure enough, over by the reception desk, Clay Finch and several of his colleagues balanced awkwardly on a circle of beanbag chairs, struggling to make small talk with Phyllis as they waited for Iggie. Clay somehow managed to look stiff even when sunk into the purple vinyl of his beanbag, and his legs were so long that, with his size-sixteen feet planted on the floor and his rear planted only a few inches higher, his knees were bent up around his ears. I gave him a big smile and wave on the way out.

Peter and I had more than an hour between our Igobe visit and our meeting with Caro and Alex, and Abigail and Luisa hadn't participated in the Forrest family breakfast of champions, so we decided to retreat to the University Café in Palo Alto. Late on a Monday morning the café was only moderately busy, its customers a mix of student and faculty types from the Stanford campus nearby and a handful of men dressed in the local venture capitalists' uniform of khakis, button-down shirts and computer bags bearing the logos of Internet start-ups and tech conferences. "Sand Hill Road is nearby," Abigail explained as we sat down. "That's where a lot of the venture-capital firms have their offices."

Luisa and Abigail ordered pancakes and an egg-white omelet, respectively, while Peter drank orange juice. I could have chewed off the one arm I didn't devour earlier for a nice, cold, caffeinated soda, but with less than twenty-four hours to go on my dare I managed to restrain myself and demurely sip a mineral water instead. I secretly hoped I wouldn't actually end up playing tennis at noon, but if I did I wanted to be able to demonstrate to Peter that my relative level of hydration had no impact whatsoever on my athletic ability—I was useless either way.

Regardless, I'd never thought I'd look forward with such anticipation to a tennis game, especially one in which I personally was expected to play. This anticipation had little to do with my hope that the game might not take place and even less to do with the chance that this would be the day when Peter would see Caro and realize he'd preferred life with her. Instead, it was almost entirely due to how much I was looking forward to ensnaring Alex Cutler.

While Iggie's story about purposely ditching Hilary hadn't done much to improve anyone's opinion of him, it had passed Abigail's mental polygraph test. But she'd told us in the car she was equally confident he was lying about not knowing the driver of the other Lamborghini. Which, along with the ACVLLC phone number and vanity plate, further validated our working hypothesis that the driver and thus Hilary's abductor had been Alex Cutler. At least, this was the working hypothesis of everyone but Peter, who remained unenthusiastic about casting blame in Alex's direction.

"Why else would Hilary have gotten into the second Lamborghini, then?" I asked, reaching my fork over to sneak a bite of Luisa's pancakes. A couple of hours ago this would have been a perilous maneuver, but now that the nicotine gum had worked its magic, she was tamer than Spot and even pushed her plate closer so I could better help myself. "Hil might not have noticed it wasn't Iggie at the wheel until she was in the car, but once inside she never would have stayed unless she already knew the driver. She's too street-smart for that. And you introduced her to Alex yourself."

"I know, I know," he said. "But it seems premature to jump to conclusions based on some similar initials, a couple of descriptions of a 'preppie' guy, and the fact that Alex invested in Igobe. We still don't even know for sure what kind of car he drives."

"I know what kind of car he drives," I said confidently. "I'll bet you anything he pulls up to the tennis club in a Lamborghini."

"I don't want to bet," he replied.

"Are you sure? Betting is fun. Especially when I win."

"Rachel, it would be bad enough to find out Alex has done something to Hilary. It would be even worse to find that out and then owe you whatever random thing you'd insisted on betting me for."

"Why do you think I'd bet something random?"

"Maybe because the last time I lost a bet to you I ended up having to personally prepare every available recipe for pigs in a blanket so you could conduct a scientific taste test?"

"First of all, it was a small price to pay for the advancement of haute cuisine, and second of all, there's a strong argument to be made that losing that particular bet was a lot like winning."

"What argument is that?" he asked.

"Now we know for a fact how to make the best possible pigs in a blanket. We never again have to lie awake nights worrying that we're making inferior pigs in a blanket."

"By *we* you mean me, right? Because I don't recall you doing any of the cooking."

"It's simple division of labor," I said. "You're better at cooking and I'm better at taste-testing. My palate is more refined. It worked out perfectly."

"As you would say, how exactly are you defining *perfectly?*"

"Well, this is a fascinating discussion the two of you are having, but there may be a way to solve the Lamborghini question before you see Alex," interjected Luisa.

"What's that?" asked Abigail, who also seemed happy for discussion of the pigs-in-a-blanket bet to draw to a close.

"Perhaps Ben has heard from the guy he asked for a list of Lamborghini owners in the area. It's already early afternoon on the East Coast, and his contact should have had time to check by now," said Luisa.

Ben's offer of the previous night had completely slipped my mind—it was hard to keep much in there given all the space Alex Cutler, Che Guevara, Petite Fleur and the Rice-a-Roni jingle were hogging up. "That's a good idea," I said, "Let's call him again." I turned to Peter. "But are you absolutely sure you don't want to bet Alex isn't on that list before I make the call? There must be other cocktail-hour finger foods we need to perfect."

"I'll pass, thanks."

I pulled my BlackBerry from my bag and dialed Ben's number, but it went right into voice mail without even ringing. "He must have turned his phone off," I reported, waiting as his recorded voice told me to leave a message at the tone. I did as instructed, quickly summarizing our talk with Iggie and asking about the Lamborghini owners and Hilary's receipts.

My message complete, I disconnected and left the Black-Berry on the table, which I generally considered a grave lapse in cell-phone etiquette, but most of the venture-capital guys were doing it and I wanted to have it handy should Ben call back right away.

"What if Alex does drive up in a Lamborghini?" said Abigail. "What happens then?"

"*When* Alex drives up in a Lamborghini," I corrected her. "I guess we start talking about Hilary and how she's missing, and then we see how he reacts. It's probably too much to hope that he'll confess, but he might give himself away somehow. And assuming he doesn't confess, we follow him once he leaves the club. If all goes well, he'll lead us to Hilary."

After some debate, we agreed that Peter and I would drop Luisa and Abigail at a nearby car-rental agency so that they could pick up a separate car. "Call us or text us before you leave the club," said Luisa. "Then we can trail Alex, as well, just in case you lose him or he realizes what's happening and tries to lose you."

This seemed to be as good a plan as we were going to come up with, and it was nice of Luisa to offer to sacrifice her trip to the mall. The nicotine gum seemed to be bringing out the best in her, even if I worried that it couldn't be healthy to go through nearly two packs of the stuff in as many hours.

It was after noon, so we paid the check and prepared to leave. As I picked up my BlackBerry, I saw that the little red light was flashing, indicating I had a new message. At the same moment, Luisa's phone started buzzing from within the depths of her oversized handbag.

I peered at the BlackBerry's screen. The new message was a text, from a number with a four-one-five area code. I recognized it immediately: it was the number from which Hilary had sent her truncated S-O-S early Sunday morning. "Wait!" I called to Peter and Abigail, who were already heading toward the door.

Luisa, meanwhile, was tossing items from her purse onto the table as she tried to locate her buzzing phone. "Aha," I heard her mutter as she finally pulled it out of the bag along with a silver compact, two pairs of sunglasses, a Spanish-language paperback of Borges essays, a silk scarf, a wool scarf, three lipsticks, a fountain pen, and a Filofax bound in shiny crocodile.

My awe at what Luisa kept in her bag was almost enough to make me forget the message waiting for me on my own phone. I clicked it open.

False alarm. I am in love!!! Hope I didn't worry you too much. Will explain all later. ☺ H

I read the text three times over in disbelief. *A false alarm?*

Luisa was staring at the screen of her own phone, a furrow of annoyance creasing her usually smooth brow. She muttered something else, and while I had never taken Spanish, I knew enough to recognize it as the sort of word that didn't get taught in high-school Spanish classes. At least, not the sort of high school in which I'd been enrolled.

Worldlessly, she lifted her gaze to meet my own, and wordlessly, we exchanged phones.

The message on Luisa's screen was identical to the one on mine.

21

"It's a very good thing Hilary hasn't met with foul play," said Luisa, "because I'm looking forward to killing her myself."

"Only if I can help," I said. I couldn't remember when I'd last been so exasperated. Between trying to impress Peter's family, being blindsided by revelations about his romantic history, and worrying that the prized piece of business I'd brought in might turn out to be just the thing to take me permanently off the partner track, I would have had plenty to keep me neurotic over the last couple of days without having to chase around on misguided rescue missions.

To their credit, neither Peter nor Abigail seemed to resent the way we'd been wasting their time.

"It's been fun," said Peter with a shrug.

"And I got an extra vacation day out of it," said Abigail. "And maybe even a raise. Right, Peter?"

Peter hesitated, but not about the raise. "I know I'm the last person who should be bringing this up, but aren't you two at all worried that the messages came from the ACVLLC phone?"

"We know Hilary doesn't have her own phone with her, so she has to use someone else's," said Luisa reasonably. "The ACVLLC phone must belong to her new man—the one with the Lamborghini. Perhaps it was somebody else from the party, and the initials are just a coincidence."

"And the new man could still be Alex Cutler," I pointed out. "We were only suspicious of him because he has so much to gain from Igobe's success. But now that we know Hilary's all right, there's no reason to be concerned about him. If anything, we should be concerned *for* him, given Hil's track record."

"If it is Alex, then why didn't he mention it when I spoke to him?" asked Peter.

"They could be trying to keep things quiet for a while," offered Abigail. "You know, while they're in the honeymoon phase of their relationship."

"Has Hilary ever kept anything quiet before?" asked Peter.

Luisa laughed. "It's usually radio silence for the first few days when there's a new man in the picture. I'm surprised we heard from her at all. But she's never been in love before, either. I guess there's a first time for everything."

"Remember when she disappeared with the guy she met on the chair-lift in Colorado? We didn't hear from her for a week after that," I said.

"But I don't know if I really see her and Alex together," Peter said. "I mean, he just doesn't seem like her type." He was understandably reluctant to face the possibility that his planned match for Alex wasn't going to work out, and while it would be easier for him to win Caro back if she wasn't involved with somebody else, he still hadn't admitted to himself that he wanted to win her back in the first place.

"Hilary's never had a type," I said. "Other than male. And we don't know for sure it's Alex. She could have met Mr. Lamborghini in the elevator at the Four Seasons. I wouldn't put it past her."

"She's picked up men in far more exotic locations," agreed Luisa. "At least this one has good taste in cars, even if it is a bit flashy."

There was something anticlimactic about this latest development, but I was willing to welcome any anticlimax at this point. It wasn't as if all of the uneasiness I'd been feeling had completely dissipated—in fact, plenty remained. But now I could focus on my own personal life, and my professional life, too. If I concentrated hard enough over the next twenty-four hours, I just might be able to retrieve my normal status from the Dumpster into which it had been so callously tossed by recent events.

It would have been considerate of Hilary to have sent her message a few hours earlier, because then I would have had sufficient time to invent a reason why tennis was out of the question on this particular day. But it was officially too late to weasel out of the game now, and while the debilitating stiffness I'd felt when I'd first awakened hadn't worn off completely, it had worn off too well to serve as an excuse. I began mentally steeling myself for what would certainly be both a mortifying and physically unpleasant episode.

Since we no longer needed to trail Alex Cutler it no longer made sense to rent an additional car. Instead, Peter and I dropped Luisa and Abigail at the mall, promising to pick them up after the game, and headed to the tennis club. The drive from the mall took less than five minutes, but it was still enough time for Peter to start humming again. Even worse, I found myself humming along. At least with the Rice-a-Roni theme, I knew the words, but now I was held captive by this nameless, unknown piece of jazz, and if it didn't stop soon, an exorcism of some sort might be in order.

The clubhouse was an understated California mission-style building tucked at the end of a narrow road not far from the Stanford campus. Peter and I pulled up to the front of the building and entrusted the Prius to the care of a valet. I was still curious as to just what Alex Cutler would be driving, and the valet assured us that neither he nor Caro had yet arrived, so we decided to wait for them outside. From the courts behind the clubhouse we could hear the ominous thwacks of balls meeting racket strings accompanied by the occasional grunt or shout of a particularly zealous player. Peter seemed to be inspired by this, taking practice swings with his own racket as we waited. Meanwhile, I scanned the cloudless sky, hoping for signs of a sudden torrential downpour or locust infestation.

I wasn't sure what, exactly, I expected of Alex's and Caro's respective means of transportation. I probably thought there was still a good chance Alex would drive up in a Lamborghini, although I was also glad Peter hadn't agreed to bet me on that point. And I was reasonably certain Caro would drive up in a hybrid of her own, in a nice, sporty but feminine color like pale blue or maybe seafoam green.

Of course, I should have known better. When they did arrive, each within a minute of the other, there were no Lamborghinis, nor were there any hybrids. There weren't even any cars.

They were both riding bicycles.

And not just any bicycles. These were fancy, multi-geared racing bikes, with complicated levers on the handlebars and little slots for water bottles and tire pumps. After Caro embraced me as if I were her long-lost Siamese twin and Alex said hello all around, I endured a lengthy discussion of the bikes' special features, the best hundred-mile rides in the area, and the relative merits of road biking versus mountain biking. I was almost grateful when Alex pointed out we should hurry if we didn't want to miss our court time.

The two of them were already wearing their tennis whites, and Caro looked every bit as blond, tanned and glorious as I'd feared. I thanked her for the clothes she'd brought to lend me, charmingly packed in an L.L. Bean tote she'd strapped to the back of her bike, and Peter and I went to change. In the ladies' locker room, I unpacked the bag's contents and spread them out on a bench. They included a sports bra in a size thirty-four C, which, short of emergency breast implants, I would never either fill or need, a white tennis dress trimmed with pink piping, and little white socks with matching pink pom-poms. There was also a note, written in a neat cursive script:

This is my favorite tennis outfit—it always brings me luck! I hope it isn't too big on your adorable little figure! Can't wait for our game—it's going to be so much fun! ☺ C

It seemed as if everyone in the Bay area, and not just the Forrest family, was confused about the meaning of the word *fun*. I took off my own clothes, storing them in the locker I'd been assigned, and donned the dress Caro had left me, at which point it became abundantly clear that *little* was the operative word for any description of my figure. The skirt should probably have hit at midthigh, but without Caro's various curves to fill it out it came down nearly to my knees, although it was hard to tell since the fabric was almost the exact same color as my skin. I pulled my hair into a ponytail as fast as I could in order to minimize any time in front of the mirror, grabbed the racket Caro had described as "one of" her spares, took a deep breath and went to join the others.

I knew that the odds of my having developed any athletic skill or eye-hand coordination since I'd last been forced to play this game were minimal, so I felt it was important to set everyone's expectations suitably low. "In case Peter didn't tell you," I announced to Caro and Alex as we walked onto the court, "I really suck at this."

Caro laughed. "I'm sure you're much better than you think. And we're just going to play a friendly game. Nothing to worry about."

"And it's doubles," said Peter. "I've got you completely covered."

We spent a few minutes hitting back and forth, with Peter and me on one side and Caro and Alex on the other. I managed to avoid most of the balls that came my way, but the one I did hit made it over the net, although it wobbled a bit on top before falling over. "See," said Peter encouragingly. "You're a natural."

And then the match began for real.

If this had been a movie, the next hour would have been condensed into a montage set to something peppy and upbeat, with snippets of Peter and Caro and Alex expertly sending the ball across the net interspersed with snippets of me for comic relief. There would have been shots of the ball flying off the tip of my racket and onto the next court, the ball zooming past me as my racket hit nothing but air, the ball zooming at me as I jumped out of its path, and at the shining climax, the moment when I swung at the ball so hard I lost my grip and my racket flew from my hand, soared twenty feet up into the air and nearly decapitated Peter on its descent.

It didn't help that everyone was so nice about my stunning ineptitude. Then things got even worse when, with one set over, we switched partners for a second set. Peter and Caro played together as a seamless team, a tennis *pas de deux,* fielding the balls with the sort of ease that comes only with years of shared practice. And while Peter had, against all odds, seemed to find my gaffes endearing, Alex Cutler found them less so, though he did do his best to hide his annoyance. My screwing up also appeared to be contagious; Alex's own skills deteriorated as the game wore on, and I noticed he was limping slightly.

"Is your leg all right?" I asked. It was his serve, and I was handing him the balls I'd collected from the net. It seemed only fair to do the collecting since I was the one who'd sent them into the net in the first place.

"Oh, it's fine," he said. "I bumped into something the other day, and my knee's a bit sore. That's all."

"Are you sure you want to keep playing?" I asked, trying

not to sound as hopeful as the prospect of an early finish made me feel.

"It's no big deal," he assured me. Sadly, I returned to my position at the net.

Behind me, I heard him bounce the ball a few times and then call out the score. I didn't really understand tennis scoring, but I understood enough to know that we definitely weren't winning. Then his serve came whizzing by me, and Peter scrambled to receive it. Fortunately, he hit long and deep and to Alex's side of the court. Alex returned it, also scrambling, and lobbed the ball high in the air. I heard him swear as he stumbled on his bad leg.

"Got it!" yelled Caro, sighting the ball as it arced up and over the net. She stretched her racket behind her head, waiting for just the right moment to bring it forward with a snap.

If this were still that movie montage, what happened next would have been in slow motion. Of course, if it had happened in slow motion, I would have been able to get out of the way. Instead the ball sprang off Caro's racket strings with such power and speed I barely had time to register it hurtling toward my face.

The next thing I knew, I was flat on my back and the blue sky above me was filled with spinning silver stars. There was also something warm and sticky pouring from my mouth, and I had the unfortunate feeling that that something was blood.

"At least you didn't lose any teeth," said Peter.

A crowd of onlookers had gathered around us, either drawn by the excitement of unexpected violence or eager to take a break from their own games. One woman had come running from an adjacent court, announcing that she was a doctor and bending down to take my pulse and check that my jaw wasn't broken. It wasn't, and my tongue was still intact, too. But the ball had split the corner of my lower lip, which was what accounted for all the blood. I'd never known a lip had so much blood in it and I would have been happier not finding out.

The doctor and Peter debated for a bit about whether I needed stitches, but after she'd made liberal use of an antiseptic that stung so badly I nearly did bite my tongue off, she assured me I'd be fine. "There will be some swelling, but that should go away in a week or two," she said.

"Or two?" I asked feebly. It hurt to move my mouth, and judging by the muffled way my words came out, my lip was already well on its way to swollen.

"Three at the most," she said, packing away the first-aid kit somebody had brought her from inside the clubhouse. "Be sure to put some ice on it."

The crowd began to disperse, probably disappointed by the relatively tame nature of the injury I'd sustained, and Peter helped me up to my feet.

"Rachel, I'm so sorry," said Caro who'd been hovering to one side, her eyes filled with concern. "I really didn't mean to hit you."

"I know you didn't," I said. And I did. She was too thoroughly nice and wellmannered for even her subconscious to consider doing such a thing.

"Come on," she said, leading me off the court. "Let me help you get cleaned up."

There were a couple of women leaving the locker room as we walked in, and they looked at me with a combination of sympathy and revulsion. Once I saw myself in the mirror, I could understand why. My lower lip was several times its usual size, blood streaked my chin, neck and the previously pristine front of my borrowed tennis dress, and most of my hair had escaped its ponytail. Some strands were plastered to my forehead with sweat, while others corkscrewed out from my scalp in a number of unlikely and less than attractive directions.

"Ack," I said, first at my reflection and then to Caro, indicating the red stains on her dress. "I've ruined your lucky outfit."

"Don't worry about it," she assured me. "You only proved

it's not really lucky. Now, while you're rinsing off I'll go find something cold to put on your lip."

I undressed and stepped into the shower with care, soaping up as best I could. When I emerged, wrapped in a big white towel, Caro was waiting. "Here," she said, smiling and extending her hand. "This is just as cold as ice, and it won't drip."

It was as if the gods had decided today would be a good day to torture me. She was holding a can of Diet Coke.

The only reason I managed to restrain myself from opening the can and drinking the soda down in one magnificent gulp was that my ability to drink anything without a straw had been severely compromised. Instead, I held the sealed can up to my lip and prayed it was possible to absorb some of its contents through osmosis.

Caro insisted on staying with me as I dressed, just in case I caught another glimpse of myself in the mirror and grew woozy at the sight. And while this was considerate of her, knowing she was watching me made me self-conscious. Some people— Hilary, for example—had sufficient body confidence that this sort of thing didn't bother them, but I'd never been the type to strut naked around a locker room, particularly not in front of my fiancé's ex- and probably future-girlfriend. Mostly I did everything I could to avoid locker rooms altogether.

"I love your clothes," Caro said to my exposed torso as I pulled my top over my head. "They're so…*New York*."

I was wearing jeans, a cotton tunic and ballet flats. It was hardly an outfit I'd describe as especially urbane, but I could see how anything that couldn't be purchased at a sporting goods store might be described as "New York" in this environment.

"Peter really seems to love it there," she continued.

"Where? New York?" I asked, surprised. There had been a few rough patches when Peter had first moved east, and it would be premature to say he'd accustomed himself to Manhattan living as yet. And seeing him back in San Francisco had made it all too clear how much he missed its outdoorsy lifestyle. Central Park was a pretty spot, but it couldn't match the countless nature-based activities available in Northern California.

"I'm sure it's just as much you as it is the East Coast. I've never seen him so happy. The two of you make such a great couple."

I'd moved over to the mirror, where I was trying in vain to fix my hair without actually looking at my face, but I could see Caro reflected behind me. Her expression was completely free of guile.

"You think so?" I asked, wondering where she was going with this.

"You complement each other so well," she said.

"Sometimes it seems like we have nothing in common," I confessed, marveling as I did that I was admitting this to her, of all people.

"But that's what keeps things interesting. Take Alex, for example."

"What about him?"

"Well, I know a bunch of people think we'd be a good couple. Even Peter wants to set us up. He's trying to be subtle about it, but…." Her voice trailed off.

"But Peter's not so good at subtle," I supplied.

"No," she said with a laugh. "Peter's definitely not so good at subtle. He's too much of a straight shooter. He tried to act like organizing this tennis game was just a casual thing, but it was pretty obvious he was trying to play matchmaker."

I froze with one hand on my comb and the other grasping a chunk of hair. Even with everything that had happened the previous night, I clearly remembered Peter telling me it was Alex and Caro who had suggested the game. So why hadn't he admitted that he was the one who'd initiated it? If his conscious motive was, in fact, to throw Alex and Caro together, why hadn't he just told me the truth? Anxiety fluttered down from my chest to take up residence in my stomach. Maybe it was actually starting to happen: the feelings Peter had been repressing were finally escaping from the subconscious pit in which he'd tried to keep them buried, and he'd wanted an excuse to see Caro and me at the same time, the better to compare and contrast and sort out what he truly felt. That was a disconcerting thought—it was pretty obvious who'd come out ahead. In fact, if the contest had indeed started, it was probably already over, as well.

Caro was still talking, and I tried to concentrate on her words rather than my panic. "Things would never work with Alex and me," she was saying. "I can't put my finger on it, exactly, but we just don't click. We have a lot of the same interests, and we have a lot of friends in common—we've gone sailing a couple of times, and we're even in the same cycling club—but there's something missing."

"Oh?" I asked, but I wasn't surprised to learn Caro was in a cycling club. She was probably in all sorts of clubs dedicated to activities that Peter would love, things like kayaking and rock climbing and Ultimate Frisbee. I wasn't in any clubs, except for a book club that hardly ever met. When we did meet, we usually skipped the book and went straight for the booze.

"We carpool every so often, when there's a cycling outing or to parties, but somehow it's always hard to keep the conversation going. He gave me a ride home the other night, and it felt like the drive would never end."

I was looking for anywhere to take my thoughts but where they currently were, and typically, my mind zeroed in on the wrong part of what she was telling me—namely, that if Alex had given her a ride home from the party, then he most definitely hadn't been with Hilary. But it couldn't hurt to be sure, and trying to identify Hilary's new man was infinitely preferable to wondering how long it would be before I was in the market for a new man, as well. "What kind of car was Alex driving?" I asked. "The other night?"

"What?" asked Caro, surprised by the direction in which I was taking our little locker-room chat. "Um, an SUV of some sort. I wasn't really paying attention."

"Is that the only car he has?"

"It's the only one I've seen him drive. It's convenient because he can strap his bike onto the back."

Part of me was relieved to hear this. I didn't want Alex Cutler to be Hilary's first love. His tennis court behavior suggested that underneath the pleasant exterior lay the interior of a jerk.

"Speaking of couples," said Caro, even though we hadn't been, "What's going on with your friend Hilary and her boyfriend? His name is Ben, right? The tall guy with the dark hair?"

Caro might not have been expecting me to ask about

Alex's car, but I definitely hadn't been expecting her to ask about Ben. I gave up on my own hair and turned to face her. "I was just thinking about them. You know, they broke up the other night. At the party."

"Really?"

"Yes. In fact, Hilary's already got a new guy."

Caro hesitated. "Then does that mean Ben's available?"

"I guess so. Why?"

I thought she might be starting to blush, but she was so tanned it was hard to tell. "Oh, I was just wondering," she said, striving for a casual tone. "We started talking at the party, right at the beginning of the evening, and I felt like we were hitting it off. But then I got hijacked by Alex, and the next time I saw Ben he was with Hilary, and Peter told me they were together."

"Not anymore," I said, wondering at this new twist. Was it possible Caro was as skilled as Peter at deluding herself about what sort of man was right for her? As far as I could tell, she and Ben couldn't be less alike: she was polished and bright and outgoing, and he was—well, not polished, frequently moody and occasionally a bit slow. But Caro was interested in him. Maybe there was something about carrying a gun that had a more universal appeal than I'd realized.

"Do you know if he ever found a place to rent a boat?"

"Rent what?" I asked, beginning to collect my things and stow them in my bag. At Caro's insistence, we'd thrown away the blood-stained tennis dress, but I had the feeling it would be appropriate to buy her a new one. That wouldn't have been a problem if I had even the faintest idea as to where to begin shopping for such a thing.

"He was asking me about places where he could rent a sailboat for a day or two. I can't remember how it came up, but I'd mentioned that I sail."

"I didn't know Ben was a sailor," I said. Then again, there was a lot about Ben I didn't know.

"He was thinking it would be fun to get out on the water for an afternoon," said Caro. "I suggested a couple of marinas where you can rent boats, and I even offered to lend him mine."

"Uh-huh," I said distractedly, stealing a surreptitious glance at my BlackBerry. The little red light was flashing again.

"I don't use it as much as I'd like, and it's a pity for it just to sit there, empty," Caro said, presumably about her boat.

"Uh-huh," I said again as I scrolled through the messages that had accumulated. Ben, as if he knew we would be talking about him, had sent me a text just a few minutes earlier. I clicked it open.

Sorry I missed your call. Still waiting on list of L'ini owners and haven't gotten to receipts yet. Following up on hunch now. Will check in later. ☺ Ben

Belatedly, I realized we'd neglected to tell him Hilary was safe, although, from his perspective, it might be better for her to have been abducted than gushing with unprecedented excitement about the new man in her life. And his message served as a vivid reminder that he should have known better than to think things would work out with Hilary—she would never be able to sustain a long-term relationship with someone who used emoticons.

I was in a mean mood now, and this was a mean thought on my part, but it wasn't the meanness that gave me pause. In fact, it was more than a pause—it was an epiphany. The realization washed over me with abrupt clarity, leaving me amazed at how long it had taken to arrive.

Hilary could never have written that text.

All of Hilary's friends knew there was a long and varied list of things for which she had little patience, but the message Luisa and I had received included several items near the top of that list: an immoderate use of exclamation points for starters, not to mention gushing professions of love, and, most importantly, emoticons. Falling in love might have given her newfound patience when it came to gushing, and perhaps even about exclamation points, but nothing was powerful enough to overcome her passionate distaste for emoticons.

But Luisa and I had both been so eager to get back to our own lives that we'd accepted the text as legitimate and dismissed Peter's concerns without a second thought. I couldn't help but groan.

"Are you all right?" asked Caro.

"What? Oh, I'm fine, thanks." But perhaps some degree of osmosis had indeed occurred, because my mind was suddenly working with a speed and precision I hadn't felt since my last Diet Coke, and it was pointing me in an entirely new direction. I knew with absolute certainty what had happened: Hilary's kidnapper must have found the phone she'd used, seen the SOS texts she'd sent early Sunday morning and was now trying to counteract them via the same medium.

Which meant Hilary was still missing.

Which also meant we were back to Alex Cutler. Only, we couldn't be back to Alex Cutler, because I also now knew he'd given Caro a ride home from the party, and not in a Lamborghini but in an SUV.

Which meant we were back to square one, which meant Iggie. But Abigail was confident Iggie was telling the truth about having left Hilary at the Four Seasons, and something told me she was right. Being married to a person provided excellent training in lie detection. Or so I'd heard. The way things were going, it was unlikely I'd ever find out for myself.

Which meant we were back to whatever came before square one.

And that's when I had another epiphany, and this one was also well overdue.

We'd been overlooking the most obvious suspect.

What if Hilary's disappearance had nothing at all to do with Igobe or her magazine article? If that were the case, then we'd ignored the very first person we should have considered, the very first person it was customary to consider when something happened to a woman: namely, her husband, boyfriend or significant other.

And in this case, that very first person was Ben.

23

I tried my best to hide my impatience as Peter and I said our goodbyes to Caro and Alex, enduring another painfully detailed discussion of sporting equipment with what would have been a fixed smile if my lip hadn't been too swollen to make smiling possible. Once in the car, however, I wasted no time laying out my newest theory.

"Think about it," I told Peter. "Think about all of the things we've accepted as fact, when they're really just what Ben told us. He could have made it all up: what he saw on the security camera tape, the registration for the phone Hilary used to send her SOS texts—everything. And he said he'd passed out when he got back to the hotel on Saturday night, but did you notice that the bed was still made Sunday, even though the Do Not Disturb sign was on the door of his room? It definitely didn't look as if housekeeping had been there. And then there are the times he's been off doing things on his own. Like last night, when Abigail and Luisa were having dinner, and then again today. Where is he? What hunch is he following up on? And if it's such a good hunch, why didn't he tell us about it in the first place?"

While it had some holes we couldn't completely fill, Peter liked my theory, possibly because it managed both to validate his own suspicions about Hilary's most recent text and to direct my suspicions toward somebody other than his dream date for Caro. Who, it turned out, wasn't exactly Caro's dream date, but Caro didn't realize that the man she thought *was* her dream date had been recently voted Most Likely to Be a Bad Guy. On the bright side, the renewal of Hilary's MIA status meant I could once again postpone worrying about which relationships were and were not everyone's respective destinies, and I knew enough to appreciate any silver linings that came my way.

We'd called Luisa and Abigail as we were leaving, and they were waiting for us as we pulled up. Judging by the shopping bags they piled into the hatchback their outing had been successful.

"Guess what?" I said, turning around to bring them up-to-date as they slid into the backseat.

Abigail stifled a gasp, and Luisa recoiled. "Good God, Rachel! What happened to you?"

I quickly explained about my little collision with a tennis ball. "But that's not the important thing."

"Face forward, then. Do we have to look at you while you're telling us what the important thing is?" said Luisa, as if my fat lip was some sort of purposeful assault on her refined sensibilities.

"Do you need more nicotine gum?" I asked patiently. Given the circumstances, I considered my concern for her well-being extremely noble.

"I have plenty of gum, thank you, but it's going to take a lot more than gum to make you less scary."

"It's not that bad," said Peter.

"See, Peter doesn't think it's that bad," I told Luisa.

"He's either lying or he's living proof that love is indeed blind," she replied.

"What's the important thing you wanted to tell us, Rachel?" asked Abigail, who was growing skilled at moving discussion forward on those occasions when Luisa and I fell into a conversational rut.

Peter turned the car toward the highway as we told them about my various epiphanies and Alex Cutler's alibi.

"You're right," said Luisa as I explained about the fake text, the realization washing over her just as it had washed over me, except without the self-recrimination. That was my personal area of expertise. "But do you really think Ben is behind everything?"

"Who else could it be?" I said.

"But then why did he wait so long to send the second text?" she asked. "Why didn't he text us yesterday, so we wouldn't have been concerned or looking for her at all? In fact, why didn't he use her phone in the first place?"

"There are a couple of pieces we can't get to fit," admitted Peter. "Maybe something was wrong with her phone, and then maybe he couldn't find the phone she used to text us—maybe he dropped it wherever he stashed Hilary, and he went back to that place today and found it. It seems like he could have done that yesterday, but maybe he was worried we'd notice." What he left unsaid was the assumption that Hilary had been "stashed," rather than done away with on a more permanent basis. None of us was willing to entertain that thought, and the simple fact that Ben hadn't left town seemed to indicate he was still attending to her in some way. At least, that's what we hoped.

"Then what about the second Lamborghini?" asked Abigail. "And the blonde who came out of the hotel and got into it? And its ACV vanity plate? Ben didn't tell us about that—the doorman did."

"That's the other piece we can't figure out," I said. "It could have been a coincidence, just like Iggie said. A driver he didn't know, and then a different blonde altogether. Ben might have seen them when he watched the tape from the security cameras, which is how he also would have known about the other driver's vanity plate. Then he could have improvised about the phone registration having the same letters."

This explanation was also a stretch, but if all went well, we'd be able to get the answer from the horse's mouth soon enough, assuming Ben was the horse in this case and that we'd be able to corral him or lasso him or whatever the appropriate extension of the metaphor might be. We discussed calling the police, but it was still unlikely our reasons for worrying about Hilary would make sense to an outsider. The texts Luisa and I had received that day would have reassured anyone who wasn't aware of Hilary's distaste for emoticons—they'd even temporarily reassured us. It seemed as if we would waste valuable time getting the attention of the authorities, and then telling our story could take hours.

We agreed that our time would be better spent tracking Ben down on our own.

Even so, we didn't want to call him again—he probably wouldn't pick up, and we didn't trust ourselves not to sound too curious about his whereabouts, thus letting him know we were on to him. Instead, we sent him a text telling him we'd heard from Hilary and asking him to call us, hoping this would have the combined effect of letting him think we'd fallen for his ploy while leaving enough left unexplained that the natural thing for him to do if he was trying to act innocent would be to get in touch. In the meantime, we'd return to the hotel and attempt to retrace his steps from there.

It was still early in the afternoon, and traffic was much lighter than it had been that morning. We zipped north at a steady pace, the road clear before us and the occasional glimpse of sun flashing on the waters of San Francisco Bay to our right. The drive would have been entirely pleasant if we weren't worried anew about Hilary's whereabouts, and if we weren't now all humming the song Peter's father had been playing the previous night. Even Luisa and Abigail had fallen under its sway, and a sing-along of our favorite numbers from *Annie* did nothing to clear our heads—moments after we finished the final bars of "You're Never Fully Dressed Without a Smile" the unknown, insidiously tenacious tune was back, and soon we were all humming in unison.

"How can we make this end?" demanded Luisa. "I don't think I can take it anymore." She was halfway through a third pack of Nicorette, but it no longer seemed to be working its magic.

I wasn't in the best of moods, either, between my own continued withdrawal, my recent facial disfigurement and my newest set of concerns about Peter, which persisted no matter how diligently I tried to shunt them aside. "There's only one cure," I said. "We need to hear the song all the way through."

"How can we hear it all the way through when we don't know what the stupid thing is?" said Abigail. She wasn't going through any sort of withdrawal, but the humming was apparently enough to make her cranky, too.

"We have to find out," said Peter, who also sounded unusually grumpy. "And I know exactly who to ask." His cell phone rested in a cradle on the dashboard, and he reached over and pressed a couple of buttons that activated its small speaker phone and then speed-dialed a number.

"Dr. Forrest's office," answered Charles's receptionist.

"Hi, Mitzie, it's Peter."

"Peter!" she said warmly. "How are you, sweetie?"

Sweetie was almost closer to forty than to thirty, but that was beside the point. "I'm fine, thanks. And you?" We all listened as Mitzie gave Peter the update on her husband, children, and, from what I could glean from the conversation, a pair of erratically behaved lovebirds named Joe and Judy.

"Is my dad around?" asked Peter once Mitzie had finished discussing how Joe and Judy were flourishing now she'd changed their brand of birdseed.

"Sure. He just finished up with a patient, and I'm sure he'll want to talk to you. Hold on a sec."

A moment later, Charles's voice boomed out of the tiny speaker. "Peter? Everything all right?"

"Everything's fine, except I seem to have a song stuck in my head. What were you playing last night? When Rachel and I got home?"

"Last night? That was Sidney Bechet. You must know Sidney Bechet—he was a contemporary of Louis Armstrong. Not as famous, but every bit as talented. Some would argue he was even more talented. One of the great jazz musicians of all time, and a real legend on the soprano sax." This was practically more than Charles had said during the course of the entire weekend, and it was definitely the most I'd heard him say at once.

"Do you know which song was playing? Right when we came in?" Peter asked.

Charles didn't remember, which meant Peter was reduced to humming it to him, but since Peter was nearly tone-deaf the rest of us ended up humming along, as well.

Charles seemed oddly delighted to be on speaker phone with us all. He chuckled. "I can't believe you don't recognize it—I've played that record hundreds of times. It's one of Bechet's most famous works. Some would even call it his signature piece." And then he began to sing, in a surprisingly melodic tenor he had neglected to pass along to his son. The words were in French, which meant they mostly mushed together, but one phrase stuck out.

"*Au jardin de mon coeur,*" sang Charles, "*une petite fleur.*"

"What was that?" I interrupted.

"*Au jardin de mon coeur,*" he sang again, "*une petite fleur.*"

"Petite fleur?" asked Peter.

"It's the name of the song. 'Petite Fleur.'"

With a rush, disjointed memories of the previous day

came flooding back: first sitting in Union Square as the sounds of a distant saxophone wafted over us, and then the lone musician at the Martin Luther King memorial, playing the saxophone for the handful of people scattered across the grassy lawn.

"That's it," I blurted out. "Now we know for sure. Marxist Santa and Petite Fleur are the same person."

"What did you say, Rachel?" asked Charles.

"Oh. Uh, nothing." I had no intention of giving him yet more reasons to think I was idiosyncratic.

"Dad, thanks. This has been really helpful," said Peter.

"Yes, thank you," the rest of us choroused.

But as soon as Peter had disconnected the call, I explained. "Marxist Santa or Petite Fleur or whatever we want to call him—he was nearby, watching us, both when I received the keychain and then again when we found the iPod. But we didn't notice him, because he was playing the saxophone. We thought he was just a regular street musician."

"So we're looking for a jazz aficionado and saxophone player who's also a hacker and a Marxist and is trying to screw up Igobe and its IPO?" summarized Peter.

"Exactly," I said.

"But we're not looking for that person," Luisa reminded Peter and me, her tone stern. "We're looking for Ben, because we're trying to find Hilary, and the two things have nothing to do with each other. You both need to focus."

"Right," I said, trying to focus.

"I know this isn't about Ben," said Abigail apologetically, "but I still keep thinking about Leo. It's as if Petite Fleur is channeling him from beyond the grave."

Luisa did not remind Abigail to focus, which seemed like a blatant double-standard. "What makes you say that?" she asked instead.

"Leo played several different instruments, including the saxophone, and he was a huge jazz fan. He even named his dog Scat," said Abigail.

I started to turn around in my seat, but Luisa made a threatening noise low in her throat, so I faced forward again. "What does naming a dog Scat have to do with jazz?" I asked.

"Scat's a type of jazz singing, isn't it?" said Peter.

"Yes," said Abigail. "But instead of singing real words, you sing made-up syllables."

"Like *bop* and *bap?*" I asked.

"*Bop*'s a real word," said Luisa.

"Not when people sing it that way. And *bap* isn't a real word, either," I said.

"It might be, in some other language."

"But that doesn't count, because if you're singing in English and then you sing *bap*, it's not supposed to mean anything."

"But it would count if you were singing in the other language," she insisted.

"But we're talking about singing in English."

"Of course we are, since you don't speak anything besides English. You really should consider broadening your cultural horizons."

"My horizons are broad," I protested.

"How are your horizons broad? Give me one example of how your horizons are broad."

"I speak excellent pig latin."

"You two aren't going to start up again, are you?" asked Peter through gritted teeth. "Because we still have a good ten or fifteen miles to go, and you really don't want to be walking on the highway once it's dark."

24

We had to grovel a bit, but ultimately Peter didn't make us walk the rest of the way, so half an hour later we were back in the lobby of the Four Seasons. Fortunately, Natasha was on duty at the front desk, and she remembered me from the previous day and still thought I was Hilary. She also must have been trained in not registering disgust at the appearance of hotel guests, although she did ask what had happened to my lip. I explained about the tennis ball, thinking as I did that I should come up with a more interesting excuse. If I was going to look like a special effect from a horror film, I should at least have a story that could better withstand repetition. One with more drama and even a hint of intrigue.

We took the new keycard Natasha coded for me and headed up to the room Ben had been sharing with Hilary. We knocked, just to be safe, but there was no answer, and the Do Not Disturb sign no longer hung from the door-knob, so I used the keycard to open the door. Then I drew the security bolt on the inside so we wouldn't have to worry about Ben walking in on us if he suddenly decided to return from whatever shady activities he'd been pursuing.

Hilary's belongings remained in the modified state of dis-order in which we'd left them the previous day, and more importantly, Ben's suitcase was still there. We took this as a positive sign, but the pile of receipts I'd left on the desk also looked as if they hadn't been touched, which only reinforced our hypothesis that Ben wasn't actually playing on our team. He had no need to recreate Hilary's itinerary if he already knew where she was.

With a collective sense of déjà vu, we began searching the room yet again, but this time we concentrated on Ben's belongings rather than Hilary's. His neatness seemed com-pulsive when contrasted with Hilary's mess, which was compulsive only in its need for chaos. It was a miracle their relationship had lasted as long as it did.

Peter hoisted the suitcase up onto the carefully made bed and unzipped it, and we all began rifling through its contents. This felt vaguely unethical, and it was probably illegal, as well, but if desperate times did, in fact, call for desperate measures, then we were well justified. But that didn't mean we found anything but dirty clothes stuffed into a plastic laundry bag and clean clothes folded alongside. A search of the bag's in-ner and outer pockets proved equally fruitless, as did an ex-amination of the lining for any hidden compartments. There were no papers, no maps with a convenient X marking a spot, or even a handy Palm Pilot or calendar.

Luisa began repacking the bag as Peter and Abigail started on the dresser and closet. Since I'd been so successful the first time I'd searched it, I went into the bathroom, where Ben's toothbrush stood in a glass by the sink next to his Dopp kit. Going through this felt even more invasive than going through his suitcase; there was something more personal about a man's deodorant and dental floss than his spare socks. But I unzipped it anyhow and began removing the items one by one. As far as I could tell, it was the usual assortment of toiletries and grooming items, but I kept digging, hoping I would come up with something revealing rather than anything disturbing. And, depending on one's point of view on these matters, what I did come up with could have been either.

I reached into the very deepest corner of the canvas case, and my fingers landed on something small and hard but covered in soft fabric. Its very shape and texture aroused my apprehension, and my yelp of shocked discovery brought everyone running.

"Are you all right?" asked Peter, who arrived first.

"Is that what I think it is?" asked Luisa, her eyes landing on the box cupped gingerly in my palm. It was covered in dark velvet and had a tightly hinged lid.

"I haven't looked inside yet." I gave the box a gentle shake, but nothing rattled. It could contain cuff links of the nonrattling variety, but as much as I wanted to believe this, Ben didn't seem like a French cuffs sort of guy.

"Do you plan on opening it?" asked Luisa. "Or are we all just going to stand around and stare at it?"

But opening the box only confirmed our darkest fears.

Inside, nestled into a satin pillow, was what was unmistakably intended as an engagement ring. The modest stone was an emerald, not a diamond, but its deep green would have matched Hilary's eyes perfectly.

"What was he thinking?" asked Luisa, incredulous. "Engagement rings aren't Hilary's style."

"Neither are engagements," I said. "Or marriage, for that matter."

"I had no idea he was so serious about her," said Peter.

"I don't think she had any idea, either," said Luisa.

"It must have made it even worse for him when she ended things," said Abigail.

We weren't sure what to do with the ring, so for lack of any better ideas we restored it to its original hiding place and returned to the other room, where we resumed searching the various drawers and shelves.

Luisa was the next person to find something of interest: a sheet of hotel stationery on the bedside table, covered with a handwritten list of phone numbers. "Are any of these familiar?" she asked, passing the piece of paper around so we could all take a look.

Each number had a local area code, but otherwise none was immediately recognizable. "Well," she said, "it shouldn't be too hard to find out what they're for." She sat down on the bed, managed to retrieve her phone from the depths of her purse without incident and began dialing as the rest of us continued with the task at hand.

The desk was the only unsearched area somebody else wasn't already searching, so I began sorting through the items on its surface and in its drawers, listening to Luisa's repeated inquiries as to whom she had called. I found nothing I hadn't already seen the previous day, and most of it had been provided by the hotel—the room-service menu, a sheath of writing paper and postcards and directions on how to access the broadband network—so I took a moment to leaf through the receipts. Regardless of Luisa's lecture about focus, I couldn't help but be curious as to where and when Hilary was supposed to meet Petite Fleur. At least now I understood why she'd been reading a book on jazz and didn't have to worry about staging an intervention.

There were several little slips of paper documenting taxi rides to and from local addresses, but the receipts were the kind the cabdriver fills out by hand rather than prints from a meter, and even the ones that included a date lacked time stamps, so they were only moderately useful. I also learned that Hilary had been a frequent customer of a Seven-Eleven on Market Street during her stay in the city. There were a couple of credit-card slips for more expensive lunches and dinners, and I set those aside, thinking I would examine them more closely later. Then I came to the last receipt.

"That's more like it," I said as a puzzle piece clicked into place. It wasn't part of the puzzle we were trying to solve, but it was still satisfying.

"What's more like it?" asked Luisa, glancing up from the list of numbers.

At nine-sixteen on Friday night, Hilary had paid six dollars and forty-two cents for a Glenlivet.

This in itself was unremarkable. Hilary had always appreciated single-malt Scotch, preferably served neat, although it didn't mention that on the receipt.

What was remarkable was the name of the establishment: Chez Bechet. An hour ago the name would have meant nothing to me, but now I knew better. It sounded exactly like the sort of place a guy who called himself Petite Fleur would hang out.

Of course, at this point figuring out where Hilary had planned to meet Petite Fleur was a purely intellectual exercise, and Luisa was quick to point that out. "The more pressing question to answer is what Ben was doing with a list of phone numbers for marinas and boat clubs."

"Is that what the numbers are?" asked Peter, turning from his inspection of dresser drawers.

"Every single one I've reached so far," she confirmed. "But I don't know why he was calling them. What was he trying to accomplish?"

"I can answer that," I said. "He wanted to go sailing. Caro said he asked her about places he could rent a boat when she talked to him at the party." And then another puzzle piece clicked into place, one that fit nicely with the contents of the little velvet box. "Unbelievable. He really should have known better."

"What's wrong with sailing?" asked Peter.

"Nothing's wrong with sailing. But Ben must have been planning a romantic outing with Hilary so he could pop the question." I sighed. "What a sap."

"How does that make him a sap?" he asked.

"Because he should have known better than to think Hilary would find sailing romantic. Hilary's the least romantic person on earth," explained Luisa. I almost felt bad for Ben. How was it possible for him to have dated Hilary for even the brief period he did and still be so utterly clueless about her?

Then I had another thought, and this one was chilling. Maybe Ben hadn't been planning a romantic outing at all, but rather an outing of an altogether different sort. "Do you think he called the marinas from the hotel phone?" I asked Luisa. Yesterday he'd said his cell-phone reception in the room had been lousy.

"How should I know and why should we care?" asked Luisa, but I was already using the phone on the desk to dial the hotel operator.

"Hi," I said when the operator picked up. "I was wondering, could you tell me if I made any calls from my room Saturday, yesterday or today?"

Just as Natasha had been trained not to show shock when a guest showed up looking like the victim of an overzealous round of collagen injections, the operator had been trained not to let on whether he found a question stupid. If I'd been on his end of the phone, I would be wondering why I couldn't remember my own calls. "If you'll hold on for a moment, I'll pull up the records," he offered instead. There was a brief, mercifully Muzak-free pause, and then he came back on the line. "Nothing Saturday, and nothing yesterday except a call to hotel security, but you placed several calls today. In fact, just a couple of hours ago. All to local numbers."

"A couple of hours ago?" That wasn't good.

"Yes, ma'am. A couple of hours ago."

"Could you give me the numbers and the exact time of each call?"

"Sure," he agreed, without commenting on what could

only be interpreted as either amnesia or a propensity for blackouts on my part. As he read them off, I motioned for Luisa to hand me the slip of paper. Each number he gave me was on the list, and he read them in the exact same order as Ben had written them. The final number was one toward the end of the list. It had been dialed only an hour and thirty-six minutes earlier, and on closer inspection I could make out a faint check mark alongside. "That's it," said the operator, even though there were still a few numbers left on the piece of paper we'd found.

I thanked him profusely, wondering as I did if he was going to use me as an example the next time somebody asked him about guests' strange requests, and hung up the phone.

"What does that mean?" asked Luisa after I shared what the operator had told me.

"It means he wasn't planning a romantic outing to pop the question," I said. "At least, not anymore. He made these calls well after Hilary broke up with him and went missing."

"But then why would he still want to rent a boat?" she asked.

"Because now he might have something far less romantic in mind," said Peter. "That's what you're worried about, isn't it?"

I nodded.

"I think you're right to be worried," said Abigail. She'd pulled a chair over to the closet while we were talking, apparently to reach something she'd seen on the uppermost shelf. Now she stepped down lightly from the chair, and I saw she was holding another box, but this one was covered in leather, not velvet, and it was considerably larger than the one I'd found. "If this is what I think it is, and if it's as empty as it feels, then he definitely had something less romantic in mind," she said.

She set the box on the desk and lifted the top. If we'd been hoping to discover another piece of jewelry, perhaps a necklace to match the ring, we were out of luck. The box was empty, but the molded indentations of the inner padding clearly indicated what it usually housed, and its very emptiness was cause for alarm.

It looked as if Ben had decided to take his gun with him on his little maritime jaunt.

All but one of the calls Ben had made were to marinas right in the city. The exception was the last phone number, the entry with the check next to it. This had been for the Bayside Yacht Club, a marina near Coyote Point in San Mateo, roughly halfway between San Francisco and Silicon Valley. That Ben had selected a relatively out-of-the-way location couldn't be a promising sign, and it also seemed logical to assume that it was the last number Ben had dialed because he learned this marina could meet a need the other marinas could not. And while none of us wanted to think too hard about precisely what need it met, we agreed that the best course of action would be to get to Coyote Point as soon as possible.

Maddeningly, the highway we'd taken back from Palo Alto passed right by Coyote Point, and, even more maddeningly, the brief window when there wasn't rush-hour traffic in the Bay area had closed while we'd been searching Ben's room and tracing his phone calls. Soon we found ourselves sitting again in the Prius, stuck once more in heavy traffic and heading south at a plodding pace over ground we'd already covered twice that day. We were learning from experience just how good the hybrid's gas mileage was.

"Ben can't be that far ahead," said Peter, who'd been trying to reassure us ever since we found the empty gun case. "First of all, if he's smart, he'll wait until dark, when there's less of a chance anyone will see him doing anything out of the ordinary. And even if he doesn't wait, it's not like he could take a taxi or public transportation if he's trying to move Hilary from wherever he had her hidden to the marina. He probably had to rent a car, which meant finding a rental agency and then dealing with the paperwork. That must have added at least half an hour and probably more like an hour to his trip, and then he still had to pick her up. Who knows? We might even beat him there."

"But what if he'd already made arrangements for a car before he made the calls to the marinas?" asked Luisa. "He might have rented a car days ago, and that's what he used to take Hilary wherever he took her in the first place."

She had a point, and it wasn't a terribly comforting one.

According to the GPS, our destination was less than twenty miles away, but those miles were ticking away far more slowly than the minutes, and the mood in the car was tense. If we'd had any songs stuck in our heads before, this latest turn of events had wiped them clean, though I doubted any of us was able to fully appreciate the lack of a soundtrack.

"I just don't understand. What can Ben possibly be thinking?" demanded Luisa suddenly, interrupting the silence into which we'd lapsed. "Is he really planning to get Hilary onto a boat, take the boat out to sea, kill her, dump her overboard, and then simply hope nobody either saw him or finds her body? All because she broke up with him?"

"I guess so," I said. It sounded irrational, but except for the breaking-up part, somebody had tried to do something similar to me just a few months earlier. I hadn't enjoyed the experience, but now I was wondering if my misadventure was what had given Ben the idea. Realizing I might have served as the inspiration for how my friend would be murdered was more than a little discomfiting.

"Wouldn't there be all sorts of forensic evidence? In the car and then on the boat?" asked Abigail. "Could he really get away with it?"

"Presumably Ben knows how to cover his tracks. He is a trained law-enforcement professional, after all," said Peter, who had temporarily forgotten he was trying to reassure us.

"A completely unreasonable one," grumbled Luisa. "I'm sure the jeweler would have let him return the ring."

We lapsed back into tense silence after that, inching through the traffic around the airport and continuing south. The sun was still glistening on the Bay, but it no longer looked as cheerful as it had a couple of hours ago, and its deepening slant merely served to remind us that time was passing. I tried to distract myself by counting hybrids, but I gave up in frustration after I reached fifty and discovered we'd traveled only six miles. When the pleasant, authoritative voice of the GPS finally alerted us to our exit, I felt several years older than when we'd started out.

At least traffic was no longer a major obstacle once we were off the highway and onto surface streets. A few minutes later we saw a sign for the Bayside Yacht Club painted in blue letters on a white shingle, and the GPS instructed us to turn from the road and into the parking lot before congratulating us on reaching our destination.

The slams of our doors closing echoed in the open air when we got out of the car, and in front of us, beyond the parking lot, water lapped at a narrow beach. A wood-plank walkway connected the beach with four long piers stretching into the bay, each lined with docked boats, but there was an air of weekday desolation to the place, punctuated by the occasional cry of a seagull and the low hum of traffic from the nearby highway. If a person was trying to transport a hostage in broad daylight without being seen, apparently Monday afternoon wasn't such a bad time to do it. Nobody else was in sight, and there were only three other cars in the lot: another hybrid, an SUV and a lone Ford Taurus in a telltale neutral color. I took a moment to peek inside, and the car was empty, but I could see the rental agreement resting on the dashboard, and I could even make out Ben's name at the top. Feeling self-consciously sleuthlike, I put my hand on the car's hood. The metal felt warm, though it was also parked in direct sun.

A small clubhouse stood to one side of the parking lot, and this was where we went first, hoping we'd be able to learn which of the boats Ben had engaged so we could then intervene, ideally before he left the dock and put whatever devious plans he had for Hilary into motion. Of course, what we'd hoped for and what we got were two entirely different things.

"This is a private club," said the staffer we eventually found, sounding only slightly snotty about it. "We don't rent boats. The boats here belong to our members and are not available for hire to the general public." He said *general public* the way some people say *pondscum,* and I had a feeling he lumped anyone who did not regularly dress in yachting attire into that category, but I also had a feeling we'd awakened him from a nap, so he was already disinclined toward us. Nor could he recall a man showing up and asking to rent a boat that day, let alone a man who looked like Ben. "Everybody knows this is not a rental facility."

We hadn't known it wasn't a rental facility, so what he said wasn't strictly true. Still, there was something about the way the man's nostrils flared when he spoke to us that made me worry I smelled as bad as I looked, regardless of my recent shower. When he yielded no further information we went back out to the parking lot.

"Ben wouldn't just leave his car—he has to be around somewhere," I said.

"If he didn't ask to rent a boat, he must have known he couldn't rent one before he even got here. Was he planning on hijacking somebody else's boat?" asked Luisa.

"If he managed to hijack Hilary, I wouldn't put it past him to hijack a boat," said Peter, who seemed to have given up on trying to be reassuring.

We quickly decided to split up into pairs and canvass the boats, checking for signs of either Ben or Hilary and asking anyone we encountered if they'd seen people matching their description. Knowing that Ben was armed made this a scarier proposition than it would have been otherwise, but it was unlikely he'd risk shooting at us here in broad daylight, even if he had been desperate enough to transport Hilary without the cover of darkness. After we all promised each other we would proceed with caution, Abigail and Luisa started on the pier at the northern-most end and Peter and I started on the southern-most end, agreeing to work our way to the center.

It was probably a good thing so few people were around, because I imagined most of the club members wouldn't appreciate complete strangers jumping onto their boats, checking to see if anyone was on board, and then jumping off. Peter and I made it to the end of the first pier without spotting a single other person, much less signs of either of the individuals we were looking for, although I did catch a glimpse of Abigail and Luisa in the distance speaking to a man lounging on the deck of one of the larger boats in the marina. Judging by his gestures, he was urging them to join him for a drink and potentially a sunset cruise, and judging by his Hawaiian shirt and the daiquiri glass in his hand, I wouldn't be surprised to learn he had both a waterbed and a disco ball belowdecks.

We advanced to the next pier, but this one also proved empty of humans except for an elderly couple guiding a modest craft into its slip. We lost several minutes convincing them that my fat lip was the result of an accident and not because I was unable to extricate myself from an abusive relationship with Peter. We then lost several more minutes helping them tie up, getting an entirely unwanted lesson in knot-making because Peter was too polite either not to help or to let on he already knew how to make the knots. Even so, we still managed to reach the remaining pier before Abigail and Luisa and began checking the boats there. I was growing increasingly worried we wouldn't find anything at all, and if that were the case, I had no idea what we should do next.

Then, halfway down the pier, Peter froze. He reached out an arm to keep me from moving forward. "That's weird," he said softly.

"What's weird?" I asked, matching his hushed tone.

He pointed to a small white boat a few slips ahead. Everything I knew about sailing I'd learned in the last half hour, but even I could appreciate its graceful lines and gleaming brasswork. Delicate script on the hull spelled out *The Good Sport, San Mateo, CA.* The very name should have been enough to tip me off, but I was still surprised by what Peter said next.

"That boat. It's Caro's. She must have changed marinas."

It figured that Caro would name her boat something like *The Good Sport,* but I could reflect further on that once we rescued Hilary. Instead, I flashed back to our locker-room conversation. "Caro told Ben she had a boat," I said, keeping my voice low. "And she also told him she hardly ever uses it. But she probably didn't tell him where she kept it, and that's why he was calling around—to locate it."

"Why would he want to use her boat instead of renting one?" asked Peter.

"This is better. In fact, it's perfect. This way he doesn't have to worry about leaving a record. It's one thing to explain away why you rented a car; renting a boat is a different matter. I'll bet you anything he's got Hilary on there."

"No bets," said Peter, but he took my arm, and we moved quietly up the pier.

Nobody was on deck, and we couldn't make out any sounds from the interior cabin, but this was preferable to hearing gunshots. Peter stepped aboard in one smooth motion, and the boat dipped slightly with his weight, but there was continued silence, and wordlessly he helped me up to join him. I followed as he moved with sure steps across the deck, trying not to think about how many times he and Caro must have gone sailing together on this very boat.

The hatch above the steeply pitched stairs leading down to the cabin yawned open, and we paused as we approached, listening again for any sound from within. But there was only the creaking of the boat as it rocked gently in the water.

Peter turned to me, miming that I should stay on deck and call for help if anything happened. I mimed back that I would. Then I waited thirty seconds for his sandy head to disappear inside before trailing him down the stairs.

Here I found a small living space, no more than six feet wide and ten feet long, all paneled in shiny teak. The curtains were drawn, and the cabin was dark, but I could make out a compact dining table built into one wall next to an equally compact galley. Beyond the table, a short narrow hallway led to a partially open door which I guessed led to a bedroom, and that was where Peter was heading.

What happened next happened quickly.

Just as Peter started to move into the bedroom, a pocket door in the wall slid noiselessly open behind him, and Ben walked into the hallway. His head was down, but something metallic glinted in his hand, and he was so close to Peter he could practically reach out and touch him, which was entirely too close for my comfort.

There wasn't time to ask questions, much less to think, so I did neither.

Instead, I grabbed the first thing I saw, a heavy cast-iron skillet resting on the single-burner stove. I raised the skillet high, just as Caro had raised her racket on the tennis court, and charged across the small room.

Ben never even saw me coming. The skillet made a whooshing noise as I brought my arm down, and it connected with his head with a strangely gratifying thwack.

He crumpled first to his knees, then pitched facedown onto the floorboards.

26

Peter spun around. "What—" he started to ask, but then he saw Ben sprawled behind him.

Who knew I'd be so much more accurate with a skillet than a racket? It wasn't as if I cooked any better than I played tennis, but Ben was out cold. Or nearly cold. He moaned softly, and the metal object clattered from his hand, but otherwise he looked unconscious.

I rushed to pick up what Ben had dropped, eager to move the gun out of his reach before he came to. But it wasn't a gun he'd been holding. It was a pair of scissors, and while scissors could be dangerous, this particular pair didn't look especially sharp or lethal. In fact, they were really nothing more than glorified nail clippers—I'd only mistaken them for a gun because it had been so dark, and because I was pre-disposed to think that's what Ben must have in his hand. Had he been planning on giving Hilary a manicure before he killed her?

That odd thought barely had time to register before we heard a muffled thump from the bedroom. I stepped over Ben as Peter switched on an overhead light and pushed the door open.

We found Hilary curled on the narrow bunk, uncharacteristically quiet and still, but that was because a swath of electrical tape was plastered across her mouth and around her head, and a makeshift bungee-cord harness ran from her wrists to her ankles, immobilizing her. Above the tape, however, her green eyes were flashing with a look of such ferocity it almost seemed safer to keep her tied up.

"Don't worry," Peter told her. "We'll have you out of this in no time." He started working on the knotted cords while I began picking at the edge of the tape. Yet again, my nails proved insufficient to the task, so I put the scissors I'd taken from Ben to use. I cut an opening into the tape and then managed to peel it off without taking too much of Hilary's hair or skin with it, but when she opened her mouth to speak, only a rasp came out, and we realized her throat must be too dry for words.

As Peter continued his work on the knots, I ran to the galley and found a bottle of spring water, carefully skirting where Ben lay. I tipped the bottle to Hilary's lips, and she drank half of it down as I waited, looking forward to everything she would tell us. It would be nice to be thanked for snatching her from the jaws of death and then to hear her version of events.

But the first thing she said was neither appreciative nor

illuminating. "You look like hell, Rach," she croaked. "What did you do to yourself?"

I managed to restrain myself from putting the tape back on, but that was partly because Peter had just managed to liberate her wrists and she would have only peeled it off again herself.

"That's not important," I said. "Are you all right? Did Ben hurt you?"

"Of course Ben didn't hurt me," she said, stretching her arms and legs with relief. "But what did you do to him? It sounded like a gong being struck from in here. We should call a doctor or something if he doesn't wake up soon."

I hadn't realized two days was enough to develop Stockholm syndrome; it had taken several weeks, maybe even months, to transform Patty Hearst from an heiress to a bank robber. Still, Hilary had been through a lot, and I reminded myself to be patient. Or to at least use my patient voice. "It was either get Ben or let him get Peter," I said. "Or you. He was going to kill you."

"Ben wasn't going to kill me. He was trying to rescue me."

"Rescue you? From who?"

"I think it should be *from whom*."

I clenched my jaw. "From whom, then?"

"From Iggie, obviously."

Peter went to find Luisa and Abigail while Hilary visited the head and I searched for something to put on the lump that was already rising beneath Ben's close-cropped hair. Judging by the increasing frequency of his moans, he'd be coming around shortly, and I hoped I hadn't done any permanent damage. For once my lack of upper-body strength might prove to be an asset. I located an instant cold pack inside a first-aid kit, and with Hilary's help I rolled Ben over and wedged it between the lump and a needlepoint pillow we placed on the floor. Now that we'd turned on the lights, it was even more obvious the boat belonged to Caro. The decor was sporty but feminine, and the blue-checked fabric of the curtains matched the cushions on the bench next to the dining table.

"So what exactly happened?" I was asking Hilary when Peter returned with Luisa and Abigail in tow.

"The bastard Tasered me," she said.

"He whatted you?" asked Luisa.

"A Taser's a type of stun gun," Peter told her.

"Iggie with a stun gun. Can you believe it?" said Hilary.

Abigail didn't, apparently. "It's hard to picture," she said. "Are you absolutely sure it was Iggie?"

"Of course it was Iggie," Hilary replied, biting into an energy bar. We'd found the galley well stocked with the sort of healthy snacks favored by people who preferred not to let the need to eat interrupt their exercise. "He said he'd give me an interview, but he insisted on going to his house, so he drove me to the hotel and waited while I ran up to the room for my notebook and computer. But as soon as I got back into the car he shocked me. The next thing I knew, I was locked in his stupid Lamborghini in a deserted parking garage by myself."

She took another bite, and we waited impatiently for her to chew and swallow. "Then what?" I asked.

"The doors were jammed, and I couldn't get them to open—he must have some way to override the interior controls. My purse wasn't there, so I didn't have my own cell phone, but I saw another phone on the floor right in front of the driver's seat. I guess it had slipped out of his pocket and he didn't notice. I used it to dial nine-one-one, but there was no reception since I was underground, so then I tried to send texts. I hoped that once the car reached somewhere with better reception the messages would go through."

"They did. But why didn't you tell us what had happened in the texts?" Luisa asked.

"I had just started the first message to you when I heard footsteps. I didn't have much time, and I wanted to get more than one SOS out, so I had to keep it short. I knew you'd figure out it was Iggie because people saw us leave the party together, so I sent the texts as fast as I could and dropped the phone back on the floor. Then I pretended I was still out of it. Which didn't make any difference, because the jerk Tasered me again as soon as he was back in the car. I woke up here, and I've been here since. Mostly I'm amazed he was able to carry me. Do you think he's been working out?"

"This might sound like a strange question, but are you positive it was Iggie in the car with you?" I asked. We gave her the abridged version of what we'd learned since she disappeared, explaining about the second Lamborghini and Abigail's certainty that Iggie had been telling the truth, at least about not knowing where she was.

Hilary looked up from ripping open a bag of granola and considered my question. "Well, I did have to duck my head down when I was getting into the car at the hotel. And then my eyes were closed when he came back to the car in the parking garage. But it had to be Iggie. He knew I'd heard the rumors that he murdered his partner, Leo, and he must have thought I was going to write about that, along with all of the other problems at Igobe, because I'd been asking him about Leo at the party. That's why he had to make me disappear. It just never occurred to me until he Tasered me that the rumors were more than rumors and that he could be violent. I mean, it's Iggie, for Chrissakes. I thought he was too much of a nerd to be dangerous. Guess I was wrong."

"How did you know about Leo?" asked Abigail.

"When I was researching Igobe, I came across a computer hacker who calls himself Petite Fleur, of all things. We e-mailed a few times, and then we met in person. He's the one who told me that the technology could be hacked, and he also told me about Leo and how he died."

"This is the guy you met at Chez Bechet on Friday?" I asked.

"You managed to figure that out, but it took you two whole days to find me? What were you people doing all this time?"

"Did Iggie come back ever?" asked Peter. "After he brought you here?"

"Uh-huh," she said through a mouthful of granola. "Around midnight last night. He untied me so I could use the bathroom and have a drink of water, but he threatened to Taser me again if I made any noise. I was still blindfolded, so all I could see was a little sliver if I looked straight down, but I caught a glimpse of his watch, and that's how I knew what time it was."

"And it was definitely Iggie?" Abigail asked. "Did you recognize his voice?"

"He was whispering, so it was hard to tell, but who else could it have been?"

"Could you see any of what he was wearing?" she pressed.

"Just bits and pieces. Khakis and running shoes. And maybe a fleece? I didn't get a good look, but I did manage to kick him pretty hard, right in the kneecap. Of course, then he did Taser me again, but it was worth it."

Abigail and I exchanged a glance. "So you never actually saw him when you got into the car at the hotel, or in the parking lot," I confirmed.

"And when he came back here, it was after midnight, and he was wearing khakis, running shoes and a fleece," said Abigail.

"Right," said Hilary.

"Then it couldn't have been Iggie," she said. "Not past his bedtime on a Sunday night. And not in those clothes. He doesn't own khakis. He doesn't own anything anymore that's not purple."

From the floor, Ben gave another moan, his loudest yet. "It wasn't Iggie," he said. "God, my head hurts."

We all turned, startled. Nobody had noticed him even stirring. "That's my fault," I said lamely. "Sorry."

"But if wasn't Iggie, who was it?" asked Hilary.

Personally, I'd been thinking all over again about a certain someone who probably had a closet full of khakis, not to mention a sore kneecap. And while that someone also had an alibi, as I looked around the cabin I felt another epiphany taking shape.

"It has to be Alex Cutler," Ben said. "I got the names this morning of owners of Lamborghinis registered in California, and he's not on the list, but the same set of letters from the vanity plate is: ACVLLC." He struggled into a sitting position, wincing with pain. "Then I checked with hotel security again, and this time they let me look at the videos from outside the entrances, too. It turns out they'll let you look at pretty much anything if you give them enough cash. The guy with the second Lamborghini talking to Iggie outside the main entrance was the same guy I saw getting off on our floor, and that's whose car Hilary got into. Then I checked the tape from the other entrance, and I saw him go in and then come back out of that entrance fifteen minutes later, which is when he went to our room. He must have wanted to make sure Hil hadn't left any of her notes behind. And then, just to be sure, I found a picture of Cutler on his firm's Web site. It's definitely him."

"What gave you the idea to look for Hilary here?" I asked.

"I was talking to Caro about sailing when Alex joined us. He mentioned that he'd been out on Caro's boat, and I figured that if I were in his shoes and had to quickly come up with an out-of-the-way place to hide somebody a few hours later, the boat would come to mind. Caro hadn't told me where she docked, but I got a list of marinas from the Yellow Pages, and then I called around, pretending I was supposed to deliver a new jib and was double-checking the address. That's how I figured out where to go."

"But it can't be Alex. Alex has an alibi," Peter reminded us. "He was with Caro."

I was about to tread over some very dangerous ground, and I wasn't quite sure how to proceed. "You know, I've been thinking. It's possible, if you look at it in a certain light, and this is just a theory, and you never really know—"

"Spit it out already, Rach," said Hilary.

"Maybe Alex didn't have an alibi. Maybe he had an accomplice instead."

Peter looked at me. "What are you trying to say?"

"Well, Iggie probably knew Alex was up to something. He probably told Alex about Hilary's suspicions, and that's how Alex knew to follow him to the Four Seasons. But I think somebody besides Iggie was aiding and abetting."

"Who?" asked Luisa.

"Caro," I said. "What if she was in cahoots?"

"Caro wasn't in cahoots," said Peter without skipping a beat. There was a note of warning in his voice, one I couldn't remember ever hearing before. But somehow it made me want to say more, not less.

"Then why did she lie about Alex driving her home from the party?" I asked. "She must be in cahoots."

"Rachel, I know Caro too well. She would never be involved in anything like this. And would you stop saying *cahoots?*"

"Ben, was the hatch down to the cabin locked when you got here?"

"Yeah, but picking locks is part of our basic training. It didn't give me much trouble."

"But whoever brought Hilary here in the first place must have had a key," I said.

"Probably," Ben agreed. "I didn't see any of the scratches around the lock that you usually see if somebody had already tried to fiddle with it."

"Who but Caro would have a key?" I said to Peter.

"I can't explain it, but there has to be some sort of mistake," he said. "Maybe she hides a copy somewhere on deck, and Alex knew where it was."

"Do you think she has stock in Igobe, too? She handles the company's PR, right? What if Iggie paid her in shares instead of cash? If that's the case, she wouldn't want Hilary's article to come out, either."

"Rachel," Peter repeated, "Caro doesn't have anything to do with this. Maybe Alex is involved, after all. He must be, given what Ben saw on the tapes. But not Caro. It's impossible."

There was an awkward silence as Peter and I stared at each other, and it continued even after I broke eye contact. Everyone else was studiously averting their gaze the way people do when they don't want to interfere in another couple's fight, and I found myself with nowhere to look but down. My eyes fell on the needlepoint pillow we'd used to cushion Ben's head, still lying on the floor next to where he sat. The pillow was monogrammed, which didn't surprise me. Caro seemed exactly like the type of person who'd have a lot of monogrammed belongings. But what did surprise me was the monogram.

"Peter, what's Caro's full name again?"

"Caroline. Caroline Vail," he said. "But what does that have to do with anything?"

"Does she have a middle name?"

"Caroline is her middle name. She has a first name that she never uses."

"Why not?"

"Because she hates it."

"Why does she hate it?" I asked.

"How would you feel if your name was Agnes?"

"Agnes? Really?"

"Yes. But why is that so important?" Then his eyes followed mine to the pillow. "Oh," he said.

The initials were there, stitched in red wool on a blue background: A.C.V. For Agnes Caroline Vail.

"Oh," he said again. Then, a moment later he continued a little more quietly, "It's a coincidence. That's all. It has to be a coincidence."

And another awkward silence fell over the room.

Hilary didn't have much patience for silences, awkward or otherwise. "What time is it?" she asked.

Ben checked his watch. "A little past seven."

"We can argue about accomplices later," she said. "Right now I need to go. There's somewhere I have to be."

"Where do you have to be? We need to figure out how we're going to catch this Alex person and bring him to justice," said Luisa.

"Can we figure that out on the way? I promised Petite Fleur I'd be at the club at eight. And he's an elusive guy—I wouldn't want to miss him."

"I'd like to meet Petite Fleur," I said, glad of the diversion. "Maybe he can even help us with more than your article."

"I'd like to meet Petite Fleur, too," said Abigail.

"Does this mean we're all getting back in the car?" asked Peter. His voice had almost returned to normal now that we'd tabled the accomplice question.

"I guess so," I said.

"All right. But we need to lay down some ground rules first," said Peter.

Given Ben's recent head injury, it didn't seem safe to let him drive, so he left his rental car in the parking lot and all six of us piled into the Prius. It was a bit cramped as a result, but Luisa should have known better than to agree to do Rock Scissors Paper with me to determine which of us was going to squeeze into the hatchback.

The return trip to the city took nearly as long as the trip to the yacht club, but it was far less stressful now that we weren't worried about anybody killing anyone else in the immediate future, and since Peter's first ground rule was that Luisa and I weren't allowed to speak directly to each other while in the car, there was no bickering. Instead we spent the time brainstorming about ways to prove what had happened since we lacked the hard evidence or eyewitness testimony we needed to officially incriminate anyone. It was good to have Hilary back, but that didn't mean we should let her abductor and any coconspirators he might have get away with everything.

"Hilary," asked Abigail as we neared the city, "just out of curiosity, what does Petite Fleur look like?"

"Skinny and bald," Hilary said.

"How old would you say he is?"

"I'm not sure. His face is pretty young-looking, but you

don't see a lot of people under forty with so little hair. And it wasn't like his head was shaved or anything. He was seriously bald."

Abigail was clearly thinking about Leo again, but even when he'd been alive there was no way anyone could have described him as skinny and bald, at least not based on the picture I'd seen. If anything, he seemed like the poster child for hirsute. Still, it was easy to understand how a teenaged skateboarding enthusiast would label anyone an "old dude" if he looked the way Hilary had described Petite Fleur.

Once off the highway, we were only a few minutes from the Mission neighborhood, where Chez Bechet occupied a small storefront on Valencia Street. Posters in the window promised live jazz, which under normal circumstances would have been enough to keep me far, far away, but tonight something else in the window made equally sure that nothing would keep me from going inside: a hand-lettered sign advertised a two-for-one drinks special lasting the entire month of June.

Two drinks for the price of one had an unquestionable appeal, but it wasn't the prospect of a bargain that drew me in, or the fact that the offer was written in big block letters in a hand that was becoming as familiar to me as my own. It was the occasion for the special that caught my attention—namely, Che Guevara's birthday, some eighty years ago this month.

We filed through the door into the sort of dark interior that would have been smoky if smoking were allowed in public establishments in California. A bar area occupied the front of the club and then opened up into a floor crowded with small tables and chairs, all facing a compact stage at the end. It was early still, and it was also a Monday night, so we weren't surprised to find the stage empty and only a scattering of patrons taking advantage of the Che birthday special.

"He was sitting in the back the last time I met him," said Hilary, leading the way past the bar. "I got the sense he's a regular. Everyone seemed to know him, and he mentioned that sometimes he performs here, too. I think he may even be one of the owners."

We hadn't advanced more than ten feet when a dog began barking, and there was something familiar about the bark. A moment later, a Great Dane bounded up from the rear of the club, and there was something familiar about him, too. Dogs the size of small ponies aren't that common, and his white coat with its black markings was distinctive. I realized I'd seen him before, being walked by a bald man on the sidewalk in front of the Forrests' house.

More importantly, the dog had evidently seen Abigail before and seemed to know her well. He made a beeline for her, rising up on his hind legs to lick at her face and then circling her excitedly, bumping up against her hips and barking.

Abigail, meanwhile, had gone as pale as a ghost. In fact, she looked as if she'd seen a ghost. As far as she knew, she had.

"*Scat?*" she said faintly. She was rewarded with another round of licks and barks.

And then she looked up to see the skinny bald man now standing in front of us.

"*Leo?*" she asked.

It turned out that if you wanted to fake your own death, it helped to be a hacker.

"But what about the dental records?" asked Abigail. "And the bone fragments?"

We'd joined Leo at his usual table in a back corner of the club, and since the first jazz combo wasn't scheduled to go on for another couple of hours, it seemed like as good a choice of venues as any for the time being. He shrugged in response to Abigail's question. "The dental records were my dad's—I hacked into my dentist's network and replaced the files of my own X-rays with his. When he was sick, he lost some of his teeth. It happens with certain types of cancer. I saved the teeth after he died, and I also had the remains from when both he and Scat's mother were cremated. That's what they found after the cabin burned."

This was gross but apparently effective.

"But why?" asked Abigail. "If you wanted to leave, or change your life, or whatever you were trying to do, why didn't you just do it? Why go to all the trouble of faking your own death?"

"Because someone wanted me dead. Iggie had been threatening me, and while it was hard to take threats from Iggie seriously, I had a couple of close calls that made me think it would be better to make myself scarce."

"Like what?" I asked.

"Like getting home to my apartment and smelling gas. Somebody had left the burner on and blown out the flame. I don't cook, and I hadn't used the stove in months, but if I'd lit a match—man, the entire building would have blown up. And then another night I was up at the cabin and Scat started going nuts, barking like mad. I ran outside just in time to see someone take off, but he was on a bike and I couldn't catch him, and it was too dark to get a good look at him. The next morning I found a can of gasoline and a bunch of old rags by the side of the driveway."

"On a bike? Do you mean a bicycle or a motorcycle?" I asked, just to be sure.

"A bicycle. And the cabin was at the end of a long road, at the top of a steep hill. Whoever it was had to have pretty good endurance to pedal up there with a big can of gasoline. He must have had it strapped to the back of his bike somehow, or maybe he carried it in a knapsack."

"Then it definitely wasn't Iggie," said Abigail. "I don't think he could ride a bike that didn't have training wheels, much less up a hill in the dark with all of that added weight."

"But Alex Cutler is in a bike club," I said. "He probably would have enjoyed the challenge."

"The venture-capital guy?" asked Leo. "You think it was him?"

It took only a few minutes to tell him about what had happened to Hilary, and to confide our suspicions about Alex.

"It all fits," I said. "And it explains why he would have freaked out when he heard Hilary was digging up the rumors about your death. He was worried about more than her screwing up the IPO—he couldn't let her find out he'd tried to kill you."

"But he didn't. I burned the cabin down myself. And I'm not dead."

"He doesn't know that, and even if none of his attempts were successful, the last thing he'd want is anybody looking into what happened all over again."

"I never did like that guy," Leo said. "He was always talking about rates of return and exit strategies. He could care less about what the technology actually did as long as his investment paid off."

"Why didn't you just call the police?" Ben asked. "When you thought someone was trying to kill you?"

Leo shrugged again. "The software I created was to keep big brother from looking over people's shoulders, not to invite him in. I don't trust the police now and I didn't then. I didn't want to be a billionaire, either, but I also didn't want people trying to kill me. I just wanted to live my life. Do my work and play my music and hang out with my dog. That was all I wanted."

"So you staged your own death?" said Hilary.

"Better to have people think I was dead than to have them coming after me. It wasn't such a sacrifice. I was sick of the entire scene. But then it turned out I was sick of more than the scene. I had cancer, too. Hodgkin's."

"Is that why you look so—?" Abigail started to ask, but then she stopped herself, worried he would take offense, or perhaps remembering that her appearance had also undergone considerable change.

Leo laughed. "Bald, you mean? Don't worry, it doesn't bother me. My hair never grew back after the chemo, and I lost a lot of weight that never came back, either."

"But how could you get medical treatment if people already thought you were dead?" asked Peter.

"It's easy to make up an identity for yourself if you can access the right computers, and it's just as easy to set yourself up with a health plan. Living off the grid isn't a problem when you know how the grid works, and I got a kick out of sticking it to big insurance."

"Here's what I don't get," I said. "If you were so willing to walk away from your old life, what are you trying to do now? Why do you care about Igobe and its IPO enough to stop it?"

Leo reached over to scratch behind Scat's ears. "Well, that's the irony of it. I thought I didn't care, but there's nothing like thinking you really are going to die to make you realize what you care about. The technology I developed can do a lot of good, and the money to be made off it can be used to do more good."

"And that's why you were leaving the clues for the other bankers and me?" I asked. "You wanted us to help you figure out how to divert the money from Iggie and his investors to do good?"

"Exactly. I got all the information about the people Iggie was scheduled to meet from his own network at Igobe, and I left clues for them all. But you're the only person who made it this far. You'd have to have a decent grounding in social justice to put the clues together. Power to the people, right?" Leo clinked his glass of orange juice against the lemonade I'd ordered, which had turned out to be a bad choice since the citrus made my cut lip sting.

"Did it occur to you to just call us, instead?" I asked, trying not to sound impatient. I knew he'd been through a lot, but he'd also made my weekend far more complicated than I would have liked.

"What would be the fun in that? And this way I could make it a test, you know? You were the hardest to track down, since you weren't staying at a hotel. I had to hack into your office's systems, too, to find out where you'd be this weekend, but that only took a couple of extra minutes. So. Can you help me?"

I was sure my colleagues at Winslow, Brown would be less than thrilled to learn how easy it was to breach our corporate firewalls, but right now I had to answer Leo's question. "I wish I could, but that's not what investment bankers do. It's not like we're all morally bereft or anything, but you don't make partner by playing Robin Hood. Legally, the company and any money to be made off it belong to its shareholders."

"Well, I used to be a shareholder in the first company, before Iggy reincorporated it as Igobe. But it would probably be a real production to stake any claim now everyone thinks I'm dead, and by the time I prove that I'm not dead and get everything straightened out, it will be too late, won't it?"

"Probably," I admitted. "You'd need to get a lot of lawyers involved, and you'd be looking at a pretty lengthy legal battle. Especially since we still have no way of proving that Alex tried to kill you, or that Iggie was involved in any way—it's not as if we can charge them with anything criminal that would throw a wrench into the IPO process."

"Then I guess I'll just have to go to Plan B."

"What's Plan B? What are you going to do?" asked Luisa.

"Are you going to hack Igobe's technology?" asked Peter.

"If you hack it, there won't be any money to be made for anyone or for any cause, however good," I pointed out. "Security software is worthless if it's not secure."

"No worries," said Leo. "I've got it all figured out."

"Will you tell me about it?" said Hilary. "So I can put it in my article?"

"Sure. But you might want to think about publishing your article online, and you might want to do it quick. Because twenty-four hours from now it will be old news."

28

Tuesday morning dawned cool and cloudy, except for my skin, which dawned fluorescent with sunburn. My lip hadn't been the only casualty of yesterday's tennis game. My face and arms were now a startling shade of magenta, as were my legs from where the tennis dress I'd been wearing had ended down to where the tennis socks began. I was almost tempted to put on my new pink outfit rather than introduce a color outside of the cranberry family into the day's look.

We'd spent the better part of the previous night with Leo, watching as he prepared to put Plan B into motion and helping out as best we could. Fortunately, Peter's parents hadn't been expecting us for dinner, nor had they been waiting up when we'd returned home a little after three in the morning, too tired to do anything but fall directly into bed. This was also fortunate because while we hadn't discussed my suspicions of Caro any further, and while Peter slept wrapped around me in his usual way, I still felt as if the tension between us was almost palpable.

Our flight home was scheduled for early that afternoon, and we packed quickly upon waking. I spent a few extra minutes in front of the bathroom mirror, experimenting with powder and concealer as Peter carried our bags downstairs, but the cosmetics just made everything worse, so I rinsed my face clean again before joining him in the kitchen.

He must have warned his parents about my appearance, because they showed only concern rather than shock, and Susan pressed a tube of aloe vera cream on me. "We'll have to make sure you're more careful the next time you're here," she said, apparently unaware that the odds of there being a next time were slim.

They both had early appointments at their respective offices, so the goodbyes were hurried. "Are you sure we can't take you to the airport later?" asked Charles.

"That's all right," Peter told him. "We've got a ride lined up." Susan hugged us both, and Charles shook his son's hand and patted me awkwardly on the shoulder.

I felt a pang of sadness as they left. They would have made nice in-laws, at least as far as in-laws went, but it seemed unlikely that I'd ever know for sure.

Abigail picked us up in her car, and then we stopped at the hotel to collect everyone else. Hilary and Ben added their bags to Peter's and mine in the trunk, filling it to capacity, but Luisa was carrying nothing but her purse. The look on her face silently dared any of us to comment, but we were too preoccupied with the morning's agenda to give her the teasing the situation would have demanded under other circumstances.

I was beginning to feel as if I knew every leg of the journey south to Silicon Valley better than I knew the two blocks from my Manhattan apartment to the nearest subway stop, but familiarity didn't make the miles pass any more quickly. We reached Igobe's headquarters right on schedule, just before ten, and Abigail slid the car into the same visitor's spot we'd used the previous day.

Sprinklers were busily irrigating the Igobe logo in front of the entrance, and we took a moment to review our plan before stepping through the sliding-glass doors. Phyllis seemed no more pleased to see us than she had yesterday, and she flinched when she got a good look at me, but at least today I was officially on Iggie's calendar and had arrived at the appropriate time.

"But why did you bring Biggie and these other people again?" she asked from beneath her Igobe visor. "Where are your colleagues from Winslow, Brown?"

My colleagues from Winslow, Brown were safely going about their business in New York, as I'd made the executive decision to disinvite them shortly before they were due to get on their San Francisco-bound flight last night. There was no reason for anyone to rack up additional travel expenses in pursuit of a deal that was never going to happen. I only hoped the partners would remember more about how I'd saved the firm from involving itself in a business disaster than about how I'd been the one pushing to get involved in the first place. I told Phyllis I'd be representing Winslow, Brown on my own this morning but that my companions would be sitting in on the meeting.

"That's highly unorthodox," she said with a sniff.

I couldn't disagree, so I simply nodded and attempted a smile, knowing full well that between the state of my lip and the boiled crimson of my skin, this was the visual equivalent of poking her in the eye.

She flinched again. "Igor's running a few minutes late—he had to take another meeting unexpectedly—but why don't you all wait in the conference room?" she suggested, making no effort to hide her eagerness to have me out of her line of sight. "You know how to get there, don't you?"

We assured her we did and headed for the glass-walled room where we'd spoken to Iggie the previous day, glad to have the chance to get everything set up beforehand. Peter fiddled around with the equipment we'd brought, and in a few minutes he'd hooked up a Webcam to face us down the length of the conference table. Behind the Webcam, he projected the display from his laptop, complete with a live Internet connection, onto the large white screen that hung on the far wall. "We're all set," he said.

"Now we just need them to show up," said Hilary.

"I wonder what Iggie's 'unexpected meeting' was," mused Luisa, her tone dry.

"I think we could all hazard a pretty good guess," I said.

And a few minutes later we knew for sure. Through the glass and across the floor, Iggie appeared around a far corner, and he was accompanied by Alex Cutler. They had their heads close together, talking as they walked, and even from the distance it was evident neither was terribly happy. If everything went as planned, they would soon be even less happy.

"Do you think Alex told Iggie everything?" asked Abigail.

"Just because his little kidnapping plot backfired doesn't mean he's going to give up on keeping the whole mess from getting out," said Hilary. "He might have been trying to limit Iggie's role before, but now he needs all the help he can get, and Iggie's got a lot at stake here, too."

As we watched, the two men paused and turned as if they'd heard their names being called, and Iggie waved at someone. Caro was making her way through the maze of cubicles to join them, dressed in a neat navy pantsuit. With her attaché case and her blond hair pulled back into a chignon, she looked every bit as much the public-relations expert as she had the tennis star the day before. Accomplice or not, I'd had a feeling Iggie and Alex would call on her—they would need her to spin any bad news that might leak. Of course, they had no way of knowing that they were facing a deluge, not a leak.

The three of them huddled together out on the floor, and their discussion appeared heated.

"We need to get things moving," I said, glancing at my watch. Our timeline had only limited flexibility.

"Leave it to me," said Hilary. She pushed open the door of the conference room and gave a yell. This got the attention of everyone in a ten-mile radius, but she crooked her finger in the direction of our targeted threesome. "Come join us!" she called, a broad smile on her face. "There's something in here you're going to want to see."

Alex's face went pale beneath its tan, and Iggie looked like he might throw up. They might have already discovered Hilary had escaped from Caro's boat, but that didn't mean they'd expected her to show up here. Caro, however, answered Hilary's broad smile with one of her own.

"Hi, there!" she called brightly. She headed our way, with Iggie and Alex following reluctantly in her wake.

"What a nice surprise," Caro said, still smiling as she entered the conference room. "What brings you all here?"

"Iggie and I had scheduled a meeting to talk about Igobe's public offering," I said, which was the truth, if not the whole truth.

"Great!" she said. "You know, I have a few shares myself, and I've been looking forward to cashing in. There are a couple of local charities that could really use more financial support, and I'd love to send some extra funds their way."

She really had the whole sweetness-and-light act down to a science, I thought, incredulous.

Hilary, meanwhile, ushered first Iggie and then Alex into the room. "Whoops," she said, as Alex let out a yelp of pain. "How clumsy of me. I didn't mean to step on your foot. By the way, have you met my friend, Ben? Ben's an FBI agent. And he has a gun. Will you show them, Ben?"

Ben obligingly pulled open his jacket and displayed his weapon, cased in its shoulder holster, as Hilary closed the door and flipped the switch to make the glass walls opaque.

"Hey, Rachel," said Iggie, apparently too stressed to use anything but my real name. "Could we postpone our meeting? Some stuff has—uh—come up, and I really need to spend some time with Alex and Caro."

"This will only take a minute," I assured him. "And

Alex and Caro are welcome to join in. In fact, we'd prefer that they did."

With Hilary and Ben blocking the way out, they had little choice but to sit down.

"Ready?" Peter asked, poised before his laptop.

"Absolutely," I said.

"Here goes," he said, and he pressed a few buttons. On the screen, the Web browser loaded a new page in which a square of video played. It displayed an empty seat in a room filled with technical equipment: computers, servers, scanners and cables. In one corner of the room, a Great Dane could be seen, dozing on a cushioned dogbed of plaid flannel.

"What is this?" asked Iggie. "Rachel, are you sure we need to do this now?"

"Shh," I said, as a man walked into the frame and took a seat on the chair. He leaned over, typed something into the keyboard on a table next to him, and then he leaned back and looked up directly into the lens of the Webcam on his end.

"Hello," he said.

Iggie gasped. *"Leo?"*

"That's right," said Leo.

"But—how?" asked Alex.

"It turns out I'm not dead. I know, man, it's a real shocker. But we can catch up on old times later. Right now there's something I want you to watch."

We could see his hands moving in toward the camera, and then the images on the screen blurred as he rotated the camera to face his own computer screen. "This is all live, by the way. Just in case you were wondering," Leo said over the tapping of his fingertips on a keyboard. "Now, I'm pulling up a Web site I set up myself. It's called www.leolovesyou.org. Catchy, don't you think?"

"What is this?" asked Alex, his surprise giving way to impatience.

"You'll see," said Leo. The image on the screen in front of us blurred again as he adjusted his camera, and then it settled into focus, revealing a snapshot of Scat alongside a short message:

Welcome to LeoLovesYou.

The security software available from this site is free to all users, but contributions are welcome and will be used to support a range of worthy causes, from eliminating poverty to eradicating disease.

This software is superior to anything on the market today, including Igobe's. In fact, it was created by the same developer who developed their software. But it's better. And unlike Igobe, it's absolutely free.

So download it and contribute what you can. And spread the word.

Peace out and power to the people.

"What have you done?" cried Alex, jumping up from his seat. He rushed to stand before the screen, rereading the words in disbelief.

"This can't be happening," moaned Iggie. "I can't believe this is happening."

Leo ignored them. "I've put in a counter, right there," he said as his finger swam onto the screen and pointed at a box in the corner. "To track how many people download the software. The word should be starting to get out—I announced the launch on my blog a few minutes ago. Let's watch, shall we?"

Eleven, read the number in the box. But then it turned to twelve, and then to thirteen. Then, right before our eyes, it jumped to eighteen, and from there to thirty-five. A moment later, the count had passed two hundred, and a moment after that it topped a thousand. The digits began moving so quickly they were barely legible.

"Make it stop," said Iggie. He'd pulled his knees up to his chest and was rocking back and forth in his chair. "Somebody make it stop."

"Have I mentioned this is live?" Leo said with a chuckle. "I bet we'll be at a million before the day is over, and ten million in a week."

"Are you insane?" shouted Alex Cutler, at Leo presumably.

Leo considered this. "No, I don't think so."

"You've ruined everything!" Alex's future bank account was declining in direct proportion to the rate at which the number in the box, and his heart rate, increased.

"Do you need me to explain it again?" Leo asked, his voice calm. He moved his finger, pointing to another box on the screen. "Check this out. It looks like people are making donations, too."

$25,412, read the number in this box, but only for a second. In a flash it was closing in on $40,000, and this was just the beginning.

Alex let out a bellow of rage. "That's my money," he yelled. "You've stolen my money."

"I wouldn't call it stealing, and it's all going to good causes," said Leo reasonably.

"Call him off," said Alex, his eyes darting around the room. "Somebody call him off. We'll do whatever he wants us to do. Just call him off."

"Too late," I said with a shrug.

"And too bad you can't Taser him from here, isn't it?" added Hilary.

"You—" said Alex. His hands clenched into fists, and he lunged for her.

She shoved an empty chair at him, and it hit him hard, right in the knee. Judging by his cry of anguish, it was the same knee she'd kicked before.

"That must have hurt," Hilary said with a delighted grin.

"You—" said Alex again, bending over, his face twisted in a grimace of pain.

"What are you going to do now?" Leo asked him from the screen. "Kill her?"

I didn't know whether it was the lost fortune, the second blow to his knee or the taunting that pushed Alex over the edge, but over the edge he went.

"I was waiting for when I would have time to take the boat out far enough to dump the body," he raged. "I couldn't kill her before then. The body would have started to smell. But I shouldn't have waited. I should have killed her. And I should have killed you when I had the chance, Leo. Then you would have been really dead. I should have known you'd spoil everything if you could."

"Was that a confession?" asked Luisa.

"It sounded like a confession to me," said Hilary.

"It was definitely a confession," I said. "Good thing we're recording this. You got that, right Leo?"

"Got it," he confirmed, tilting the camera to show the screen of another electronic device. We could see red letters displaying Recording before Leo turned the camera back to his computer screen.

Iggie, meanwhile, continued to rock and moan, and the numbers on the screen ticked higher.

Alex looked wildly around the room, momentarily speechless as he absorbed what he'd just done. With a roar he picked up a chair and threw it at the screen. The chair bounced and tumbled to the floor, leaving a dent on the screen where it had hit, but the numbers in the boxes continued their steady upward climb.

"Alex, Alex," said Leo. "Haven't you learned by now that violence solves nothing?"

Apparently he hadn't, because that's when all hell broke loose.

Alex picked up a second chair, and he threw this one at the Webcam, knocking it onto the floor before picking up yet another chair. This one he pitched toward the head of the table.

"Get down!" yelled Peter, and everyone dived for cover. The chair crashed into one glass wall, splintering it, and Alex followed it up with another chair, and then another and another. Shards of glass flew around the room as the barrage continued.

Then I heard Ben cry out. There was a thud, and the room went suddenly still.

A second later, rough hands grabbed me around the neck and pulled me out from where Peter had pushed me under the table. Alex yanked me into a standing position, and I felt something cold and hard against my temple. Then I heard the unmistakable noise of a gun being cocked.

"Everybody just shut up and back off," he yelled. "I need to think."

I could understand why he needed to think, but I didn't see why he had to do it with a gun pointed at my head. Ben was out cold, yet again, which was how Alex had managed to steal his weapon. Between getting dumped and then being clobbered over the head twice in two days, Ben might end up winning the prize for the worst San Francisco visit ever.

"Uh, Alex," I said, as politely as I could under the circumstances. "Do you really want to add a successful murder to the various attempted charges you've already racked up?"

That probably wasn't the right thing to say, because he only tightened his grip around my neck, jabbed the gun harder at my temple, and began edging toward the door.

"Rachel and I are going to go somewhere to think," said Alex, dragging me backward. "As long as nobody bothers us, nobody will get hurt."

Personally, I didn't find this promise credible. Neither did Peter, because he slowly eased up from the crouching position he'd assumed. "Alex, look, it's not too late to get everything straightened out," he said, making the smallest of movements in our direction.

Alex lifted the gun from my head and pointed it at Peter. "Don't take another step," he said. "Not even an inch. And that goes for the rest of you, too," he added, training the gun on the assembled group.

Peter held his hands up, palms out. "Why don't you take me with you, instead?" he said. "We've got a history, after all. I could help you talk everything through."

"Peter, you can't just switch places with me," I said. "You might get hurt."

"Better me than you," he said.

"Dude, it's not your choice," said Alex. "I'm the one

with the gun, remember?" As if to remind us, he jabbed it against my temple again.

"What do you care which hostage you have as long as you have a hostage?" Peter asked.

"Well, for starters, you're a lot bigger than she is. Don't take this the wrong way, Rachel, but as hostages go, I'd rather have a weakling. No offense."

"None taken," I said.

"But I'd make a better shield," Peter pointed out. "Since I'm bigger. If somebody tries to get at you, they'd have to get through me, and there's more of me than there is of Rachel."

"I'm not going to stand here arguing about who I'm taking hostage," Alex said.

But all of this debate had distracted him. I saw movement from the corner of one eye, and then I heard the sort of grunting battle cry I'd only heard before in Jackie Chan movies.

I would have ducked if Alex didn't have me in a headlock. There was a whir of navy pant-suited limbs, and the gun went flying in one direction and Alex went flying in another, slamming against the conference table. Miraculously, I hadn't been touched.

"Ooof!" said Alex, right before one of Caro's legs whipped out and caught him in the abdomen. Then her other leg whipped out to catch him in the same sore knee, and he gave a tortured groan.

Caro made the Jackie Chan noise again, and with a final flying kick, she finished him off.

Of course, I thought, watching as Alex fell to the ground. Caro would be a black belt, too, on top of everything else.

30

Perhaps the biggest miracle was that we made it to the airport with plenty of time to spare. The chaos hadn't ended with Caro overpowering Alex, but things calmed down once the police had taken him and Iggie into custody and began taking statements from us all. After they finished with me, I went to the ladies' room to make sure I didn't have any broken glass still caught in my hair.

Under the harsh fluorescent light, my sunburn took on a violet tinge, but that might also have been because everything in the room was purple, from the stalls to the tiled walls to the sinks. I wasn't sure what they'd charge Iggie with, but I had a feeling he'd end up doing some jail time along with Alex, and I doubted he'd be happy exchanging his purple wardrobe for whatever color inmates were wearing these days.

The door swung open, and Caro walked in.

"Hi," she said with a smile. "How are you holding up?" I noticed that neither the light nor the purple surroundings seemed to have any effect on her flawless skin tone, and even after her awe-inspiring display of martial-arts proficiency, her hair was smooth and her suit completely unwrinkled.

"I'm fine," I said. "But I don't know how to thank you."

"Thank me? For what?"

"For coming to my rescue like that. It was really impressive." And surprising, but I didn't say that aloud.

"Oh, it was nothing," she said, running her hands under the tap. "Anybody would have done the same thing."

"Not many people *could* have done it," I insisted. "I couldn't have."

"It wasn't a big deal." She smiled at me again and turned off the water, and I handed her a paper towel from the dispenser.

I hesitated, unsure how to ask what I needed to ask, and also unsure whether it was wise to do so without anyone else around. But the building was now swarming with policemen, so I was probably safe enough for the time being, and it was important to get the answer to my question, not only because I was genuinely curious but because it would play a critical role in determining my romantic future. I decided to throw caution to the wind and go for the direct approach. "You know, I'd thought maybe you were in on everything."

Caro had been touching up her already perfect lipstick, but now she turned from the mirror. "Whatever gave you that idea?"

"Yesterday you told me Alex gave you a ride home the other night."

"I guess I'm going to have to find a new ride for the next

cycling-club outing. Who could have known Wednesday would be the last time we ever carpooled?

"Wednesday?"

"We meet every Wednesday during the summer. It's great to fit in a ride after work when it stays light out long enough."

"Oh," I said, as the first in what would likely be multiple waves of embarrassment washed over me.

"Did you think—?"

"You said 'the other night,' and I guess I just assumed—"

She started to laugh. "You assumed I meant from the party."

I fumbled for words, but she wouldn't let me even begin to apologize.

"Trust me. I'm flattered. Nobody ever suspects me of anything—it makes me worry I'm dull."

"You're not dull," I assured her. "Nobody who did what you did to Alex Cutler could ever be dull."

Part of me was glad to know she hadn't been Alex's accomplice, but a more selfish part of me almost wished she had, because now I absolutely had to say what I said next. There wasn't going to be a better time, even if it took every drop of willpower I possessed. I took a deep breath, said a mental goodbye to happiness and spoke.

"Caro. You should take Peter back."

"What?"

"You should take Peter back," I repeated.

"I thought that's what you said. Are you serious?"

"It's obvious that you two belong together. I don't know why you broke up with him in the first place, but that must have been a mistake."

Her expression combined shock and amusement. "First

of all, I didn't break up with him. Not really. And second—we were awful together. Just plain awful."

"He said you broke up with him."

"I guess I was the one who finally said the words, but things would have dragged on for another fifteen years if I hadn't ended it. Peter couldn't stand being the bad guy. And now he keeps trying to set me up with other guys, because he still feels responsible." She laughed again. "He's going to really do a number on himself for having tried to foist Alex on me."

"But you and Peter—" I began haltingly. "I don't get it. You're so alike. You're a perfect match."

"But don't you see?" she said. "That's exactly it—we're exactly alike. It was one thing when we were eighteen and didn't know any better, but after a while, well—" She paused, thinking about how to phrase it. "It was too *smooth.*"

"What's wrong with smooth?"

"Everything's wrong with smooth. It's too easy, too comfortable. Everybody needs some friction. That's what keeps things interesting." She paused again. "But speaking of smooth, what's the deal with Leo? Do you know if he's seeing anyone?"

Abigail drove us all to the airport. Ben and Hilary were booked on a different airline, so she dropped them off at one terminal and Peter and me at another. Ben's attempts to convince Hilary to give their relationship another shot hadn't met with much success, but Luisa made no mention of her own return plans. She said goodbye to us at the curb and then got back into the car with Abigail. I wondered how long she'd be extending her San Francisco stay.

Peter offered to get our boarding passes at the electronic

kiosk while I went to the newsstand to stock up on reading material. There was a refrigerator next to the rack of magazines and paperbacks, and I realized with a jolt that I couldn't remember when I'd last thought of caffeine. It had been an eventful day, packed with distractions of all sorts, but this was still unprecedented. My dare was over, and my arm reached out of its own accord for a Diet Coke, but something in my brain stopped my hand before it made contact. I wasn't sure how things would untangle themselves when we were back in New York, and Caro's words had made me think, but I still thought there was a chance I'd lost a fiancé on this trip. At least I'd be able to say I lost a bad habit, too.

The line at security was long, but I spent the wait catching up on the e-mails and voice mails that had filled my Black-Berry, and Peter checked in with his office. I followed him down the concourse while typing out answers to the most easily addressable queries I'd received from work colleagues, and I continued to type as he shepherded me onto the plane and into my seat.

The doors to the jetway closed, and a flight attendant came down the aisle, asking all passengers turn off their electronic devices. I powered down the BlackBerry and stowed it in my bag.

"So," said Peter. "That was quite a trip."

"It certainly was," I said as the plane pulled away from the gate.

"What do you think was the best part?" he asked.

I cast my mind back over the last three days, unsure which part I would describe as *best*. Mostly there'd been a lot of stress and racing around interspersed with intervals of physical and emotional torment.

The pilot's voice came on over the intercom before I could craft a diplomatic response. "We're next in line for takeoff, ladies and gentlemen, and we're looking at clear skies. It should be smooth sailing all the way to Las Vegas. Flight attendants, please take your seats."

"Wait." I grabbed Peter's arm. "Stop them. We're on the wrong plane."

"No, we're not."

"But this plane is going to Las Vegas."

"So are we."

"But we're supposed to be going to New York."

"There's something I thought we could do in Vegas, first."

"What do you want to do in Vegas?" Had Peter developed a gambling problem without my noticing? Or a strange need to see Celine Dion in concert?

He reached over and took my hand, and then he cleared his throat. "Well, I thought we could get married."

"You mean, elope?"

"Uh-huh. It'll be fun."

I looked at him, stunned and temporarily speechless. "One thing I learned this weekend is to be very, very nervous about anything you think will be fun."

"This won't involve any physical activity, I promise. At least, not the sort of physical activity you're worried about. And you can wear your new dress."

"Have you learned nothing this weekend?" I asked. "Peter. You don't want to marry me. You just don't realize it yet."

"Of course I want to marry you. I'm in love with you. I

thought we had that all settled. Have you changed your mind? Don't you want to marry me?"

"No, I do. It's just that I'm so wrong for you. You need someone normal."

He stared at me in amazement. "Why do you think I love you?" he asked.

"I have no idea," I admitted.

"Do you know how normal my life was before I met you? With my normal family and my normal friends and my normal job? It was like living in black-and-white. Until I met you. Suddenly I was living in color, and I don't want that ever to end."

"Really?"

"Really," he said.

He leaned in to kiss me, and the plane thundered down the runway, gathering speed before lifting off the ground.

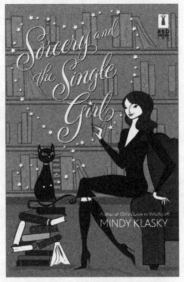

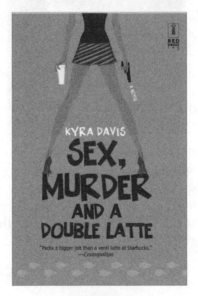

They don't believe in magic, but the
Wednesday Night Witches cast a mighty spell!

Lee Nichols

Eve Crenshaw and two friends ditch Manhattan for
a seaside cottage but soon realize they're getting more
than they bargained for. A stormy night and a strange
bottle of liqueur somehow lead to life getting better for
the Wednesday Night Witches, but everything else on
the island starts going to hell....

Wednesday Night Witches

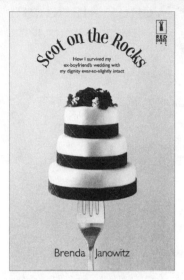